WHAT ROSE FORGOT

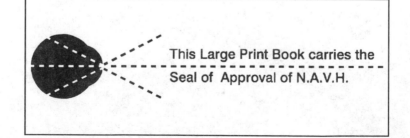

This Large Print Book carries the
Seal of Approval of N.A.V.H.

WHAT ROSE FORGOT

NEVADA BARR

WHEELER PUBLISHING

A part of Gale, a Cengage Company

GALE
A Cengage Company

Farmington Hills, Mich • San Francisco • New York • Waterville, Maine
Meriden, Conn • Mason, Ohio • Chicago

GALE
A Cengage Company

Copyright © 2019 by Nevada Barr.
Wheeler Publishing, a part of Gale, a Cengage Company.

LIBRARY OF CONGRESS CIP DATA ON FILE.
CATALOGUING IN PUBLICATION FOR THIS BOOK
IS AVAILABLE FROM THE LIBRARY OF CONGRESS

ISBN-13: 978-1-4328-7087-4 (hardcover alk. paper)

Published in 2019 by arrangement with Macmillan Publishing Group, LLC/St. Martin's Publishing Group

Printed in the United States of America
1 2 3 4 5 6 7 23 22 21 20 19

For Brooks

CHAPTER 1

Rose's head drops, jerks, and she's awake. *I've fallen asleep meditating,* she thinks. It's been a while since she's done that. Over the years, an ease of concentration has incrementally developed. Staying awake is — was — easy. Eyes still closed, she circle-sweeps her hands overhead, breathing in. The inner elbow of her right arm burns like a cigarette has been stubbed out on the flesh. Her muscles complain as if, instead of their own weight, each arm carries a twenty-pound dumbbell. Hands together, she touches her forehead. *Clarity of perception,* she thinks ritually. Then, hands to mouth, she thinks: *Honesty in what I say and do.* Hands to heart, she bows: *An open and compassionate heart toward all beings.*

Ritual done, she takes a moment to center herself, to be aware of being aware, before ending the session. The smell of forest loam, damp and earthy, fills her nose. Mixed with it is the faint exciting odor of burning leaves in autumn.

Rose's eyes snap open. Golden leaves scatter a small patch of earth around her folded legs. Scarlet foliage shivers like flames on an enclosing hedge.

"What the . . ." Rose is not in her meditation room. It is not August. She looks up. Above her stretches the trunk of a slender pale-barked tree. Yellow leaves, the shape and size of coins, clatter like falling rain as a breeze plays them against a deep blue sky.

Coins begin to spin, the edges of blue growing dark. Rose drops her head into her hands, waiting for the vertigo to pass. Through her fingers, she sees her legs crossed in a half lotus. They are fish-belly white and skinny, shins knife-sharp, skin falling away in crepey folds from her thigh-bones.

In August, at the age of sixty-eight, fit and fine, Rose sat on her meditation cushion. Now she is a hundred and three, no place she's ever been before, and it is autumn.

Holy Rip Van Winkle, she thinks.

Raising her arms, she studies herself. Inside her right elbow, sore and ripped at the center, is a raw puncture wound. Several healing jab-wounds orbit it. Tracks on her arms, like a junkie. She looks down. Her chest and belly are covered in a short blue-and-white-print cotton tunic. Tree bark chafes her lower back as she shifts position. Her back is bare.

This is a hospital gown.

Fear that has been gathering like an army on the edges of her confusion pours down in a screaming horde. Rose closes her eyes and raises her hands, palms out as if to stop the barbarian invasion.

"It's a dream," she says. Her throat is dry, her breath puffing in rasps over an arid tongue and cracked lips.

Rubbing her face vigorously, Rose breathes deeply several times, then opens her eyes again. Still autumn. Still an ancient junkie. Still in an alien land. She slaps herself, hard: cheeks, shoulders, thighs. At the same time she yells as loud as she can: "Aaaahhhhhhhh!"

Nothing changes, except now her cheeks sting and her throat is filled with razor blades and sawdust. Thirst has become more demanding than the pain in her arm, the sickening spin of leaves more demanding than fear.

This is a dream.

Rose knows this. People don't wake up on the wrong side of the rabbit hole. She rolls to her hands and knees. Slowly, achingly, her dream-body convinced it is that of an emaciated centenarian, she readies to stand. Arms around the tree, she pulls herself to her feet. The bark is smooth. A breeze blows cool on her bare buttocks.

Awfully specific for a dream, she thinks. This thought injects another dose of terror into her brain. She lets it pass. It leaves a trail of broken glass in her psyche. Rose has had many dreams where she knows she is dreaming. So many, she has devised a surefire test. When Rose is dreaming, she can fly. Letting go of the tree, she raises skeletal mottled arms to the sky.

Rose cannot fly.

She's back on her knees, sticks and leaves pricking her bare legs.

Asleep, awake, in her meditation room, or in the Land of Nod, she has to have water. Never before has she been truly thirsty. This is it. Water becomes the only thing that matters. After she drinks, she will figure out what is happening.

In the ring of flaming leaves surrounding her, there is a break, a dark triangle big enough for a child — or a shriveled old woman — to crawl through.

Rose crawls through it.

On the other side is a long narrow meadow. Sun touches the grasses. They

10

sparkle with their offerings of dew. Cars honk in the distance. Traffic hums faintly. Beyond the trees, across the cleared area, she sees roofs tucked into the riot of fall color. Rose has never been here before.

No past, no future, the present a mystery, she is groundless, a spark of life in a chunk of meat, part of the duff and twigs. This is the eternal moment of Now. Somehow, she'd imagined it would be more enlightening, less creepy.

Laughter, gay and careless, percolates through the gap in the foliage screening her from the meadow.

Holding to fistfuls of the supple branches, she totters out of her meditation lair. She pulls herself to her feet, stands swaying and blinking in the morning sun. Two boys, perhaps twelve or thirteen, both wearing small backpacks, are walking bicycles down the green. They don't notice an ancient skeleton in a hospital gown wobbling in the shrubs.

In the side pocket of one boy's pack is a red plastic water bottle.

In another incarnation, she might have said, "Excuse me" or "Good morning." What she does is point and croak, "Water." A cartoon, the tattered old prospector crawling across the desert sands toward a

11

mirage boasting a single coconut palm, unrolls in her mind, and she laughs, a dusty "Huh, huh!"

The boys stop.

"Did you hear that?" says the boy with the water bottle.

"Gunga Din," Rose says, and wishes she hadn't. It will be incomprehensible — insane — to a modern boy.

"There!" The other one points a finger at Rose. "Hey, lady, were you the one screaming?"

The nearness of water gives Rose the initiative to let go of the bush. She takes two staggering steps toward the boys, both frozen, mouths agape, eyes round. Reflected in those eyes Rose sees herself as the boys must see her. Hair uncombed, leaves clinging to a filthy stained hospital gown, gaunt and wobbly and batshit crazy.

"OMG," says the nearer boy, a nice-looking kid with shiny brown hair falling over his forehead, his wiry frame covered in the ubiquitous baggy cargo shorts and a green T-shirt. "You okay, ma'am?"

Rose can think of no short answer to that. She opens her mouth to say, "Could you please let me have a drink of water?" What comes out is "Unh, unh." A withered arm with a bony hand claws at the air. The boys

12

flinch back.

"Aden," says the boy who has the water, "you go tell the people at the nursing home one of their patients got away. I'll stay here and make sure she doesn't get more lost."

"You sure?" asks Aden, eager to get away from the specter that is Rose.

"Pretty sure," the water boy says.

Aden straddles his bicycle.

Nursing home? Got away?

"No," Rose cries feebly. "Help me!" Her knees give way. As she falls to all fours, the hospital gown parts in back and slides down her elbows, leaving her naked.

"Go! Go! Go!" she hears the water boy yell, then the sound of bicycle tires throwing gravel as Aden leaves.

No longer able to hold her head up, Rose stares at the grass, panting like a dog.

A tentative hand lands on her shoulder. "Water, ma'am. I'm sorry there's not much." Gripped in a brown young hand, the bottle appears beneath her face, the spout near her mouth. Rose wraps cracked lips around it and sucks.

"You have to bite down to get the water to come out," the boy says.

Rose bites down and, like a suckling calf, works her throat. A couple of tablespoons of tepid water reach her before a gurgle lets her know the bottle is empty. She keeps sucking convulsively until the boy gently pries the spout from her lips. There isn't enough water to reach her throat, but her tongue is sufficiently wet. It no longer feels like beef jerky.

"Can you stand up?" the boy asks.

Rose nods. With his help she makes it shakily to her feet.

"Let's get you fixed up," the boy suggests. Matter-of-factly, he draws the hospital gown up around her shoulders. Moving behind her, he says, "You've got yourself all undone."

Her gown is tugged straight as he ties the two ties in the back.

"Amazing boy" is all Rose can manage.

"When Dad's aunt Clara got bats in her belfry we kept her at home," he says. "There. Good as new."

"My belfry is emptying. Bats are flying the coop. Mixed metaphor," Rose says. "You — somebody — tell me where this is." Rose feebly waves an arm and feels the gown pull open over her bottom. "This is so weird . . . It's not summer. What — I don't know . . ."

"You'll be okay. Aden is going to get people to help you. Want to sit down?" the boy asks kindly.

Rose doesn't want to sit down, but realizes

she can no longer stand up. He helps her to a boulder near his fallen bike. Without his hand gripping her arm, Rose would collapse.

"Hey!" comes a shout. Two men in white coats burst out from an arch of trees a hundred yards away. "Hold her!" one of them shouts as they trot toward her and the boy.

"White coats," she murmurs. "Where are the butterfly nets?" Terror slams into her, snatching the breath from her lungs. "No! No," she begs, and clutches the boy's hand. "There's been a mistake. Don't let them take me."

"You'll be okay now," the boy says soothingly. "They'll get you some water to drink, and get you all set."

The men arrive. Both panting, both overweight, alike to one another as Tweedledee and Tweedledum.

"I think she's super dehydrated," the boy says. "I gave her some water, but it wasn't much."

"Thanks, kid," the nearest Tweedle says. "We'll take it from here."

Rose can't run. She can barely stand.

Expertly, they flank her. Each takes an elbow and a grip on the corresponding shoulder. Effortlessly, they lift her until her toes are skimming the ground, not like she's a person, but like she's a sack of lawn clippings being dragged to the curb.

"Wait," Rose wails, kicking as ineffectually as a baby. "Damn you! Put me down!"

They pay less attention to her than they would to a yapping dog. In a practiced two-man scuttle, they cover ground rapidly, rushing her toward the gaping hole in the foliage from whence they emerged. The tops of Rose's feet scrape along the ground. She bends her knees, lifting her feet to stop the damage. The men don't notice the extra weight. Rose tires; her feet are dropping. She tries to run between them, but they are moving too fast.

The three of them shoot through a tunnel of leaves. On the other side are houses, lawns, sidewalks. Half a block away two police cars and two sedans, one white and one gold, are double-parked in front of a one-story brick building with wide glass entrance doors. A discreet sign bolted to the brick reads LONGWOOD MEMORY CARE UNIT.

Two uniformed men and four women, one in pale green scrubs, are standing on the sidewalk as if waiting for the delivery of Rose. One is an impeccably dressed woman in her seventies, tall with a straight back

16

and determinedly brown hair. Her arms are crossed tightly, as if she is afraid a word will shatter her. Next to her is a diminutive redhead in her forties, hair blunt-cut across her eyebrows.

"I know you!" Rose screams. "I know you!" She laughs with relief. Her throat is so dry, the laugh sounds like a growl. Names, Rose needs their names, but nothing comes. The handsome older woman is a blank. When she looks at the small redhead, all that comes to mind is "bad boob job." Trying to pull her arms free of her captors, Rose shouts again, "I know you!" The tall fragile woman turns her face toward Rose, her glasses flashing in the sun.

"You know me! Help me! For God's sake, help me!" Rose tries to plant her feet, stop the parade. The men don't slow.

"Gigi!" comes a call from behind. Twisting painfully in the orderlies' grip, Rose manages to look back. Hair shining in the morning sun, strong tan legs flashing as she runs, a girl races up the sidewalk from the direction of the tree-lined arch.

"Grasshopper!" Rose shouts. She knows this girl, loves this girl. Rose is so happy, she babbles, unable to stop herself. "I'm dreaming. Or I'm Rip Van Winkle. How old am I? This is so crazy. I sat down. Then I woke up and — and, and I'm so glad to see you!" She laughs from sheer joy at the sight of the beloved face of her granddaughter.

"What are you doing here, Mel?" Boob Job demands.

"Just what I was going to ask you," the elegant woman says to Boob Job.

"Did you Uber, sweetie?" the woman in green scrubs asks too loudly, too brightly — a woman trying to defuse a difficult situation.

"I was searching the greenway for Gigi," Mel says. Rose wants to hug her granddaughter, but Dee and Dum have such short arms. "Our house backs up to it, you know."

"Of course I know," snaps Boob Job. To Rose she says, "You've caused quite a commotion. We've been looking for you half the night. We had to call the police."

"Stella," says the older woman repressively, putting a manicured hand on the younger woman's arm.

"Well, sorry that I still care! Sorry that I think she's still family," Stella says hotly.

Her name is Stella. Never trust a woman with big boobs and slitty eyes. Still, Rose shouts, "Stella!"

Mel — Grasshopper — comes around in front of where Rose sags between the two

18

men. Her eyes, her roguish smile, are so familiar, so comforting, that Rose's eyes burn with tears.

"Don't, Melanie," the older woman says. "Seeing you upsets her."

Rose is going to protest, fight the Tweedles, but a sturdy black-haired woman in a Santa-red power suit, fingers sparkling with rings, shoves a large plastic cup filled with ice and orange juice under Rose's nose. The sides are beaded with condensation; a bent straw sticks invitingly out of the plastic top. Everybody and everything disappears. Rose latches her lips around the straw and sucks until her cheeks cave in, swallows, and sucks some more.

"I bet she got pretty dehydrated," says Ms. Red Suit cheerfully. "First the flu, then the night's adventure."

The juice is nectar. Cool and sweet, it flows over her tongue and down her parched throat. Rose has never tasted anything so good. Afraid it will be taken from her, she drinks as fast as she can. The straw slurps in the ice cubes at the bottom. Liquid painfully swells her shriveled stomach. Still, she gasps, "More."

"More?" asks Red Suit. Suddenly Rose is hypnotized by the woman's eyebrows. By their artistry. They are gelled and brushed

19

and painted until they are as exquisite as the antennae of a luna moth. Then Rose flies out of her body, sees it slump, lifeless in the hard male hands. From above, she sees herself as a rose mandala sand painting. Wind comes. The sand eddies, blows into tiny tornados, the pattern scattering.

"Poison!" she screams, juice running down her chin. "They are poisoning me!" With a gust of sand that resembles a human arm, she slaps away the plastic cup and watches it fly in slow motion from the beringed hand.

"Just a mild sedative," the sturdy woman says. "She is so agitated. I was afraid she might harm herself."

Wind takes all that is left of Rose, trailing it in pale blues and pinks and golds. Then all of it is gone. Rose is gone.

CHAPTER 2

Out of a coil of snaking dreams an answer rises, floating into a window as small and dark as that of a Magic 8-Ball, a child's toy. Rose doesn't know what the question was. The answer is consciousness. Rose is conscious.

Barely oblivious, she thinks vaguely.

Fog curls around the tiniest thread that is her and carries it away into the darkness.

An hour, a day, a year later, voices call her back. Not by name, but by shared humanity. Or maybe merely noise different from the humming of her brain.

Voices in her head.

Voices in one's head is always bad.

Open your eyes, she thinks, and tries. No dice. Panic lends her strength. With a mighty effort, she wins a narrow slit of vision, red-rimmed top and bottom and sliced by blades of black, as if she peers through a prison window at sunset. Above is a colorless sky. Glare from an unseen source backlights tombstones leaning precariously over her. Rose considers screaming, but can't remember how that is done.

"How in hell did she get out?" a woman asks.

"She wasn't in lockdown. They moved her to general when she got the stomach flu," another woman answers. "Her medications got flushed from her system. She must have woken up and decided to leave us."

"See that it doesn't happen again."

Not markers of the dead, these are people. The voices aren't in her head. This is a good sign.

Rose feels as if she should recognize the speakers. They are somebody. Who exactly drifts in the fog clogging her mind. Turning from the slit of vision, she closes her eyes, trying to penetrate the mist. Each tentacle of thought unravels like smoke in the wind.

"Too bad it didn't turn into pneumonia, the old person's friend."

"Stomach flu rarely turns into pneumonia," a woman says dryly. "The point is, she vomited up her meds. These don't stay in the system long. They need to be kept to a certain level. Besides, these things can happen too fast and too often. We need to be careful of our special needs patients. When

22

we get her back in the Secure Community, and get her medications stabilized, I'll be a lot more comfortable."

Rose collects a few available words and attempts speech. Air whispers over the cracked desert of her tongue, puffing like dust between stiff lips. "Thirsty," she tries to say. The knack of speaking eludes her; she only manages a small sighing sound.

"She's coming around."

"I've been here too long as it is. I need to get back to the office."

Rose wanders back into the clouds roiling in her skull.

When the Magic 8-Ball again turns up consciousness, Rose opens her eyes to an op-art nightmare of shapes: hangmen's nooses, sharps, bulbous-eyed heads. The texture of panic is not ice cold and ice blue. Instead of carving through her cranium, this terror leaks, filling gaps in the mist with nauseating sludge as thick, black, and evil-smelling as tar.

Breathe, she tells herself. *Relax into the moment.* Inch by inch her breath reclaims mental real estate, blows fear back into the corners.

Right View: She is in a hospital bed, looking at a ceiling in a hospital room, side-lit from lights in the hallway. "I am confused and disoriented," Rose whispers. "I am in a hospital. I am back in the hospital again."

Right View: Not a hospital. A nursing home. Like scraps of shredded paper, images flutter behind her eyes: people slumped in empty sacks of wrinkled skin, staring, spittle at the corners of their lips, the stench of urine and hopelessness.

Right Intention: Get out.

Rose had gotten out. Now she is back in.

She tries to lift her hand to scrub the sand from her eyes. The motion is aborted; her hand jerks like a little dog reaching the end of its leash. Her other hand meets the same fate.

Breathe in, calm the mind. Breathe out, calm the body. She can breathe; a cause for happiness.

Inner clamor and confusion lessen. Monsters on the ceiling are a simple play of light and shadow. Craning her head up until her neck aches, she can see her hands. Both wrists are cuffed to the sides of the bed with wide soft bands. The cuffs are tethered to the rail.

They have tied her down.

Rose's eyelids glow orange. Daytime. The sun has risen. *Miracles abound,* Rose thinks groggily. She forces her eyes open a little.

People. People she should know. She is beginning to hate this. That she hates it means it has happened before. Emotion attached to thought equals memory.

"Good morning." A man in a white coat and tie — a doctor, Rose supposes — smiles down at her. "You're looking much better."

Rose isn't feeling better, but, she realizes, she is feeling. Before there'd been numbness, gray featureless brain-scapes.

"Wanda, what kind of meds do we have her on?" the doctor asks.

"Just antidepressants," Wanda replies. Rose recognizes Wanda. It is she of the luna moth eyebrows. She works here. Not a nurse. Her teal pantsuit screams management.

"She will have purged any medications with the vomiting," the doctor says. "Now that she's out of the woods as far as the flu goes, and back in a secure environment, get her levels back on par slowly. Half for a day or two, then, if she's doing well, up them."

Rose doesn't want her levels back on par. She had gotten out because her levels were below par, because, pathetic as the process is, without the "meds" she can think. She is thinking now. Not clearly, but, with concentration, she can feel her way from A to B.

The doctor and Wanda leave the room.

With more effort than she would have expected, Rose manages to keep her eyes open. She needs to see her body if she is to remain in it. An IV is plugged into her right arm, the long metal sharp taped down to her right wrist. Her eyes move to her crotch. White and gray, a hilly landscape of blankets obscures her body. Her feet are two hillocks away.

Risking the sirens' song of oblivion, she lets her eyes close and focuses on the sensation between her legs. Moving her hips slightly, she feels a sting and a tug. A catheter, she guesses, its tube taped down to her leg to minimize irritation.

Fog slips into sinuous shapes, trying to lure her back into the deeps. Opening her eyes again, she takes in a breath, then sighs some of the mist out, winning a clear small space. Holding herself in that space, she studies her left wrist.

The padded cuff is firm but not tight. Gently she begins working, pulling her elbow up until the tether is tight, then, thumb tucked to palm, fingers gathered to a point, she twists her hand back and forth.

Right Intention: Free herself.

As her mind clouds and her vision grays, Rose clings to that with the desperation of a drowning woman clinging to a log.

Time flaunts its versatility, flying, passing in a petty pace, racing, standing still. Rose's arm wrenches and turns. Rose remembers and forgets, pulls, twists, remembers, forgets.

At some point she realizes her left hand is free.

With a hazy sense of triumph, she lifts it and holds it before her sticky eyes. Behind spread fingers a monitor flashes a shard of green light.

Kryptonite, she thinks. Lex Luthor is keeping her prisoner with kryptonite.

Willing strength into that left hand, that free agent, she moves that marvelous hand across her body and watches as it pulls the tape off her right arm, then eases the needle from her flesh. Clumsy fingers claw at the buckle, scrape at the strap, and her right hand is free.

Exhausted, Rose lies back, eyes resolutely open, and waits for a semblance of focus to return to body and mind. Intention. Isn't there something she is supposed to be doing? The Land of Nod calls seductively.

"No," Rose whispers. A hand gripping the rail to either side of the bed, she drags herself into a sitting position. The room slides sideways, does a half turn, then settles. Her brain is clearer than when she was lying on her back, with it flattened in her skull like Silly Putty left too long in its egg.

Silly Putty. A fragment of memory tries to tug a smile from the corner of her mouth. Before she can catch it, it vanishes. She scans the room, trying to pry the real from the unreal with the force of her gaze. Bedding, rails, hoses, bags, metal trees, monitors: her eyes wander over them. Apparatus are on her and in her and around her, attached to one another, attached to her. She and the machinery inter-are.

All phenomena are devoid of a separate, individual self. Empty.

This is not helpful.

Moving slowly, lest she and the medical detritus should interfere with one another, Rose peels back the bedclothes. The rest of her white-and-blue hospital gown is crumpled in her lap. Extending from beneath it are legs so pale, fragile-looking, and unbelievably bony, it takes her a moment to realize they are hers. White-and-blue-striped socks cover her feet.

For an inestimable time she sits holding on to the rails. Why she sits, why, much as she craves rest, she is afraid to lie down, slips from her mind.

She can't remember why she is where she

is, how she's gotten here.

Who are you?

Rose Dennis.

When were you born?

1952.

What day is it?

I don't know.

Who is the president of the United States?

I don't know, but I know I hate the son of a bitch.

A litany from somewhen.

Rose squeezes her eyes shut and rubs them with her fists. That had been a test for sanity. Evidently Rose had failed.

Right View: Nursing home.

Right Intention: Get out.

For long moments, she considers that intention. The shackles are off. But the doctor said she was back in a secure environment. There will be locks and watchers. No walking out.

Rose lowers herself back to the bed and painstakingly buckles her wrists back into their cuffs. There is nothing she can do about the IV. They'll just have to work that mystery out for themselves.

Fear is all around her, fear that this place, these people, are keeping her against her will. Perhaps for her own good. Perhaps not. Rose does not like people imposing unpleas-

29

ant things on her "for her own good." Until she has a plan, one that will carry her farther than a couple of football fields from this place, she will play possum. She will watch. She will be mindful.

She will resist having the level of her meds raised to par. Her mind must be allowed to clear. Then:

Right Action: Very carefully and mindfully get out.

CHAPTER 3

Rose is wearing a nightgown and robe.

"Up and around." Wanda, the woman with the luna moth eyebrows, leads her from a hallway into a waiting room. "Is it good to be home, Ms. Dennis?"

Rose is Ms. Dennis. This is home. On one side of a large room is a couch. A nurses' desk is on the other. Three brown Barcaloungers line the far wall. An old man and two old women in nightgowns and robes crumple like deflated dolls on the furniture.

"Ms. Dennis is officially out of the woods," Wanda says cheerfully.

"You had quite an adventure," says a woman behind the desk.

"Stomach flu is nobody's idea of fun. Her meds got purged — along with everything else," says Wanda. They laugh. Rose does not.

"She's sedated now, but it will wear off. Be sure she gets her meds at dinner. Give her her lunch meds as well. We need to restore her levels as soon as we can."

That's not what the doctor said. Rose can remember. He said slowly restore her levels.

"Of course," says the nurse. She comes from behind the desk. Rose is handed off.

Package delivered, Rose thinks. The Rose Dennis package has been delivered "home."

"Thanks, Wanda," the nurse says.

Wanda presses a plastic card against a black plastic square beside the door. It slides open. She leaves, heels clicking on the vinyl flooring.

"Someone will sure be glad to see you," says the woman who now holds Rose's elbow. "Let's get you settled with your friend, then get some dinner in you." The nurse prattles as she guides Rose around the chest-high desk and through a wide arch into another room. "You are skinny as a scarecrow. We'll get some meat back on those bones."

The second room is dominated by a long scarred wooden table. At the far end, an ancient man in pajamas and a white cotton robe like the one Rose wears puts a puzzle together.

"That's Mr. Buschbaum," the nurse says. "Mr. B, Rose is back on her feet."

Mr. B does not look up or respond.

The nurse pulls out a chair and seats Rose in it, patting her into place as if she's made of Play-Doh. In the center of the table are a mug of colored markers, several pairs of children's snub-nose scissors, and sheets of paper with the outline of a sailboat. One is colored green with a blue sail.

The nurse whisks out.

Rose wonders if she is supposed to draw a picture.

"She's right in here, Chuck. I know you've been worried." The nurse returns, leading a man by the elbow. "This is your friend Chuck Boster," the nurse says as she maneuvers the man into a chair beside Rose. "See, Chuck, Rose is well and back among the living."

Chuck is six feet tall, Rose guesses, and thin. Beneath the loose skin is a defined musculature. His hair is thick, with lots of salt, and cut short. He would be handsome if lax muscles weren't dragging down his cheeks and his eyelids. He isn't much older than Rose is.

Than Rose was. She doesn't know how old she is now.

Smiling at the two of them, the nurse says, "Chuck has been missing you. Haven't you, Chuck?" Chuck does not respond. The nurse turns her happy face to Rose. "Since

33

you've been sick, he's moped and asked, 'Where's the rose?' half a million times."

Uncertain what to do, Rose does nothing. The nurse doesn't seem to notice. She pats Chuck's upper arms as if fluffing up a pillow. "You two get reacquainted. Dinner in a minute. Good to be home?"

The question is aimed at Rose. She feels it hit, but doesn't know what to do with it.

The nurse walks away.

Side by side, Rose and Chuck sit staring at the pens in the coffee mug. Rose doesn't know Chuck; still, she feels a knowingness, an ease, familiar, pleasant. Concentrating hard, she digs words out of her brain and offers them one at a time. "How long have you been here?" Her voice is barely above a whisper. The phrase feels out of place, but it is all she has.

Chuck moves his gaze from the mug to her face, mild concern livening his features. "Where is this?" he asks.

"I don't know," Rose admits.

Chuck reaches over and takes her hand from where it lies on her knee. Rose doesn't snatch it back. The gesture feels as if it has happened before, and no harm has come of it. He folds her hand in his and sets them both on his own knee. His grasp is gentle, his skin warm and dry.

34

Rose is comforted. Tears fill her eyes. She cries because she hadn't known how desperately she needed comforting, and because there are so many people in the world with no warm hand to hold.

"You are Chuck," she says, trying the words out for hidden memories. There are none.

He nods. Again he asks, "Where is this?"

Again, Rose has no answer. "I am . . . I am the rose?" she asks.

"You grow here," he says.

Rose hears that. Tears tumble from her bottom eyelids. "I guess."

"My good wife loved roses," Chuck says, giving her hand a squeeze.

After that, they don't speak. Chuck holds her hand, and though parts of her mind skitter along the misty track that led to this room, more parts stay in Chuck's hand, averse to disturbing him, the way she is averse to disturbing a sleeping cat on her lap.

Pushed by an orderly in a white shirt and trousers, a cart rattles into the activities room. Tweedle, Rose thinks, and remembers being dragged along the sidewalk. Moving her feet in her slippers, she can feel the irritation where the tops scraped along the ground.

The sedatives are wearing off. The "meds" have been purged from her system.

"The puzzle will still be there after dinner," the orderly says to the old man impersonating a hank of hair and a bag of bones. With practiced ease, he moves Mr. Buschbaum to another chair, then sets a plastic tray with a rectangular plate divided into segments in front of him. Identical trays are placed in front of Rose and Chuck.

"Mr. B." The orderly sets a tiny paper cup containing blue pills in the puzzler's hand. "Mr. Boster." Another little cup with two red capsules is put in Chuck's hand. "Ms. Dennis." Chuck releases her hand. She watches as it floats up, nearly transparent but for the veins, and takes a paper cup with four red capsules in it.

Mr. Buschbaum dumps blue pills into his mouth. Rose stares at the capsules, pretty as drops of blood on snow.

"Dry, aren't they," the orderly says. "This'll help." He holds out a small plastic glass filled with orange juice.

Rose takes it. The juice sloshes, catching light from the window.

Poison. The word clangs, a clapper banging against the bell of her skull. Orange juice to wash down her "meds." She puts the capsules in her mouth. Lifting the glass to

36

her lips, she pretends to drink, then swallow. Clumsily, she sets the orange juice back on the tray, spilling half of it.

The orderly sighs and walks heavily from the room. Rose scrapes the dry capsules from her tongue and closes them in her fist.

Stumping back with a handful of paper towels, the orderly mops up most of the spill. A couple of tablespoons of juice slop into the mashed potatoes. Rose thinks *poison* and stares out a window half obscured by a hedge. Beyond are parked cars, a street, and houses. Rose presses her fingertips to the pills in her palm. A plan is beginning to form in her mind.

The orderly continues around the table. He pours orange juice into a cup for Mr. Buschbaum, then for Chuck. It's all from the same pitcher. This orange juice is not poisoned.

The red capsules are poisoned.

Rose eats her food and marshals facts in her mind. She had the stomach flu. She was moved to general population. She woke up and wandered off. She was caught and returned. She is ancient, frail, and in a home for old demented people.

She has been here long enough to make a friend.

She will not be staying long enough to make another.

CHAPTER 4

Dinner eaten, Rose and Chuck are parked in side-by-side loungers facing a large flat-screen TV over the sliding glass entrance door. A big woman, KAREN, her name tag reads, comes in bearing a can of Diet Pepsi.

"How many does that make for today, counting the one you probably drank in the car on your way to work?" a nurse wearing the name SHANIKA asks, vacating the chair behind the desk.

"Five. I'm trying to limit myself to eight a day. They help me stay alert on the night shift," Karen replies.

"I read —" Shanika begins.

"Don't bother. I've heard it all. Diet anything causes cancer, heart failure, car crashes, and female erectile dysfunction," Karen says.

"See you later," Shanika says, letting herself out. Karen waves.

Rose looks at the television. Cartoon

characters infect the screen. Grotesques, they would once have been called. Since the Muppets, children's fiction has gotten surreal. Why cartoons? Why not the news? Dementia as a second childhood?

A woman on the couch slips a few more degrees right of center. The man in the third lounge chair snores. Chuck struggles up out of his chair.

"Where are you off to, Chuck?" Karen, the big nurse, asks pleasantly.

"Home," Chuck says.

Karen gets out of her chair and tugs the top of her scrubs straight. "I'm headed that way. Can I walk with you?" She takes Chuck's arm. Rose watches from the corners of her eyes as Karen, chatting companionably, walks Chuck into the activities room, around the table, and back to the abdicated easy chair. "What a long walk! You must be as tired as I am, Chuck. Oh, look, what luck, your favorite chair is right here waiting for you." Without taxing her strength, she helps Chuck to sit. He lies back, eyes closed. He looks like a corpse.

Rose watches a sponge in boxer shorts cavort on the television screen.

At seven thirty, Karen emerges from behind the desk to place her keycard onto the black plastic. The glass security door

40

opens. A young woman carrying a tray of snacks, boxes of juice, and a Diet Pepsi comes in.

"You do love me!" Karen says as she takes the soda and puts it on her desk.

The young woman is really a girl, no more than fourteen. She wears a pink-striped dress. *Candy striper.* A snippet of memory, a snapshot out of the dark, coming from nothing and leading to nothing, flickers in Rose's mind.

The girl gives each resident a box of juice, helps them to skewer a foil hole with a tiny straw, then unwraps their snack-packs of crackers and cheese.

Rose sips and munches along with the others, eyes fixed on the television. Mentally, she notes the comings and the goings, trying them against her nascent plan.

Shanika returns. Residents are being carted away, down a short hall with six doors opening off of it. Shanika comes to Rose's chair. "Are we ready for a shower?" she asks cheerfully.

Wisdom — or animal instinct — keeps Rose from responding either in words or looks. Instead, she stares passively at nothing while the nurse helps her out of the chair and shepherds her down to the second door on the left. The room has leaf-green

41

walls. An old rocking chair sits beneath the single wire-reinforced window. A coverlet, printed with roses, covers the bed. It is accented by a flounced throw pillow. Rose recognizes these things. They are her things. This is her room.

Shanika shuffles Rose into the bathroom and efficiently eases her onto a stool in the shower.

"A shower will make you feel a lot better. It always does me. Of course, I'm a bath girl at heart. I like nothing better than a good long soak in a hot tub." While she talks, the nurse strips off Rose's gown. It is pink with puffed sleeves and has tiny flowers machine-embroidered on the yoke.

"Good girl!" Shanika exclaims. "You didn't wriggle out of your panties."

Rose keeps her face impassive as Shanika lifts her an inch off the stool and, with a practiced move, slips her undergarment off.

Diapers. They are soiled.

"You see," Shanika says. "Because you didn't take them off, you are all clean and dry. Diapers are our friend."

The nurse steps on a lever to raise the wastebasket lid. The offending article is dropped inside.

With great gentleness, telling Rose what she is going to do before she does it, Shanika shampoos Rose's hair, then washes her body.

The water feels so good, Rose is too grateful to suffer any but the slightest embarrassment. Shanika makes her feel cared for, as if she is a human being who actually exists. Rose is tempted to say, "Thank you," but she doesn't. Drugged orange juice, toxic red capsules, and capture are now part of her limited stock of memories.

In bed, in the same nightgown and a clean diaper, Rose realizes the simple act of moving from bath to bed has completely robbed her of physical reserves. When Shanika is gone, and the hall lights are dimmed, she forces herself to get up. Retrieving the day's capsules from the pocket of her robe, she looks around the room, then hides them behind a box of latex gloves in the drawer of the bed stand. Exhausted, she creeps back between the sheets.

"Do you want to see her?" Wanda is speaking in the hall on the other side of the half-open door to Rose's room.

"Not necessary." Another woman, the one who wishes she had died of pneumonia.

"I think we've gotten her stabilized," Wanda says reassuringly.

"Good. Her family is afraid she may not last much longer."

"Are they?" Wanda asks.

"Yes, very afraid. Absolutely terrified that she may not even make it through the week."

Rose listens, her head cocked to one side. They don't say anything more. She hears the subdued hush of the security door swooshing shut like the sound of distant surf.

Absolutely terrified that she may not even make it through the week.

Hackles, residual from time in the jungle, prickle on the back of Rose's neck. She runs her fingers through her hair, scratching her scalp to get the blood flowing. Is she paranoid? Or delusional? People with delusions can become violent if those delusions are attacked.

It occurs to Rose that normal people do the same thing. No one changes their mind. No one ever says, "Thank you for pointing out what an idiot I am, and how smart you are. From now on I'll be a better person." Tears start to flood Rose's eyes. She wills them back into their ducts.

Not even make it through the week.

A threat? An old lady stops breathing in the middle of the night, or trips over the rug in the Alzheimer's ward, breaks a hip, and dies of complications, no questions are asked. Rose's mother died in Rose's living room. No police came asking if anyone had put a pillow over her face. Old people die. Her mother was senile. She was old. She died.

Though the room is cool, sweat trickles between her breasts in a slow chilling crawl.

Whether she is delusional or visionary makes no difference, Rose decides.

Sobs boil up her throat. Shoving the corner of the pillow in her mouth, she stifles the noise.

Pad, pad, pad. "You okay, Ms. Dennis?"

The night nurse. That is who will come if she cries. Rose takes a deep cleansing breath and sighs it out.

Crazy or not, she will rescue herself. Working out the details of just how that will be accomplished, she falls asleep.

Rose wakes early, climbs out of bed, and puts her diaper back on. The orderly, not the one from the previous night, but the other one, brings breakfast. Scrambled eggs and sausage; Rose eats every scrap. Rest and food are making her stronger, cleverer, more human.

Shanika comes to remove the tray. "You're looking much better today, Ms. Dennis." Rose says nothing, and does not make eye contact, afraid she will reveal a hidden streak of sanity or, worse, give in to the nearly overwhelming urge to explain things, set the matter straight, talk through all this nonsense.

It is hard to remember that in this place, Rose is a confirmed lunatic. As recently as yesterday — she is pretty sure it was only yesterday — she ratified that diagnosis by behaving like a madwoman, drinking the orange juice, and toppling back into oblivion.

Did she need sedating to keep her from mad killing sprees? Rose doesn't think so. This is not a hospital for the criminally insane.

While Shanika putters about, straightening the room, Rose imagines talking to her.

"You know, I'm not actually demented," Rose would say casually.

"Not demented! Isn't that good news. Who should I call to come get you?"

"I don't know," Rose would admit. *"But, you see, I was a bit off —"*

"And that's why they found you meditating in the bushes without any underpants on?"

"There was a reason for that," Rose would say with a smile. *"I was resting on my way . . ."*

"On your way where?" Shanika would ask kindly.

"I don't know, but that's not the point. The point is, those red capsules you give me — and the orange juice — are what make me seem demented." A nice smile here.

"You drank your orange juice this morning," Shanika will note.

"Not all the orange juice, just some. Never mind the orange juice." Rose will be so patient. *"Here's the thing, since I've stopped taking the red capsules, my mind has gotten much clearer. I think I'm being intentionally drugged."*

"For how long?"

"Yesterday, of course. Before that . . ." There is no before that. Not yet.

"Is that why you hid in the bushes all night?"

"No. I must have . . . I must have needed something. So I . . ."

"Why didn't you just press the bell so we could come help you instead of running away in a backless hospital gown?"

"I don't know. Look." She'd show Shanika the track marks, the capsules in the bed stand.

"You're off your meds!" Shanika would say. *"Let me get my supervisor."*

Rose is shaking her head back and forth on the pillow.

"Are you okay, Ms. Dennis?" Shanika asks.

Rose nods. She comforts herself with the

47

knowledge that sanity is only a perspective agreed upon by social consensus. A handful of people thinking that when they die Hale–Bopp will beam them up is crazy. Ten million thinking Jesus will beam them up is the Rapture.

A short stretch of the Noble Eightfold Path opens before Rose:

Right View: Her mind works better when she does not take the red capsules.

Right Action: Don't swallow red capsules.

Focus on a plan.

Lunch is over. Rose is parked in the activities room. Four more red capsules have been added to her cache in the bed stand. With food, and without drugs, her body and mind are continuing to gain strength and acuity, but complex ideation is laborious. Trains of thought are difficult to keep between the rails. The difference between thinking and dreaming is not yet always crystal clear.

Mr. Buschbaum is working on his puzzle. Chuck and Rose have been given computer printouts of a lighthouse, and colored markers. The markers have a wide brush-like tip at one end and a fine pen point at the other. The colors are jewel tones: emerald, ruby, lapis, cobalt, tourmaline, amethyst. Rose is drawn into the play of light and color and space. Around her life fades. Vaguely she is aware of people talking.

"My, what a busy bee."

"That's pretty incredible."

"Mr. B, you've knocked it all apart."

"I heard she was this big-deal painter when she was younger."

"Cookies and juice?"

"That is too amazing. Are you sure you've given her all her meds?"

Light changes quality, grows dimmer, is replaced by the unlovely glare of an overhead.

"Got to clean this up, Ms. Dennis. Time for supper." A thick-fingered, slug-pale hand drops on Rose's.

Color, space, and light kaleidoscope, then shatter. Rose looks around, blinking like an owl. Chuck's lighthouse has three red stripes. A scribble of blue represents the sky.

The paper in front of Rose is covered with ink. A storm front looms up from a tangerine blaze that slashes a sea flecked with whitecaps. The lighthouse is limned by the glow from the drowning sun, the near side black in shadow. A salvation of yellow-white light cuts from the tower beacon to die in the bloated belly of the clouds.

Stunned, Rose stares at it. Since she was

six, she has had what her mother called "artistic trances," fugue-like states when she does her best work, when her mind slips free of language and opens to a clarity that is either integral to her DNA or channeled from a pure space, depending upon which teacher her mother asks.

Rose remembers that she is a big-deal painter.

Color and light and shadow are not the only things that have come together. As often happened in the past, while her conscious mind is absorbed by the composition of a painting, her subconscious mind works on other problems.

She now knows how she will escape.

CHAPTER 5

Rose opens the bedstand drawer, takes a tissue from the box, and spreads it flat on the rolling table. Six red capsules, a little over half her cache, are pinched out from their hiding place behind a box of latex gloves. Ears tuned to any sound of encroachment from the hall, she opens each capsule and pours the minuscule white spheres onto the tissue. That done, she herds the tiny balls into the crease, folds the tissue in half, then folds the edges closed on three sides. The empty capsules are flushed down the toilet. Hopefully, using the toilet all by herself is on the list of acceptable behaviors.

The tissue envelope is carefully placed in the pocket of her robe along with a pair of kindergarten scissors pilfered from the activities room. Putting on one slipper, she shuffles dead-eyed out to the common room. *Diddle, diddle, dumpling, my son John, one shoe off and one shoe on,* beats a refrain in the back of her mind. One shoe off and one shoe on; is she doing this to fool the nurse, or is this what crazy looks like?

Sitting on the couch beside the woman whose internal plumb bob is on the fritz, Rose stares alternately at the television and nothing. When thoughts arise, pleasant or unpleasant, she breathes them out, staying alert and in the moment. The plan depends on timing. At seven thirty the door opens. The diet-cola-loving night nurse comes in, takes her place behind the desk, and pulls the tab on her drink can. The day nurse goes home. The girl in pink stripes enters with snacks.

Eight P.M.

Karen leaves her cola to help the candy striper put the residents to bed. When both health workers are occupied in the rooms off the short hallway, Rose stands. Moving as quickly as she can, she rounds the desk to where the nurses sit. Gingerly she removes the tissue envelope from her pocket, unfolds one end, and pours almost a full day's dose of her drugs into the soda. Taken all at once, she hopes, they will make the night nurse drowsy enough, or inattentive enough, that Rose can get away. A few granules scatter over the top of the can. She blows them off, then scurries back to the couch.

The act has been witnessed by two people who neither notice nor will remember. Rose is short of breath and trembling, horrified by what she has done, what she risks, who she might be beneath the fog and the pretending. Is her mind really clearing, or is it merely that she thinks it is? Would a clear-minded individual poison a nurse? What if six capsules are enough to kill the woman? Tears well up and run down her face. She thinks about overturning the poisoned Pepsi.

She stays on the couch. If she is crazy, she consoles herself, it is appropriate to do a crazy thing. If she is not, they deserve what they get.

The idea of failing isn't as awful as it was when this escape plan first came to her. Now, both succeeding and failing are equally terrifying. In a day, or a week, will the thought of leaving become more frightening than staying, going madder and madder? More frightening than the thought — or the paranoid delusion — of being drugged, then killed by voices in the night?

The candy striper comes for the leaning woman. Like the Grim Reaper in scrubs, Karen resurrects one of the reclining-lounger corpses and escorts it away. Growing old is like an Agatha Christie play: And then there were five. And then there were four.

The girl in the striped dress stands in front of Rose. "Ready for bed?" she asks too loudly, smile too wide. Rose doesn't want Pink Stripes. The girl will go off duty when the last of the elders are tucked in bed. The candy striper is useless to Rose.

When the girl reaches to help her up, Rose bats her hands away. The child's face crumples as if she might cry. Rose hardens her heart. Hand in her pocket, clutching the purloined scissors, she waits for Karen, the cola-loving nurse.

The girl turns to the leaning lady. Ms. Tilted allows herself to be helped up and, zombie-like, is led away.

Karen arrives, towering over the sofa, blotting out the light. Rose's heart is pounding so hard, she is scared the nurse will hear it. Amped up as she is, Rose is amazed Karen doesn't feel the anxiety pulsing through her as she grasps Rose's upper arm and helps her to her feet.

Jittering with nerves, Rose has difficulty moving slowly, with the demeanor of a bovine mind. Not jumping out of her skin is hard. They turn from the hall into her room. Rose threads her thumb and forefinger through the handles of the scissors in her pocket.

Let the games begin, she thinks, then nearly giggles. This is insane.

Don't think about it.

Karen maneuvers Rose expertly until her back is to the bed. "All you got to do is bend your knees, sweetie, and you're there," she says.

Instead of sitting, Rose pitches forward, throwing her arms around Karen's neck as if for support. The scissors are tight in her right hand, blades aiming downward.

"Whoa!" the nurse mutters, stepping back a little. Rose holds the neck of Karen's scrubs with her left hand. Rose is shaking, time is playing tricks, the light seems to pulse and fade. The hand with the scissors wavers as she struggles for a good position from which to strike.

"I've got you," the nurse says. "You're okay." Hugging Rose with her meaty arms, she mashes Rose's face against her chest. Neatly, Karen waltzes her back to the edge of the bed.

The surgical grab-and-slice Rose had envisioned is in reality blind fumbling.

Karen lowers her until Rose's bottom is securely on the mattress. "There we go," the nurse says, laying Rose back on the bed. Desperately Rose releases her grip on the scrubs and clamps a hand on the nape of the nurse's neck, clinging like a monkey. Fingers not trapped in the handle of the scissors scrabble at the woman's flesh.

"What's gotten into you, Ms. Dennis? This is as bad as putting a three-year-old to bed." The nurse bends over, lowering Rose to the pillow.

Then Rose has it! The strap is hooked over her left thumb. Scissors in position, she cuts down. The nurse lets go of her. Rose falls the last three inches, arms crossed on her chest. Immediately she rolls onto her side and curls up in the fetal position, terrified by her crime — terrified that she's actually done it, and terrified that she'll be caught.

Silence.

Rose squeezes her eyes shut. A blanket and a heavy sigh settle over her shoulders.

"Sleep tight, Ms. Dennis. Don't let the bedbugs bite." Rubber-soled shoes squeak softly from the room.

The cola-loving nurse is going back to her poisoned beverage. Guilt pours ice-cold into Rose's pounding heart and slows it. Karen is so nice. *Where is Nurse Ratched when one wants her?*

It will be okay, Rose tells herself. If the pills

are antidepressants, they won't hurt Karen. If they are toxic, well, then the nurse has it coming.

"We all have it coming," Clint Eastwood says from some neglected corner of her cerebral cortex.

For a while, Rose remains in the fetal position waiting for the outcry.

None comes.

Eventually she dares to inspect her prize. The scissors are still in her right hand. In her left, held so tightly her fingers cramp, is the cola-loving nurse's keycard, ribbon ends trailing from the severed lanyard.

Rose hides it under the pillow. Lying back, she gazes at the ceiling, trying to calm herself. She has poisoned a soda pop, deceived a medical worker, committed physical assault and theft.

Her family is afraid she won't last long . . . absolutely terrified . . . won't last out the week.

That hardly sounds like a threat anymore. It sounds like a family member, worried that Grandmother's delusion has taken a severe turn for the worse, sharing her concerns with medical staff.

Negative thoughts equal negative emotions. Negative emotions equal suffering, Rose reminds herself and lets the thought go.

An hour passes. Nine o'clock; not nearly

57

late enough, but Rose can no longer stand the suspense. She maneuvers around the safety rail and out of bed. Padding to the door, she peeks out. Showing no visible signs of mental impairment, the nurse is at her desk studying her computer screen, the poisoned Pepsi near to hand.

Refusing to ponder what that means about pills, paranoia, or her chances of escape, Rose takes off the white cotton robe. The bedclothes straightened, she lays the robe out flat on the bed, the sleeves extended. She begins cutting. The scissors are made for four-year-olds, the blades dull, the tips blunt. They don't so much cut the fabric as chew it. Before she has one sleeve severed at the elbow, a blister forms at the base of her thumb.

Every few minutes, she stops, moves to the door, and listens to see if the muffled sound of scissors munching cloth has penetrated to the nurse's desk. She doesn't peek out again; should the nurse glance up and see one of her charges out of bed, it will warrant an immediate visit.

Both sleeves shortened, Rose drops into the room's one chair and rests. She longs to soak her hands in cool water but doesn't dare risk the sound of the tap.

Sleep effortlessly overtakes her. When she

wakes it takes several minutes to put herself, the place, and the plan back together. Outside it is still night. Rose hasn't been asleep too long. At length, she rallies and attacks the body of the robe with her pathetic instrument, cutting it off at what should be just above the waist.

Again she interrupts her task to listen at the door: snores, the muted tick of the wall clock, the air conditioner roaring on and dying off, nothing from the nurse.

On her umpteenth visit, Rose dares a quick look.

Still in front of the computer, the nurse rests her chin and cheek in her left hand, elbow braced on the desk, the plump cheek pushing up in a roll above the fingers.

Rose can't tell if she is resting, cogitating, or napping.

She goes back to work. Another blister forms on her index finger. The one at the base of her thumb is oozing blood. Each snip seems to do more damage to her than to the robe.

Around midnight, drenched in sweat and biting back whimpering noises, Rose finishes the final cut. As she is tiptoeing to the door to listen, she hears a loud thump. Rose peers around the jamb.

The cola-loving nurse has vanished. Her

chair is rolling away from the desk into the archway to the activities room. Rose wants to scream. After ruining her hands and becoming a criminal, something tipped the nurse off. She's bolted.

Without her keycard? That is hidden beneath the pillow on Rose's bed.

Stepping out into the hall, Rose takes a better look. Fingers. Four of them lie on their backs, looking like fat pink sausages against the vinyl. They are protruding from behind the desk.

The night nurse is down.

A rush of relief buoys Rose up. She wasn't mistaken. The pills are a drug, and a powerful one. The night nurse weighs close to twice what Rose does in her newfound scrawniness.

From the heights of relief, Rose plummets to the depths. The cola-loving nurse looks fairly dead.

"I've killed her," she whispers, and stumbles down the hall, her legs wobbly as a new colt's. The nurse is on her left side, one arm stretched out. Her legs tangle around each other. Her eyes are not quite shut; narrow crescents of white show above the red of the lower lids.

"No, no, no," Rose murmurs. She drops heavily to her knees. Snatching up the woman's outflung arm, she feels desperately for a pulse. Her own heart is beating so wildly, she can't tell if she feels the other woman's or not.

"I'm a murderer," she gasps. Her karma is going to suck for all eternity. "Please, can you hear me?" she whispers urgently into the ear below the dead eyes.

Rose will be buckled into a straightjacket, dragged from the Alzheimer's ward, shut in a hospital for the criminally insane, and chained to a radiator in a sooty cinder-block building with Mrs. Jeffrey Dahmer for a cellmate.

As gently as she can — the woman is a seriously large individual — Rose rolls the nurse onto her back. One of Karen's Crocs-shod feet bangs the metal desk as her legs uncross. Plugging one ear with her forefinger, Rose presses the other to the woman's chest. Fear renders her deaf for a second. It spikes, then begins to recede. She hears the steady thump of what, to her, sounds like a strong regular heartbeat.

But what does she know?

Nurse Karen might be dying.

Rose glances at the black desk phone with the line of buttons down one side. All she has to do is push one of those buttons and cry for help. In seconds someone will come.

In minutes the nurse will be on her way to a hospital to get her stomach pumped. Rose will still go to prison, but only for attempted murder.

She reaches for the phone. Her hands are shaking so badly, the handset knocks over the soda can. Brown liquid pours out like Texas crude to soak into papers stacked neatly by the mouse pad.

The night nurse has consumed about two-thirds of the drink and is out cold. Not even a full day's dose for a sixty-eight-year-old woman, weighing one hundred and ten pounds, has dropped a woman a quarter of a century younger, and nearly a hundred pounds heavier, as if she's been struck between the eyes with a sledgehammer.

Paranoia, my foot, Rose thinks. She pats the nurse's cheek softly. "Sleep tight. Don't let the bedbugs bite."

Rose trots back to her room. Free from the constraint of silence, she snips the edge of the bedspread, then, with a satisfying ripping sound, tears off a four-foot-long, eight-inch-wide strip. Her slippers are beneath the bed. Using blue and green markers, Rose scribbles the toes until they look more like colored flats than hospital shoes. Not great, but at a glance they will pass. The strip of flowered bedcover she wraps twice around her waist, then tucks the ends in, fashioning a colorful cummerbund over the nightie. The flower-and-vine motif picks up the blue-green of the slippers and the pink of the gown.

Once on, the mutilated bathrobe serves as a three-quarter-sleeve short jacket. Up close, if anyone really looks, it will be obvious there is something distinctly odd about the ensemble, but at least any passing kid on a bike won't pick her out for a lunatic escaped from the asylum.

Ideally, before the sun rises, like any self-respecting murdering night creature, she will be hidden away, safe from the light of day.

Rose studies her reflection in the mirror over the bathroom sink. There is no full-length mirror. Perhaps this is a kindness in an old folks' home. All the glass shows is her head and shoulders. Short, white, wavy hair in need of a cut; Rose runs water over her hands, then pokes and fluffs until it resembles a sane woman's hair. She's always had good hair. Her face is gaunt and pale, but her hazel eyes are clear.

"Tally ho," she says to her reflection. The woman in the mirror does not smile.

Pilfered keycard in hand, she leaves the room. The cola-loving nurse has not moved.

Passing the desk, Rose notices Karen's purse in a half-opened bottom drawer.

Rifling through another woman's purse is distasteful, but once one has drugged and stolen from her, perhaps it is inevitable. The wallet contains a credit card, a debit card, a driver's license, and seven dollars in cash. Rose dares not take the cards and would not stoop to stealing such a paltry sum of money. The wallet is returned to the bag.

Car keys with a tiny LED flashlight on the ring are in a side pocket. Rose takes the flashlight. Tissues, pens, notebook, comb, reading glasses, aspirin, lipstick: Rose takes the lipstick and uncaps it. The shade is pinker than she likes, but what the hell.

Using the wall mirror behind the desk, Rose puts a bit of the color on her cheeks, then carefully paints her lips. The woman in the mirror smiles. Amazing how a touch of lipstick can cheer a person up. She drops the recapped lipstick back into the purse and closes the drawer with a slippered foot.

On the far side of the desk, she straightens her makeshift dress, tugs her jacket straight, takes a deep breath, and flattens the key-card against the black plastic reader.

Her prison door hisses open.

CHAPTER 6

Rose steps over the threshold into a blank-walled hall that doglegs into another short hallway. This opens into the entrance foyer. The reception desk is unmanned, the double doors locked. Rose presses the cola nurse's keycard against a reader to the right of the doors. They silently slide apart.

Night air, warm and soft, sinks into her, a balm for a sore body and a troubled mind. Filling her lungs, she feels as if she drinks life, as if the conditioned air of the lock-down unit is merely oxygen to sustain the body. Fresh real air is sustenance for the spirit, filled with life-affirming qualities scientists will never discover in windowless laboratories.

For the first time in her mutilated memory, Rose feels completely alive, totally present. To her right a hedge of autumn leaves, psychedelic pink under the unearthly glow of a streetlamp, points the way. Dropping the nurse's keycard into the cacophony of color, she turns right. Walking quickly — but not suspiciously quickly — she heads toward the dark arch of trees where the sidewalk ends.

Mel said that she came down the greenway looking for Gigi; that their house opens onto the parkland, and it isn't far.

The darkness in the tunnel of trees is absolute. Path rough, Rose stumbles. Déjà vu. She stumbled in the same place on her last, doomed, escape attempt. Or is this the same attempt, a memory relived in a delusional brain?

Rose walks into the moonlight on the other side. *This is new,* she thinks. *Check out the stylish clothes.* A giggle escapes her lips. Given her questionable mental stability, chortling alone in the dark is not comforting.

The moon is still close to full. A good omen for a lunatic, Rose decides. In silence and silvery light, the gravel path leads away to the left and right.

If she has ever known what Mel's house looks like, she doesn't remember it. She was hoping she would see a familiar landmark, her memory would be jogged, and, abracadabra, she'd know where she was, and what to do next. No memory is jogged.

That isn't the only flaw in the ointment. Rose doesn't know from which direction Mel came. She doesn't even know which direction she herself went the last time she was on the lam, as it were.

She has a fifty-fifty chance of going the right direction. She goes right.

Anywhere a garden meets the greenway, Rose abandons the path, slogs through the grass, and stabs into midnight yards with Karen's tiny flashlight. Though it's small, and the radius of the beam pitiful, it is surprisingly powerful.

Homes up on low bluffs, or with no gate onto the greenway, she writes off. The worst are where the foliage is too dense to tell if there is a gate or not. Forcing herself through the underbrush, she keeps losing her slippers; her makeshift wardrobe catches and rips; scratchy dark and patchy light play tricks on her. Trees loom, menacing. Confusion spins her around until she is dizzy, then spits her out to wonder again whether to turn right or left.

After a time thirst becomes a factor, and she forgets if this is then or now. If this is now, wouldn't she have remembered to bring water after what happened then?

The moment is the moment, she tells herself, and trudges on.

The houses beyond the trees grow smaller and shabbier.

No bells ring. No lightbulbs come on. Though she can't remember Mel's house, she is sure that it is big and nice.

Right was wrong. Refusing to cry, she sits down on a fallen log and looks back the way she has come. The path dwindles away to infinity, then is snuffed out by the night.

Her head swims.

Her legs shake.

Her feet hurt.

Is this what old feels like? Fatigue, confusion, and pain? Rose doesn't remember feeling old. Though her memory is blasted, she is positive this rickety old carriage is not her body, not the one she'd had. This one has not been kept up, the oil not changed, the tires not checked. This one is a wreck.

Sitting on the log, everything aches. Bone grinds against bone. Flecks of black vie with leaf shadows in her peripheral vision. Should a four-week-old kitten pop out of the underbrush and pounce on her, she'd be dead meat.

Stoically, she retraces her steps. By the time Rose makes it back to the tunnel of trees leading to the sidewalk, she is drenched in sweat. Her legs are so rubbery that twice she has gone down on one knee simply because it buckled under her. Dizziness plagues her. If she doesn't concentrate, she walks like a drunken woman.

She stops at the arch of trees and looks toward the sidewalk.

Go back, a voice she scarcely recognizes as her own murmurs in her ear. An old woman, in a costume made of her nightie, bathrobe, and bedspread, wandering around in the dead of night, looking for a sign because she believes "they" are coming for her. An old woman dies of dehydration, her emaciated body found half-chewed by raccoons.

Bon appétit, Rocky, Rose thinks, and follows the path not taken, lifting one foot, then setting it down and lifting the other. She keeps on doing that. The moon sets behind the trees. Grasses turn dark. Shrubs hunch like bears, in the corners of her eyes. The needle-beam of her light scratches lines of green in the bushes.

Cyclone fence. Picket fence. Rail fence. Nothing shakes loose in Rose's memory. Tears are dripping off her jaw. Pitiful whimpering cries that have been irritating her for a while are coming from her own throat. She is lost to everything and everyone. Lost to herself. Deep shadows beckon, enticing her to crawl beneath the bushes and die in peace like a worn-out old cat.

A faint wisp of path, leading through the grass to her left, then disappearing into a stand of laurels, calls her name. Leaves are rose-gray in the moonlight and smell of the last breath of summer. She follows the trail through bushes edged with the strange luminescence of a city night.

The path ends at a pint-sized door with a round top and a tiny brass grate for peeking through.

Memories download into Rose's skull with all the nuance of a dump truck pouring rocks into a hole. Not collated, alphabetized, or arranged by date, a heap of images, sounds, and emotions hits so hard, she sits down with a bone-jarring thud.

When the dust settles in her psyche, she is still looking at the gate, which seems transfixed in time by the beam of her light. Rose remembers.

It is summer, hot and humid. Mel is a long-legged little girl of seven. Harley, Rose's husband, white hair glued to his forehead under a battered straw hat, draws a claw hammer from the leather tool belt around his waist. Mel, practically dancing with excitement, smiles and holds out sixpenny nails for her granddad, her palms up as if making an offering to a god.

Izzy, Mel's mom, and Rose sit on a blanket in the shade laughing. It's a hobbit gate, Izzy tells Mel. "Like in *Lord of the Rings.* When you go through it, I'll bet you'll be in Middle-earth."

"That's silly," Mel says, her maturity offended. Then she turns to Rose. "Isn't it, Gigi?"

"Stranger things have happened," Rose says with a wink at Izzy, her step-daughter-in-law.

"Daddy?" Mel calls on the ultimate source of what is real and what is not. Flynn, Harley's elder son and Rose's stepson, is several yards away talking on his cell phone. "Whatever your mom says, punkin'."

"This is so you can look out and see who's there," Harley says, fitting a mesh he's made of copper strips into a rectangle cut in the wood at Bilbo Baggins's eye level. "That way nobody can come in that you don't want to. See. You just slide this little door open."

Mel slides the minute copper door aside and peeks out through the little mesh window.

"Do you see Gandalf?" Izzy calls.

Rose neither moves nor breathes for fear

the door will vanish. A moment passes, and another. The door does not disappear into Middle-earth. She stands, curls her fingers around the handle. It is real, cool against her palm. She presses the thumb lever down. A prosaic click of metal on metal lets her know the latch lifted. Mel must have forgotten to lock it. Probably she'd ridden home from the facility with someone. What with Gigi slapping orange juice all over orderlies, and screaming about poison plots, latching the back gate must have slipped her mind.

Rose's debilitating fatigue abates slightly. The pain in hands, legs, and feet no longer matters. Hope is better than opioids. She opens the gate, ducks through, closes it, and locks it behind her. Leaning against the wood, she feels momentarily safe.

She has escaped; she has reached Mel's backyard. Like a dog chasing cars, now that she has secured her goal, she doesn't know what to do with it. Flynn, Mel's father, must have been the one who put her in the facility. Her stepson has not visited her that she is aware of. He has not come to free her. The idea of putting her life in anyone else's hands is frightening. Rose decides not to expose herself, not yet.

The roof of the house is visible beyond

the gentle rise in the yard. Mel's room is upstairs. Rose tries to summon the energy to circumnavigate the house and toss pebbles at her window. As if tiny rocks striking glass will wake a thirteen-year-old who sleeps through tornado sirens and garbage trucks plying their trade.

Carrying her slippers — both worn to wads of abused felt — Rose crosses the backyard. Grass is cool and healing under her feet. As she crests the low hillock she sees a brick platform. In its center is a giant green egg, the size of a dinosaur egg, made of glistening ceramic, the grill, Flynn's prized barbecue.

Wind gusts through her cranium. Memories flutter up like dead leaves caught in a dust devil. Steaks and corn, Mel toddling, her mother laughing, a long-necked bottle of beer in her slender hand.

Crawfish. Flynn and his dad, Harley, watching the green egg as if it might hatch. Beyond them, on the lawn, Rose and Nancy — Mel's paternal grandmother and Harley's ex-wife, the woman who had come to the Memory Care Unit with Stella — playing croquet against Izzy and Mel.

Oysters, Flynn in a heavy coat and Santa hat. Harley and his ex, Nancy, helping Mel with her first real bicycle. Rose and Izzy fleeing into the house out of the cold.

Hot dogs and beans, Harley at the grill, Flynn leaning against the garage, a hand over his eyes. Rose in the playhouse holding Mel while she cries. Izzy three months in the ground, dead of breast cancer.

When Rose's eyes clear, she is standing by a playhouse, built to half scale when Mel was six. Her hand rests on the frame above the side window. To her surprise, the lights are on in the kitchen and living room of the main house, spilling white squares onto the concrete of the drive.

Sidestepping into the heavy darkness, where the garage shadow overlaps the playhouse shadow, Rose forces herself to focus. She escaped the facility after midnight. Fatigue suggests she wandered the greenway for eight or ten hours, but it was probably closer to two. Too late for the family to be up; too early for anyone to be going to work.

"You don't care!" a woman screams. "You have everything you want!" The shattering sound of glass breaking against a hard surface sharpens the words. The porch door slams open with such force, Rose flinches. From within, a humpbacked creature, with

74

an oddly shaped head the size of a garbage can lid, is vomited out.

It shoots across the patio, running straight at Rose.

CHAPTER 7

Paralyzed with fright, Rose squeezes her eyes shut and shrinks deeper into shadow, her shoulder pressing against the playhouse wall, her head tucked beneath the low eave.

Bang!

The wall shudders.

Bang!

The eave thrums against her skull.

The ungainly monster slams the playhouse door open, barges inside, and slams the door shut. Rose blinks, trying to recover a few of her wits. Night's quiet reknits around her. No more shouts or smashings come from the main house.

Silent on bare feet, she slips around the corner of the half-pint house and stands on the faded welcome mat. The door is four feet high, the small window at the level of her chest. Faded curtains, ragged at the hems, are looped back with rotting ribbon. Rustling, like a mouse burrowing in silk, can be heard through the door. With one knuckle Rose raps shave-and-a-haircut gently on the wood.

"Go away!" is shouted from within.

Rose turns the knob and eases the door open an inch or so.

"I said go away! Leave me alone!" Something soft fluffs into the door and falls.

"Grasshopper, it's me, Gigi," Rose says softly.

There is no answer. Rose opens the door. "Cease fire," she whispers. Stooping, she steps through, closes the door, and kneels. The ceiling is only five feet high, the entire house seven feet square. "Is the lady of the manor accepting callers today?" Rose asks, as she'd been instructed when Melanie was seven.

"Gigi?" An incredulous whisper emanates from a dark nest of girl, pillows, and blankets — undoubtedly the mass that formed the monster's head when Mel ran from the house.

"It is indeed Gigi," Rose says.

"Did you wander off again?" Melanie asks cautiously. "I'd better go get Uncle Daniel."

Uncle Daniel: Rose recalls Daniel is Harley's younger son, her other stepson.

The amorphous shape evolves into a girl sitting up, her legs crossed beneath her.

Adrenaline abandoning her, Rose's exhaustion hits in a rising tide. She leans back against the door, crossing her legs as Mel does. Rose has used this playhouse many times. Melanie ceded it to her as a meditation retreat when she visited. As a child, Mel was delighted with the cushions, the incense — which Rose hardly ever burned at home — and the candle. For safety's sake, the candle was only allowed when Rose was present. Often Melanie meditated with her, though seldom for more than a few minutes.

"This is heaven," Rose says, and sighs deeply.

"No," Melanie says carefully. "This is a playhouse. Let me get Uncle Daniel. Dad's out of town."

"May I tell you a story first?" Rose asks.

"I guess," Mel replies dubiously.

Rose planned the transformation of bed clothes to street clothes, the poisoning of the night nurse, the theft of the keycard, the escape, and the search for Mel's house. In all that time she never planned what she would say when she got there.

"Gigi," Mel prods hesitantly.

"It's a long story," Rose says. "Why are you hiding out in the playhouse?"

"Uncle Daniel and Stella are fighting."

Uncle Daniel and Stella — Rose remembers that after Izzy died, Daniel, chronically underemployed, would stay at the house with Mel when Flynn was managing trade shows in other cities. No warm fuzzy memories soften the few mental snapshots she has of Stella.

Not like those she has of Izzy. Izzy died. Rose had remembered that Isabelle — Izzy — was dead, but that memory was as a headline, news, no personal connection.

This remembering is visceral, a soundtrack of laughter and weeping over a flash flood of images: a lovely woman tickling a baby, choosing little dresses, leaving for work in green scrubs, blond hair in a ponytail. Then chemo and hair loss; Izzy making a game of buying and wearing wigs to help her daughter cope. Izzy being relentlessly cheerful and upbeat. Too many images to see; Rose feels them like a bloom of butterflies. Even dead, Izzy is love. Tears run down Rose's face. She is glad the playhouse is dark.

"Like there was ever a time they were not fighting," Mel continues. "But this one was *World War Z* meets *The Battle of the Titans.* Stella comes here when she gets a mad on, and I have to listen to it. You'd think by now she'd be finished ranting. Remind me never to get married."

"Daniel is married to Stella," Rose says. Stella is Rose's other stepdaughter-in-law. Another scrap of the past falling into place.

"They split up almost a year ago. Don't you remember?" Mel asks too gently.

Don't you remember? The three scariest words in the English language. Rose doesn't. "I'm remembering a lot of things," she says defensively. "Not everything, but a lot."

By the faint light from the windows, Rose sees her granddaughter tilt her head back, graceful as a lily, her face toward the low ceiling. "Well, it's old news. Or should be. Uncle Daniel left her the house. It's a rental, but she got it, and all the stuff in it, but she keeps turning up here. She wants more money. I think she's taken some of Mom's things. Little things, clothes, makeup, like that, but still . . . ," Melanie says.

Fury at Stella flushes through Rose, waking her up. It is followed by annoyance at Flynn. Nearly two years. It was time he put away his dead wife's things.

"Stella says she comes when Dad is gone because Uncle Daniel is too lazy, stupid, mean — you pick the adjective; she's used them all — to look after me. Like Stella cares for me!"

"I care for you" is all Rose can think to say.

"I know," Melanie sighs.

"I'd hide in the playhouse, too," Rose says.

"You are hiding in the playhouse." The caution is back in Mel's voice. "Gigi, are they looking for you? If you're still sick, they'll have to take you back with them."

Fear flutters in Rose's belly, but it is too tired to take flight.

"If you get me a drink of water, and promise not to rat me out yet, I will confess all," Rose says.

Mel scrabbles in the bedding, then crawls across the floor to put a water bottle into Rose's outstretched fingers. Rose is so excited, her hands are shaking. "Open it for me?"

Melanie does. Rose tips the bottle back and drinks until it is empty. "Nectar of the gods," she says with a sigh.

"Boy, you were thirsty!" Melanie says. "Want me to get you another? It won't get you out of confessing," she warns.

"No. I'm good for now, but thanks. First, can I ask you a question?"

"Ask." There is a scratching sound, then a flare as Melanie lights the candle on the miniature table beneath the window.

Rose fills her eyes with the tousled perfection of the girl. Mel is at the very end of childhood. In weeks, maybe days, she will be gone into the labyrinth leading to adulthood.

"Ask," the girl repeats.

"What's today's date?"

"October eighteenth," Melanie says.

"How long have I been in . . ." Rose doesn't want to say the words "old folks' home" or "Alzheimer's ward." ". . . the facility?"

"Actually inside Longwood?"

"Yes."

"Not that long. A month or so," Mel says.

"A month! Four weeks?" Rose gasps. "You've got to be kidding! Let me get this straight. One day I am perfectly sane, then, a month later, I'm in a lockdown ward? Didn't anybody think that was a wee bit odd?" Anger, fresh and full of energy, wells up where, for such a long time, there has been only confusion and fatigue. Pure energy. Power. Rose welcomes it.

"You'd had a shock with Granddad's death," Melanie explains.

Shock with Granddad's death. Granddad, Harley, Rose's husband, dead.

Rose remembers.

At the Hobbit gate, she'd recalled the name,

Harley, and seen a handsome white-haired man in a tool belt. Now she feels Harley, his arms strong around her. She watches the look of joy on his face as she walks up the steps in the backyard where he waits with Father Jenkins, Flynn beside him as best man. Harley hanging a swing for a toddling Mel, building a playhouse, sitting with Flynn as he drinks vodka and cries.

Then she is in the new house in Charlotte, surrounded by boxes. Flynn and Melanie come to the door. Drying her hands on a dish towel, she opens it. The moment she sees their faces, she knows.

"Do you want to sit down?" Flynn asks.

"No. Tell me."

"It's Dad," Flynn says.

Rose stops breathing.

Sitting in the candlelight of the playhouse her husband built for their granddaughter, Rose waits for grief to come and take her, as it took her when the memory of Izzy's death returned. It doesn't. There are no memories after Flynn told her the news. Harley's death is neither real nor unreal. Along with the rest of her, it is fogged with drugs. Rose has been robbed of her grief, left a widow without sorrow, only a feeling that when the other shoe drops . . .

Rose needs her anger back. She fans it. "How could anybody think that it was normal that a completely sane human being would go totally nutso-fruitso in four weeks!"

Melanie moves her gaze from Rose to the small window above the table where the reflection of the candle's flame dances.

"What?" Rose demands.

"You know, Gigi, it's not like you were really completely normal," Melanie says miserably. "You've always been, well, you know, kind of eccentric."

"I am not in the least eccentric," Rose declares. The tide of anger, though generic, is still buoying her up. "Eccentric. What a crock."

"You meditate," Melanie says defensively.

"Oh for heaven's sake!" Rose explodes. "Everybody meditates. Meditation is the new Prozac."

"You're always standing on your head everywhere," Melanie continues doggedly.

"That's yoga! Yoga is not eccentric. Yoga is so mainstream, studios have Mommy and Me classes."

"You're a painter and a poet."

"A lucrative painter. Very lucrative," Rose says holding up a finger. "And a *published* poet, thankyouverymuch. That is not eccentric, that's downright miraculous." Rose is listening to her own voice as if it were that of the Oracle at Delphi. The words are true, a verbal form of automatic writing. They bespeak her own memories, the "facts" that make up her "self." She is coalescing out of the fog, taking on form.

"Stella said you smoke marijuana," Mel says.

Rose throws up her hands. They smack into the ceiling. "It's medicinal!" she shouts. Her own noise scares her. She squirms around until she can look out of the window. Her racket has not alarmed the main house; the porch light does not go on. The screen door is not thrown open.

"You wear African pants with the crotch at your knees and carry a parasol with purple sequins on it," Mel rushes on.

"Nobody in New Orleans thinks I'm eccentric," Rose counters.

Melanie rolls her eyes. "I wouldn't use that defense in Crazy Court."

Crazy Court.

Rose thinks about that. A few hardy crickets sing. Candlelight flickers. The incomparable peace of familiarity and love settles into the playhouse. Rose's eyes grow heavy. Almost, she can believe that Harley is alive, and she has never been lost, con-

85

fused, and incarcerated.

"I'm from New Orleans," she says. She is from New Orleans.

"Were. You and Granddad moved here a couple months ago. For me. And Dad and Uncle Daniel. Now you live here." To Rose, this is not good news. To spare Mel's feelings, she keeps that thought to herself.

"You're a Buddhist, but you smoke and drink and eat meat," Melanie adds.

"I guess I'm not a good Buddhist." Rose thinks about that for a moment. A Buddhist. Things that didn't make sense before don't make sense now, but she accepts that. She slumps against the wall. For a while neither she nor Mel speaks. Both gaze silently into the candle flame.

"I smoke?" Rose bursts out.

"Not very much," Mel says quickly. "Four cigarettes a day."

"That's right!" Rose says ecstatically. "I smoke! I remember that now."

"Camel nonfilters," Melanie says.

"Aha. I am a purist."

Melanie puts her palms together, thumbs to chest. Solemnly, Rose does the same.

Bowing, Melanie intones, "Anything worth doing . . ."

Without thought, Rose finishes, ". . . is worth overdoing," and bows back.

86

"You are so wise, Gigi Rinpoche," Melanie says.

"It is so, Grasshopper," Rose says. Both laugh, and in that moment Rose believes that all the stars in the firmament do not twinkle as beautifully as those in her granddaughter's eyes.

"I think you should forget that you smoke," Melanie says.

"Nope!" Rose replies. "I love smoking. Now that I have firsthand experience of living in a nursing home I may up my intake to four packs a day. Better my odds of dying before the proverbial hits the fan. At least free, I can choose my own drugs, and they won't be mind-numbing. I can't go back."

"It's okay, Gigi."

"They were giving me something to make me seem demented."

Leaning her chin on her hands, Melanie puffs out a long breath, making the candle flame dance erratically.

"What?" Rose asks again.

"You won't like it," Mel warns, shaking her head.

"Best get it over with," Rose says. After the adventures of the last few days, she doesn't think she can be more shaken than she is already.

Of course, she is wrong.

"It wasn't just eccentricity — we're all used to that. You started acting, you know, like, demented, long before Dad got you a place in Longwood," Melanie says apologetically.

Rose feels as if she's been trampled by gnus, not only because her theory of drug-induced insanity is smashed to smithereens, but also because it is so painfully obvious. Of course she was demented before she was put in the home. Had she not been, she would never have allowed it to happen. She would have hired a lawyer, called the police, flown back to New Orleans: all the things a sane person would do when faced with unwarranted influence in her life.

Tears fill her throat. Terror freezes them. The lump is so big, it is painful when Rose swallows it. Had she been alone she would have wept or raged, torn her hair and rent her clothing. Because of Melanie, she wraps herself in a forced calm. Whatever has happened, however she's been brought to the brink, it is over, she tells herself.

"Now it's your turn to tell me what's going on," Rose says. "What led up to my — to your dad putting me in Longwood's MCU."

With the innate flexibility of youth, Melanie curls down over her folded legs, her forehead touching the floor. From this pod-like posture, she begins her tale, her voice so low, Rose has to concentrate to hear the words. "After Granddad was killed, you started acting kind of odd — I mean, we were all shocky and miserable, but it was like it went way deeper with you, changed you. No big surprise, but you got weirder and weirder."

"Granddad was killed?" Part of Rose's brain knows her husband is dead. Part of her brain does not. "As in murdered?"

"You don't remember?"

Rose can only shake her head.

"Do you want me to tell you? You totally refused to talk about it back then. You would practically run out of the room when people asked."

Rose doesn't know if she wants to remember or not, so she just shakes her head again.

Mel looks up, a pale oval in the supple crumple she's made of her body. "You told Grandma Nancy you were having trouble sleeping, that you'd wake up drenched in sweat. Your legs would kick out sometimes like you were spastic. A couple times you said you saw people walk by in the hall when there weren't any people there.

"Then you just stopped calling or coming

over. You didn't answer your phone or your doorbell."

"I don't remember any of that," Rose admits.

"Then you tanked. The cops called. They'd got Dad's cell number from your phone. They'd found you in your car, just sitting stopped in the middle of an intersection, traffic honking and whizzing all around. You didn't know where you were."

Rose bites back a sob. She sits at the edge of a midnight sea; the receding wave drags sand from beneath her.

"You quit talking. You just stared. It was totally creepy. That's when Dad and the doctors decided you should be put someplace they could take care of you. He wouldn't have done it if he didn't have to. We wanted you here, but I'm a kid, and Uncle Daniel isn't all that grown up, and running trade shows keeps Dad on the road a lot."

It warms Rose that they had wanted her.

"Longwood was close, and Dad knew about it from an advertisement they sent out. He checked it out, and that was that." Melanie returns to an upright position. Her eyes leave Rose's face after a moment and return to studying the candle flame.

That was that, Rose thinks. She'd been acting oddly, she was found confused in an intersection, did not speak, and was totally creepy.

"Should I go get Uncle Daniel?" Mel asks.

Rose does not want to put her fate in the hands of Uncle Daniel. Rose has been declared, and proved, incapable of taking care of herself. Should she be delivered back into the hands of the authorities, she will lose the fragile autonomy she's fought so hard to win.

The fact that she was cognitively impaired prior to being put in Longwood doesn't change the fact that the drugs they'd fed her felled the large cola-loving nurse.

Rose clings to that.

"Grasshopper," she says wearily, "this isn't fair to you, I know that, and if it is too hard, don't do it — I'll understand — but I'd like some time to get myself together while I can still find the pieces. Could this be our secret, at least for a day or two?"

Melanie thinks for a moment before answering. Rose loves that she considers her words before speaking.

"Would you stay in the playhouse?" Mel asks dubiously.

"Your granddad and I have a house, don't we?"

"You don't remember?" Worry tucks down

91

the corners of Melanie's mouth.

Into Rose's mind comes a snapshot: Harley, the moving van, and Flynn in front of a white house. "I do," she says firmly. "It's whitepainted brick with a dogwood in the yard. I just don't recall the address."

"I guess I could call Uber and they'd take you to your house."

Melanie, Rose recalls, has been Ubering on her own since she was eleven.

"Would you do that?" Rose asks.

"Probably we should wait until morning," Mel says.

"How about the secret part?" Rose asks. "Are you okay with that? The Longwood people, and maybe even the police, will be looking for me as soon as they realize I'm gone. You might have to lie."

"Oh, I won't mind lying to the police," Mel says.

Rose groans. She is such a horrible grandmother.

"I probably won't have to," Melanie says kindly. "I just won't be available. Nobody much cares what a thirteen-year-old thinks anyway. Ageism, hello!"

"Tell me about it." Rose sighs. "Thank you."

"You'll owe me big-time," Melanie says, and grins impishly.

"You know I love you madly," Rose tells her.

"Everybody does," Melanie replies, with a toss of her head any diva would envy.

CHAPTER 8

An hour before dawn, Melanie goes back to the big house to finish her night on the living room sofa. When Daniel gets up, he'll be sure to see her and not go looking for her in the playhouse.

Rose more passes out than falls asleep.

When she wakes, groggy and disoriented, sunlight is streaming through the child-sized windows, making bright streaks on the cushions and blankets. In daylight Rose notices the walls are a riot of flowers, monkeys, birds, and foliage.

Images of her tracing the shapes, helping Mel to paint the colors in, the both of them splotched with paint, both intent on their work, return to her. Good memories. Mel was ten, Rose sixty-five; Izzy and Harley alive.

The foggy oblivion of drugs — or something — continues to obscure the time between Harley's death and waking up on the greenway in a hospital gown. Now she is in a playhouse, in a mangled pink nightie. This is what progress looks like, she decides, and begins neatly folding the blankets and stacking them in a corner.

"Gigi, it's me." Mel ducks in through the little door, her arms full. "Breakfast," she says, and drops a package of iced cinnamon rolls and a bottle of water on the folded blankets.

While Rose eats — ravenously, as it happens — Mel talks. "Uncle Dan's gone to work. He's assistant manager at a Starbucks at the moment. Stella's gone. I don't care where, as long as she stays there."

Stella, if Rose remembers correctly, does favors for rich friends. In recompense they give her "gifts." The favors cover everything from picking up dry cleaning to driving drunken clowns home from botched children's parties.

"I got you these." Melanie unwads a pair of tattered jeans and an equally disreputable T-shirt and drapes them on the pillows. "They should fit okay, though I think I outgrew you this year."

"I shrank," Rose manages around a hunk of sugary dough.

"Flip-flops and, absolutely necessary when traveling incognito, a ball cap."

"Go Panthers," Rose says.

"This way, if any of the neighbors see you leaving, they'll think you're nobody, one of my friends."

"I'm impressed. You really thought things through. You have the makings of a fine criminal mind," Rose says.

"Crime doesn't pay," Melanie says unctuously.

"Not as well as it used to," Rose agrees.

Rose licks her fingers clean. Pinching up the ball cap by its brim, she dumps out the contents. "Underpants!" she exclaims in delight. "You wonderful child. I cannot tell you how much I have been craving a pair of good old cotton underpants."

"And just when I was beginning to think you weren't demented," Mel says. "They're — they were — Mom's."

"I am deeply honored," Rose says sincerely and, still chewing, wriggles into the panties.

"Mom's bras would be too big for you," Mel adds.

"Not to worry. I've haven't worn one of the wretched things since I burned mine in 1969."

"Did women really burn their bras?" Mel asks.

"Yup."

"I thought it was an urban legend, like

Freddy and Elm Street," Mel says.

The jeans are a little loose in the seat, but otherwise they fit. The T-shirt is a T-shirt. Dressed, Rose is amazed at how much more substantial she feels, almost capable, almost brave.

"The fashion cure," she says as she pulls on the ball cap.

"Whatever." Mel taps thumbs against the face of her cell phone. "Car in four minutes," she says, looking out the little window. "I think you should go now. You never know how long Stella's going to be gone. Mostly it's like days or weeks, but I think she pops back unexpectedly, hoping to catch me and Uncle Daniel out, so she can snoop. I'm pretty sure she copied Uncle Daniel's house key."

"I'm packed," Rose says.

"I'll come by your house later and bring you food and stuff for a couple days," Mel promises.

"Don't you have school?" Rose asks as she follows Mel out the stunted door.

"It's Sunday."

"I knew that."

In six minutes Rose is in the passenger seat of a black late-model SUV headed to 87 Applegarth Street. Mel had the address in the contacts list on her phone. To save face, Rose acted like it was familiar. It wasn't. Applegarth rang not even one tiny bell.

Rose intends to really pay attention, to learn the way from Melanie's house to hers, to remember street names and landmarks. Soon she gives up and stares out the window at an endless upscale sameness of bedroom community stitched together by trees, lawns, and spent azaleas. *The city of Charlotte must have an ordinance requiring homeowners to plant twenty percent of their land in azaleas,* Rose thinks.

"Here we go," says the driver, a nice-looking man named Andre. Andre stays silent for the fifteen-minute drive, so Rose is rather fond of him. The car turns off Laurel Street onto Applegarth. A block and a half down, on the right, is a lot twice as deep as its neighbors. Rose remembers they chose it for the illusion of seclusion. At the end of a gravel drive is a small two-story house, faintly Victorian in the sharpness of its roof and the wraparound porch.

Halfway up the long drive a police car is parked on the gravel. An officer stands talking to two women.

The scene is so like that of the orange juice fiasco that Rose's mental gears grind to a halt. Is this now or is this then? A flashback? Creaking, the gears again start to turn. Of course Longwood is searching for her. Of course they enlisted the police to bring her back. Of course they know where she lives. Of course. That's their job. Rose is a fool not to have thought of this. She toys with the idea of turning herself in, throwing her sanity on the mercy of the medical court. Not yet, she decides. Once in the machine, she will be helpless. She needs time to figure things out.

"Quite a welcoming committee," says Andre.

The driver sees them, too. Rose relaxes. Not a flashback, just history repeating itself. The tall woman is Nancy, Harley's ex. The other woman — of medium height, stocky but not fat, maybe Hispanic — is Wanda, the manager of the Memory Care Unit. Today she wears a teal power suit and matching heels. Longwood is a full-service facility.

"Stop here!" Rose demands.

Andre stops the SUV.

"You want to avoid the cops?" He sounds as if that is the most rational choice a person can make.

"Please," Rose whispers.

"I could just drive by, you know, take you somewhere else," Andre offers.

Rose considers it, then shakes her head. "We've stopped. If we go again it might . . ." She runs out of words.

"Look hinky," Andre finishes for her. "When you get out, wave a big goodbye to me. Don't stand around like you're lost. Look like you know where you're going, and have got a right to be there," he advises.

"Thank you," Rose says. "I can't tip you. I don't have any money."

"Not a problem. You have a good day," Andre says.

Rose tugs the ball cap down more firmly and climbs out of the passenger door. Smiling, she waves a cheery farewell to Andre, then walks purposefully toward the nearest house, an enormous newly built home with a wide half circle of concrete drive. Crossing it, Rose feels as conspicuous as a cockroach on a wedding cake.

Three shallow steps lead up to a landing the size of a handball court. There is a green-painted door with a brass knocker in the shape of a hand. Hoping nobody is home, Rose pretends to be digging her house key out of her pants pocket. She peeks down the drive of 87 Applegarth. No one is looking her way.

Careful not to make a sound, she scuttles off the front stoop, around the corner, and out of sight. Butterfly bushes, rich with purple plumes, edge the house. Rose forces herself deep into their embrace, tucks her knees under her chin, and tips her head down so the ball cap covers her face.

Mentally, she reviews her performance at the door. Nonchalant? Yes. Looking like she belongs? Ditto. Digging for a key . . . She hasn't got a key. Rose clenches her jaw. Mel forgot to give her a key to 87 Applegarth, and Rose forgot to ask. What an idiot! *Me, not Mel,* Rose thinks loyally. A problem for later, she tells herself. Evil sufficient unto the day and all that.

Five minutes, maybe ten, tick by on clocks all over the world while hours plod by in Rose's mind. The heat of a southern morning, against a sun-drenched wall, sucks moisture from her body. Rivulets of sweat tickle like insects on her back. Or maybe there are insects on her back.

Finally, a car door slams. A police car passes her hideout. A second car door whumps shut, no engine sound, no car passing. Like a snake made of concrete segments, Rose uncoils and squirms from under the bushes. Lifting just her head and shoulders, she peers over the flat expanse of steps. Nancy is in her white Toyota. Through the open car window, the manager of Longwood's Memory Care Unit is speaking to her earnestly. About what, Rose can't hear. Her, she guesses.

Nancy drives away, turning left where the cop car turned right. Wanda gets into a silver Corvette convertible and sedately follows the white sedan. *Probably an automatic,* Rose thinks with disdain.

No people are out mowing, or walking dogs or baby carriages. No curtains flutter. Hoping the street is as deserted as it looks, and no good citizen will dial 911 to report a disreputable individual, speckled with twigs and dirt, hanging around the fancy houses, Rose finds her feet and slinks up the drive of 87 Applegarth.

Within minutes she is behind the white-painted brick house, safe from prying eyes. The backyard is overgrown, a path worn through the grass to a single-car garage of the same brick as the house. Lacking the picturesque appeal of the front, the rear of the residence is flat with two glass sliding doors opening onto a bare wooden platform, a "patio" in Realtor-speak. Behind the glass is a great room. To the left are the dining area, a granite lunch counter, and a large kitchen. To the right is the living area, complete with a standard-issue fireplace with fake logs and a knob to turn on the gas. A couch and a big-screen TV are the only things unpacked.

Crates and boxes fill the dining area and encroach into the kitchen. No pictures grace the walls; no plants soften the line of the mantel. Rose and Harley haven't lived here long enough to settle in. They haven't lived here long enough to attend to such niceties as a hidden key for when one locks oneself out.

The upside is, they have not lived here long enough to get an alarm system installed.

Rose noses around the scraggly yard. Hatred boils up inside her. She hates the house and the city. She hates Longwood and pink nightgowns. She hates Harley for dumping her in an alien suburb, then waltzing off to celebrate his eightieth birthday and never coming back. She hates that she'll never see him again, that his remains — or what remained of his remains — were cremated and mailed to her in a box with a plain brown paper wrapper. She hates that she cannot feel the loss of him, cannot measure the hole that yawns in her heart waiting for her to tumble in.

Under a leggy azalea bush, she finds a broken brick. It will serve.

Brick in hand, she stalks back to the side

of the house. Over the kitchen sink is a paned window. Viciously, she hurls the brick through the glass. Vandalism — even on property she owns — feels good. She finds another piece of brick and, none too gently, smashes out the shards of glass embedded in the window frame. Were she not a mere shadow of herself, she would rip the frame from the brick.

Using fury to a practical end, Rose scrambles through the window over the sink, then drags her feet and legs inside. Sitting on the counter, she draws a shaky breath. Running from cops and breaking and entering take it out of a person. She sits and breathes until she is fairly sure that when she slides off the counter, she won't fall in a heap on the tile floor.

And break a hip.

Isn't that how this scene plays out?

Negative thoughts, she admonishes herself.

Though quivering like an electric wire in a gale, she manages to stand. Her body wants to rest, but her mind is restless. Wandering into the dining area, then the living room, she touches boxes, leaving finger marks in the accumulated dust. A few half-formed memories surface of the day they moved in: Harley lifting crates, the weight of which made her cringe. Flynn panicking when she climbed up onto the roof to clean out the gutters. Melanie coming over after school. Nancy bringing her son and ex-husband sandwiches.

Mostly Rose remembers that queasy feeling you get when you realize you've made a huge mistake. She remembers wondering if Harley would be too upset if she called their New Orleans Realtor and asked her to take their house off the market.

Has it sold yet?

Probably.

Using the rail more than she would have before Longwood, the flu, drugs, and possibly a mental breakdown, Rose climbs the stairs. Off a landing that takes up more square footage than it should are three small bedrooms and two baths. Two of the bedrooms are filled with boxes. The New Orleans house was considerably larger. Neither she nor Harley downsized as much as they needed to.

The master bedroom is slightly larger than the other two and has a connecting bath. This room has been made habitable. The bed is made. Rose's old duvet and shams, with the Tree of Life motif, look out of place in the square dun-colored room. They should have repainted before the furniture arrived. Uncharacteristically, Harley rushed the move.

Harley Dennis was a most considerate individual, yet he had rushed the move. Rose stops and thinks about that. He wanted to be moved in before school started. He wanted to be in Charlotte so when Flynn was working trade shows out of town, he and Rose could take Mel. Rose wonders if Harley had a premonition of his impending death. She believes in premonitions and at the same time suspects people purporting to have them of being deluded or dishonest.

Upstairs, as was the case downstairs, the blinds are lowered, and the nearly new dun-colored drapes, left behind by the previous owners, are closed. The resulting claustrophobic twilight adds to Rose's sense of dream-walking through a mausoleum. She has her hand on a drape before she realizes that, for now, this is her world. No light, no movement that might alert neighbors or police to the fact that there is a life-form dwelling within, can be allowed to escape.

Rose loves light. A darkened house is purgatory. *Purgatory or Longwood,* Rose tells herself, *pick one.*

She sits on the edge of the bed. She is free. She can walk, talk, see, smell, and feel. She has Melanie. This is a good moment. For a while she waits for that revelation to travel from her mind to her heart. It makes it about halfway, catching in her throat.

"Cheer yourself up," she says into the dusty gloom.

Leaving the borrowed jeans, T-shirt, and underpants in a trail on the bedroom floor, Rose goes into the bathroom. Turning both showerheads on, she wastes a criminal amount of water scrubbing the nursing home out of her hair and the pores of her skin.

When she runs out of hot water, she wraps herself in a towel. There is a toothbrush in a stand by the sink. Rose hopes it's hers. Picking it up, she looks for a drawer that might contain toothpaste.

Time stutters to a halt. On the counter, in a small egg-shaped bowl of blue Wedgwood, is a gold heart-shaped locket. It is the first gift Harley ever gave her. Rose lifts it and fastens it around her neck. Beneath are two rings of gold, inset with small flat rectangular diamonds: her wedding and engagement bands.

With a sense of returning irreplaceable artifacts to their proper places, Rose puts them on. Holding her left hand to her chest, she looks in the mirror at the gold locket and the wedding rings. Harley is in the next room. For the rest of her life, her husband will be in the next room. "Thank you, love," she calls lightly.

The closet is a treasure trove of brightly colored clothes. Rose chooses a knee-length white tunic with a Nehru collar and a pair of loose trousers gathered at the ankles. More strands of what she laughingly calls her "self" are restored.

Downstairs, she finds the refrigerator empty, clean, unplugged with the door ajar. She had not been expected back anytime soon. Several cans of pork and beans, an emergency staple, remain on a shelf. Standing over the sink, Rose opens a can and eats the beans cold. Can rinsed and set aside for recycling, Rose opens the dishwasher to dispose of the spoon. It has been loaded and run, but not emptied. Three plates, four coffee cups, assorted flatware, a spatula, and two prescription pill bottles that originally contained Venlafaxine, an antidepressant Rose has been on for twenty-plus years.

The food gives her the strength to climb back up the stairs. The thin wires that have kept her skinny flu-and-drug-ravaged puppet body upright and moving snap. Bones collapse against one another.

Falling back on the California-king-sized bed, arms flung wide, she stares at the ceiling fan, white and unmoving. Memories of this house without Harley trickle into her mind: Boxes she was too tired to unpack. Food she was too uninterested to cook. Thoughts she was too miserable to think. Grief sets those memories in black-and-white. Ubiquitous roaring leaf blowers make up the soundtrack. The life-form that was Harley has dissolved back into . . . whatever life is when it's not incarnate. The Harley/Rose life-form now only has one heart, one skeleton.

The house, even with her in it, is empty of life. Rose craves the sensation of being alive. She rolls to her side. A small dark object sits in the center of one of the pillows. A mouse. Rose sits up. The mouse is gray with big ears and black bead eyes. It's made of rabbit fur with plastic whiskers.

Rose has cats.

She has been gone a long time. If they've gotten out, they've run away. They are indoor cats, unused to the urban wild. Honey Cat and Laura Lei have been taken to the pound, rehomed, or killed. A sob bursts from Rose's throat. The grief she cannot access for her husband pours out for their cats. Rose wails and gulps. Tears and snot mingle. Her mouth is an open square of pain.

"It's different, Harley!" she gasps at the bedcover. "You were doing exactly what you wanted, exactly where you wanted to do it. Our kitties were captured and caged, scared to death, dumped in a kennel to wait on a cold metal table for the syringe!"

Covering her face with her hands, Rose mumbles, "Stop telling yourself this story. This is an awful story. Tell yourself a good story about the kittens being taken to a nice farm in the country where they can chase mice. No. Stop the stories. No more stories." She breathes in. This is here. This is now. There are no cats here and now. That is the truth; anything else is just an empty story to frighten or reassure herself. What happened to Honey Cat and Laura Lei will come clear at the appropriate moment.

Rose finds herself in space — she is at 87 Applegarth Street, Charlotte, NC. She needs to find herself in time. Leaping off the bed, she staggers, then catches herself on the doorframe. This body is frail. Holding on to the rail, she carefully descends the stairs. On the kitchen counter are her iPad and iPhone, both dead. Too tired to stand, she plugs her lone charger cord into a baseboard outlet and sits cross-legged on the floor, the iPad open.

Her email is clogged with ads. She begins

to delete, enjoying the delusion that she can impose order on chaos. Finally there are only four left. Two are from Greene and Associates. Rose has no memory of that firm, but the subject line reads *HDennis Will.* Rose opens the first, sent the previous day.

Greene and Associates, reads the email, *was Miller and Associates when you and Mr. Dennis did your estate planning. When Mr. Miller passed, Alma Greene inherited the firm.* Miller was the family lawyer. When Izzy got sick, she and Flynn used him to draw up their will. After Daniel's father-in-law remarried, he went to Miller to change his will to accommodate his new circumstances.

Mrs. Dennis could you please make an appointment re: Mr. Dennis's bequests.

The second email says much the same thing, adding that Rose and Alma Greene Esq. met when Ms. Greene was a paralegal. Rose remembers. She marks both "Save as New" and moves on.

The next few are from distant friends she is vaguely in communication with.

Four emails in six weeks. So few.

Rose opens the old mail file. Most are from Marion.

"Marion," Rose whispers as memories deluge her, buffeting her nerves and inundating her bones until her hands shake so much, she folds them in her lap lest she knock over the iPad.

Two little girls in swimsuits and red cowboy hats, standing in an inflatable wading pool holding hands; two girls, one towheaded, one darker, peeking from between the ears of two kittens, making little paws wave for the camera. Two green fairies in tights and leotards, wings of green netting; two teen-agers driving four hundred miles to college in a beat-up green station wagon named Sherman. Two women standing up at each other's weddings. Two women helping each other pick up the pieces after divorce. Two old women laughing so hard, the shoppers at Belk's avoid them.

Thousands of phone calls, almost all long distance; conversations with Marion are the beads woven through the events of Rose's life. Schools, jobs, men, mistakes, mundane days and glorious nights: With Marion all the memories are there in grand disorder.

Never has there been a world where Rose was and Marion wasn't. How could Rose have forgotten Marion, her older sister and oldest friend? Even without Harley and cats, she is not alone. She has family. Rose can almost feel her blood getting thicker than water.

She laughs and yells, "Marion!"

None of the personal emails is more recent than six weeks. That must be about the time Rose was incarcerated. No wonder there are so few. Marion would have informed Rose's close friends that she was non compos mentis.

Rose has to hold her right wrist with her left hand to steady her hand enough to open the most recent of the old emails from Marion.

"You're not answering your phone or email. I'm calling whatsisname."

Flynn, Rose guesses. Marion called Flynn because Rose stopped communicating.

Scrolling down, she opens another from three weeks prior.

"You were weird on the phone last night. Are you seeing anybody? I know shrinks aren't the be-all and end-all, but I think you should find one. Sooner rather than later."

A week after that: "Call me. You're scaring the crap out of me."

The next one, flagged, is from Nancy, Harley's ex.

"Stella and Daniel have issues they need to work on. Your so-called grief is bad for them at this time. Flynn's gone and you are leaning so hard on Melanie they are all coming to hate you. I don't like to be the one to have to tell you this but the entire family is absolutely vilifying you. I'm telling you this for your own good. You should stay away for <u>MANY MONTHS</u>."

"Holy smoke," Rose breathes. Nancy and Stella had email wars for a few years. Though Rose was not the Other Woman — or even the next woman — early in her and Harley's marriage, Nancy did send a few email bombs, but nothing like this. The vitriol boiling behind the words would scarify the insides of anyone holding on to it. Or char the skin off anyone who tried to grab it. It speaks of suffering so deep as to be a pathology. Rose hits DELETE.

She opens the SENT folder. Over a three-week period she sent Marion eleven emails. Rose opens them in order. They start with "I cannot get my mind around the fact that Harley is gone." And end with "I cants seem to kep it tgether/" Taken as a whole, they and Marion's replies create a picture of the decline and fall of Rose Dennis's sanity.

Rose pulls the charger cord from the iPad and plugs it into the phone.

CHAPTER 9

On the floor, legs crossed beneath her, Rose watches the dust motes going about their business in a narrow beam of sun that pushes between the blind and the window frame. She thinks of movies and books and plays where loved ones return from the dead. In fiction, it never works out well for the living.

She taps CONTACTS, then her sister's number. Five rings, then the click: "You've reached Marion's answering machine. You know what to do."

Rose doesn't know what to do. "Marion, it's Rose. Your sister?" Panic creeps up her esophagus, and she begins bailing out words as if she is drowning in them. "It's me. Please pick up if you're there. If you're not home please, please, please call me back. I don't know what my number is — oh, right, caller ID. I was in the home, this place, Longwood. I'm not there anymore. I —"

"Rosie?"

Hearing the familiar voice, Rose begins to cry. Through choking tears she gasps, "Don't hang up. I'm okay. Don't hang up."

"I won't," Marion says. "But don't cry too long. My head is about to explode." She sounds angry.

Rose laughs, mucus running out of her nose. Cell phone clamped tightly against her ear, she scrambles up, grabs a handful of paper towels, and mops her face. "Okay," she says. "I'm done with that. Thank God you answered! Better put me on speaker. This could take a while."

"Where are you?" Marion demands. "Last I heard whatsisname, Harley's son —"

"Flynn."

"Flynn emailed me to tell me you'd gone around the bend, early onset Alzheimer's excerbated by shock, and were put in a rest home."

"You didn't bother to check?" Rose is getting angry herself.

"I called the home several times. They said you were there but weren't responsive. What was I supposed to do? Dash out there with my hair in a knot, kick down the doors, and drag you out?"

Marion doesn't travel. She lives alone with seventeen cats, four computers, two laptops, an iPad, and security cameras in every room. Rose knows she will not leave her home. Though she understands, she is stung. "You could have launched an investigation," she says indignantly.

"Into what? The last few times we talked you were confused, anxious. You sounded like all the screws were coming loose. You were scared you were losing your mind, that people were poisoning you. You started nailing windows shut because you thought people or poltergeists were coming in and out of your house and moving things around. Then you quit answering the phone."

A silence follows. Rose is holding her breath. She lets it out slowly so Marion won't hear.

"I was just glad whatsisname —"

"Flynn."

"Flynn was there to keep you from playing on the railroad tracks, or whatever they have there to play on. Besides, this isn't the first time you've gone off the deep end."

"It is too!" Rose insists.

A longer pause, an eight-months-pregnant pause.

"That was different!" Rose remembers with a shock. "Okay, some bizarre behavior, but that was divorce aftermath. I've never

ever been put into a facility, for heaven's sake!"

Marion says nothing.

"That was voluntary," Rose wails. "I wasn't tied down and drugged. It was just group therapy and sing-alongs. Besides, it was nearly thirty years ago." Rose's throat is so tight, it aches. She is careful not to make any telltale sounds.

Seconds of telephone silence, the grayest kind of silence, clunk by.

A sigh whispers through the cell phone speaker. "It was," Marion concedes. "But you have to admit, you haven't always been all that stable."

"I'm as stable as you are," Rose shoots back.

"And your point is . . ."

Rose's laugh is shaky.

"Tell me everything," Marion says.

"What about your headache?" A little payback.

"I expect it's about to get worse. Sorry," Marion says. "I'd finally given up Harley for dead, and you up for as-good-as. Your sudden resurrection is — it's a good thing — it's just a lot when I was getting over losing you. Don't ever make me go through that again."

As she has done her entire life, Rose tells

her sister everything: the first escape attempt, the drugged orange juice, hiding the red capsules, the slow return of her cognitive mind, the women talking in the hallway, saying she wouldn't last the week, the costume, the drugging of the night nurse, and her final escape. Spoken out loud, for someone else's ears, her fear of being drugged, of being plotted against, sounds like more of the paranoid behavior Marion had noticed prior to her being placed at Longwood.

When she finishes, there is a bit of silence; then Marion says, "It's obvious you were drugged, but maybe it was for a reason. Didn't the manager, the woman with the perfect eyebrows, say you were agitated, a danger to yourself and others? Maybe that was true."

"It's not true," Rose says.

"For years after your divorce your dream date was Dr. Kevorkian. I thought I'd lost you then."

That is true. Rose remembers those years. "I'd never harm anyone else," she says defensively.

"Tell that to the night nurse, if she's still alive," Marion says.

A shudder runs through Rose. "If I murdered her it would ruin my whole day," she says. "I can't have. I gave her one day's dose for me, and the woman is the size of a refrigerator."

"Maybe she has drug allergies," Marion says ominously.

Rose pinches her nose tightly to keep from making sniveling noises.

"I might be able to find out," Marion says. "I'll poke around."

Marion never hacks; she swears she doesn't know how to hack. She "pokes around" and "explores." Since the Dread Pirate Roberts went down, she'd been skittish about poking and exploring.

"Thanks," Rose says. "That would be one load off my mind."

"Maybe the . . . What do you want to call it? The nervous breakdown? Psychotic episode? The incident?"

"Spell," Rose says with a smile. "Spells are such delightful things."

"Is it possible your recent spell was brought on by drugs — not theirs, yours? Sleeping pills? I remember you once lost a night to Ambien. Drug-induced amnesia."

"I don't remember."

Marion laughs. Rose loves making her sister laugh.

"Wine?" Marion asks. "During your first divorce you lost a night to alcohol."

Marion's memory is too good. Unfair, Rose thinks.

"More than usual," Rose admits. "But not blackout, not even close."

"Medication?" Marion asks. "Medication" means cannabis.

"Nothing unusual, that I remember." Rose supposes she'll be tacking that caveat onto her statements for some time to come.

"Antidepressants?"

"I suppose." Rose is too tired to sit up. She curls down on the kitchen tiles in the fetal position.

"Are you on them now?"

"No. I've taken nothing but those red capsules. I doubt they were antidepressants. They did knock the big nurse out," Rose says.

"Better call your doctor and get him to phone in a prescription for you," Marion says.

Rose hates being reminded. Twice she's tried to go off antidepressants. Both times were disastrous, complete with hallucinations and attendant psychic phenomena.

Marion doesn't push it. "Maybe the mix of the various medications, plus the shock of Harley being killed, and you living in a strange house full of boxes, in a strange town full of strange people, created a situation where you lost it for a week or two. Flynn gets you help. You get better. Does that work?" she asks.

"It is possible," Rose admits.

From Marion's end of the phone she hears a cat complaining. She aches for Honey Cat and Laura Lei. Nothing is as comforting as the feel of fur and the sound of purring.

"Tell me about Longwood," Marion says.

Rose thinks for a moment. Loathing of the place tries to force lies onto her tongue. "Longwood," Rose says slowly, "is upscale. Nice décor. The people are professional and kind. The food is good. The bathrobe was sturdy and hard to cut. The bedspread ripped nice and straight. My shackles were soft and fleecy. My drugs were powerful and quick acting. Not a dump."

"Not a dump," Marion agrees.

"How would you know?" The complacency in Marion's tone is irksome.

"I researched it online. You don't think I'd stand by while you were put in some hell-hole, do you?"

"Well, I don't believe it now," Rose says. "For a while there I was wondering."

"They have a two-year waiting list," Marion told her. "It's a happening place. Very expensive. Lots of prizes for this and that.

Harley's son had to pull in a favor from one of Harley's old board members in Charlotte, who felt he still owed him, to get you accepted."

"Damn," Rose says. "I hate hearing that. That leaves the logical person thinking I am — or was — mentally ill. With every cell in my body I believe I was maliciously drugged, and was kept there against my will. And I know how crazy that sounds."

Rose is relieved Marion doesn't add the words that stick like a chicken bone in Rose's throat: She was bonkers before Flynn put her in Longwood. "Could stress, depression — all the things we listed — unhinge a person so much, she'd wander around in a coma, lose weeks?" Rose asks hopefully.

"In the seventeenth century fugues were popular," Marion muses. "Young men from London would go missing. Weeks later they'd turn up in Paris or Prague or Moscow remembering nothing."

"Sounds convenient."

"People used to lose weeks to 'brain fever' in old books," Marion suggests.

"Amnesia, repressed memories, the vapors, being beamed up by aliens," Rose adds. "Maybe ways to describe phenomena science can't explain."

"Nervous breakdown, psychotic break —

123

the same thing," Marion adds.

"They sound scarier," Rose says.

"Things will look better in the morning," Marion replies in the voice Rose knows means she needs to get off the phone. With Marion, a headache isn't a two-aspirin event. It is a screaming red crawl-in-the closet event.

Feeling more needy than considerate, Rose asks, "Why will things look better in the morning?"

"Because I'm going to FedEx you a credit card and an ATM card tomorrow."

"I have —"

"I canceled them."

"Oh."

"So tomorrow, you get a pedicure, a haircut, a massage, whatever. When you feel up to it, you go to Longwood and turn yourself in. Call Flynn first. I'll call to check on you a couple times a day. They will get you back on the antidepressants, get your record cleared up —"

"I don't have a record."

"The nurse. There will be legal issues with that. Better to get them settled while you are officially 'under a doctor's care' than get picked up by a local rednecked cop and stuck in the police station's holding cell bleating, 'I'm sane, I'm sane,' while the hookers and drunks roll their eyes. Think about it tomorrow. *After all, tomorrow is another day.*"

Marion was right. Tomorrow, Rose will deal with things like a rational person. *I can't think about that right now. If I do, I'll go crazy. I'll think about that tomorrow.* Rose smiles at Scarlett.

"I love you," she blurts out.

"Well . . . you should," Marion says and hangs up.

CHAPTER 10

A knock at the front door startles Rose out of sleep. She lifts her head from the kitchen floor. Drool has stuck her cheek to the tile, and it comes free with a faint kissing sound. The cell phone has slipped from her hand. Touching the button, she checks the time. She's been asleep for a couple of hours. Listening to the castanet pops of knees and ankles, she climbs stiffly to her feet. Rest has been good for her. Marion has been good for her.

She has her hand on the doorknob before it occurs to her that it might not be Melanie. Rose wants to return to Longwood on her own terms, in snappy clothes, her hair expensively cut and her eyes clear. Being snatched and dragged back by the Tweedles — or the Charlotte police — kicking and screaming, with drool on her face and her hair standing on end, is not part of her plan.

She is contemplating hiding behind the

boxes in the living room, when a small voice says, "Gigi?"

Mel is carrying three grocery bags. Rose looks both ways to see if the neighbors have noticed. No one is on the street or the sidewalks. If this were New Orleans, Rose would think she'd missed an evacuation order.

"I don't have a key," Mel says. "I couldn't find Dad's. How did you get in?"

"Where are Honey Cat and Laura Lei?" Rose demands.

"Grandma Nancy took them," Mel says, walking past Rose toward the kitchen.

"To the pound?" Rose is too loud, too strident.

"No. Grandma likes cats. She adopted them. They seemed really happy last time I was over there." Mel says this like it is the most normal thing in the world.

This hurts. It is, of course, better than them being put to death in a concrete room. Still, it hurts. Nancy should get her own damn cats. Rose is grateful and relieved. Relieved is good. Grateful is not as much fun as usual. "That's nice," Rose makes herself say, but she's thinking of the email, and wondering if Nancy somehow put this whole thing in motion so she could steal Rose's cats. Rose doesn't believe this — she

127

isn't crazy — but she thinks it.

"Wow!" Mel says as Rose empties the sacks into the cupboards and the refrigerator. "You look way better than you did this morning. Way better."

"Don't flatter me," Rose says. "I don't want to get attached to my physical beauty. It's impermanent."

"Gigi, you are attached to your physical beauty. Don't you remember? You got a face-lift when you turned sixty."

Rose nods. "Like I said, it's impermanent."

"Do we just plug this back in?" Mel asks. Rose feels behind the refrigerator and plugs it in; then the two of them shove it back into its niche.

"Thanks for the food. You didn't have to do it," Rose says. "I could have run out and done some grocery shopping. But I'm glad you did. My ability to leap over tall buildings at a single bound has been compromised. By the flu — I guess."

"You're not going to like this," Mel says. "Dad sold your car." Before Rose can say anything, Mel adds, "Dad's super efficient. He said cars lose value when they sit around and nobody drives them." Mel leans her elbows on the counter.

"Careful of broken glass," Rose says. She

points to the window. "That's how I got in without a key."

Mel's smooth lips crimp slightly. "There wasn't another way?"

Rose can tell the girl is worried that Gigi is making bad choices again.

"I talked to Marion," Rose says.

"Your sister with eight computers and a zillion cats?"

"She talked me into going back to Longwood and working this out."

"Hooray for Great-Aunt Marion!" Mel crows. "I'll call Dad. You'll want backup."

"Let's wait until tomorrow. I want to sleep without diapers and shower by myself a few times before I take the plunge. Lots of loin girding on my part. You can't imagine how surreal this has been. I feel like I fell into a rabbit hole that turned into a Hitchcock movie that's being played backward."

"I'm sorry, Gigi." Mel looks so sad for her, Rose is caught up on a wave of love. She hugs her granddaughter.

"Think of the stories I'll have to tell when it's over," she says, letting Mel go.

After sunset, the house becomes aggressively dark. To push back the shadows without giving herself away, Rose lights a candle. She is sitting on the couch, one of the moving boxes serving as a table, eating the turkey-and-provolone sandwich Mel brought from Harris Teeter's, when her cell vibrates. On the cardboard it sounds like a dying locust.

Mel.

"Hey, what's up?" Rose says, phone to her ear.

"Turn on the TV," Melanie says.

The remote is sitting on the base of the TV. "Which channel?" Rose asks.

"Nine. Local news."

Rose pushes the power button. The television screen lights up. A nice-looking blonde in a lavender blouse is anchoring. Beside her is a photograph of Rose.

". . . escaped from Longwood after assaulting a nurse. Rose Dennis is considered to be a danger to herself and others. The police say do not approach this individual, but do report if you see her. The nurse remains in ICU."

The photograph of Rose was taken at an art gala in New York. Rose is in a black cocktail dress, laughing, a cigarette in one hand, a glass of champagne in the other.

"Cruella de Vil with a butch haircut," Rose mutters.

"What did you do to the nurse?" Mel wants to know.

"I gave her a dose of the medication they were feeding me every day. It shouldn't have hurt her. She was a big person."

"Maybe she had an allergy," Mel echoes Marion.

"They're making it sound like I knifed her, or bashed her over the head," Rose complains.

"Maybe she inhaled her own vomit," Melanie says. "That happened to a kid on the football team. He suffocated."

"At least she's not dead," Rose says to re-assure them both.

"Not yet, anyway," Mel says. "Cops came to the house. Regular uniformed cops, then detectives in suits. I'm glad Uncle Daniel wasn't home. He'd have totally flipped out."

Rose can believe that. Daniel is a great guy, a man not cursed with ambition. From what Rose has seen, he is happy with friends, football, and a job that pays enough for beer. He is so laid-back, it is considered a family miracle that he finally managed to ask Stella for a divorce.

"Who talked to the police?" Rose asks.

"Me. I was a confused little girl who didn't know anything. Don't worry, they bought it, and," she adds with a note of pride in her voice, "I did not perjure myself once."

"It's only perjury if you're under oath," Rose says. "But I'm glad you didn't lie for me."

"I didn't. They wanted to come in and look for you. I said Dad said not to let strangers in the house. Then I asked for their badge numbers, their names, their supervisor's name and contact numbers, and how I could call and verify they were them. When they gave me the numbers, I asked how I could know the numbers were really real and they hadn't just given me the number of a fellow conspirator who would vouch for them even though they weren't real cops. They were pretty quick to decide to look for you somewhere else."

"When does your dad get back?" Rose asks.

"Not for nine days. He's running this massive home improvement trade show in Atlanta. Should I call him now? Or you can."

"I don't know," Rose says.

"I could call Dad, say you needed him to come back. I'm sure he'd find a way to come," Mel prods.

Rose thinks about that. "Not yet," she says. "Tomorrow, first thing, I promise." Her hand is trembling so much, the little red arrow from the remote darts frenziedly around the screen. Rose manages to turn the television off. Dropping the remote onto the sofa, she says, "I'm sorry I dragged you into this."

"Are you kidding? This is more fun than I've had in ages."

CHAPTER 11

Curled up on a bed that, sans one man and two cats, feels as vast as the Smoke Creek Desert, Rose blows out the candle and lies back. After rest and food, shower and family, she is far less shaky than she was when she broke into 87 Applegarth that morning. Nevertheless she remains exhausted, underweight, with gaps in her memory, and wanted by the police.

Smiling in the dark, Rose realizes she's living in the fast lane now.

Smoke from the candle has scarcely cleared before she is asleep.

Then awake.

The clock on the bed stand reads two forty-seven. Since it is dark, Rose assumes it is A.M. Six hours of undrugged rest have banished the last — or so she hopes — cobwebs from her mind. Still, six hours is only six hours. Tired as she is, she wouldn't have been surprised had she slept the clock around. Except she hasn't. Something awakened her.

Rose lies quietly listening. Strange house, strange noises. One of the many wonderful things about having cats is that one can blame unsettling night noises on their nocturnal habits. Too bad Nancy stole them.

There is the faint clack of the overhead fan. Far away a jet flies, that or it is distant thunder. None of this wakened her. The human mind is a marvel. Even sleeping it can sort the familiar and unthreatening from the alien and threatening. Most of the time.

Swish.

Whisper.

Creak.

Cloth sliding along cardboard, Rose guesses; rubber-soled shoes on carpet, then weight on aging hardwood. Alien and threatening. A jolt of adrenaline brings her out of bed and to the bedroom door. Before she came upstairs, she'd checked all the locks, and laid a perilous trap of heaped pots and pans in the kitchen sink so any intruder larger than a mosquito would knock them down with a racket sufficient to wake the not-yet-dead.

Whoever or whatever this is did not come in via the broken kitchen window or the front or back door. Rose did not hear shattering glass or breaking deadbolts. Hoping the hinges will keep silent, she opens the bedroom door half an inch, and puts her ear to the crack.

Downstairs, the intruder is weaving through the maze of moving boxes. Not a small, light-footed individual — Rose has no trouble negotiating the boxes in the dark without brushing against them — but a careful, practiced individual, who breathes through a stuffed-up nose and, despite the probable bulk, does not bump into anything.

She could dial 911. Then the intruder will run away, and the police will arrive and arrest her. Call Mel? The courageous little creature would probably Uber over with a baseball bat. Not calling Mel. Not if her hair were on fire.

With luck, the burglar will take the television and go. That was what burglars used to do. This is a fifty-five-inch flat-screen, a lot to grab and dash with. Money? Guns? Drugs? It would be a stupid criminal who sought that unholy trinity in a small upscale suburban residence. But then small-time criminals were not noted for high IQs and long-range planning skills.

Rose eases the door closed. With the shades drawn, the room is dim, but the skylight over the bed seldom loses its urban incandescence. For a moment she stares blankly around, her mind flitting from one half-baked plan to another. Attack the intruder? Little more deadly than a coat hanger presents itself as a weapon. The bed stand would serve as a hefty cudgel. Rose could lift it up, then wait against the wall by the door. When the intruder came through, wham! Crack his skull with it.

Rose has never bludgeoned anyone with a piece of furniture. She has a feeling it is not as easy as they make it look in the movies. Hiding might work. There is the closet, and beneath the bed. Neither infuses her with a sense of security.

Decision unmade, she takes her trousers and tunic from the chair where she'd dumped them and pulls them on over her short pj's. Her feet she slides into a pair of well-worn Toms. She is damned if she is going to face another trauma without proper clothing.

Dressed, she sneaks back to the door, opens it a sliver, and listens. Faint as the hiss of a snake on sand, she can hear what sounds like a gloved hand sliding up the banister.

A landing, another eight steps, and the intruder will be upstairs. Three bedrooms, two baths. There are boxes in the other bedrooms. They might hide her for a minute or two, no more than that.

A needle of blue-white light slices across the dun-colored faux shutters over the small window on the stair landing.

Rose silently pushes the door shut. There is no lock. No matter; it's a cheap hollow-core. A booted foot will punch right through it.

No hiding.

No attacking.

All that remains is running away.

She crosses the bedroom to the window facing the street. Making no noise, she slithers behind the curtain and blind. A streetlight glares at her from across the sidewalk, throwing the roof of the wraparound porch into high relief. On the window frame, nicely illuminated and right before her eyes, is the lock. Rose flips it open, puts her fingers into the pathetic grooves on the bottom of the frame, and lifts. The windows are new and cheap. The metal in the grooves makes only the slightest hiss. Hope surges. Eight or nine inches up, the window jams.

The intruder's tread is heavy on the stair, a steady whump like Mothra stomping through Tokyo. Gathering the strength in her legs, Rose lifts again. The window does not budge. Not one quarter of an inch.

Rose hears the footsteps even out. Monster Man is upstairs.

Bending at the waist, she shoves her head through the nine-inch gap between window frame and sill. An ear is scraped raw, but she is breathing outside air. She's heard that if a person's head fits through, so will the rest of her body. This seems as good a time as any to test that theory.

The crash and snap of splintering wood help her decide to commit to the task. Monster Man did not bother with the knob; he kicked the bedroom door open. To scare her worse than he already has? If so, it is efficacious. In the instant between kick and grunt, when, Rose supposes, the door hit the wall and ricocheted back to smack the intruder, her body squeezes through the window like dried paint from an old tube.

The window delivers her feet. Rose gets them under her and pushes up. The porch roof is a couple of yards wide and slants gently downward. On one side, it curves around the house in a gentle embrace, forming the long wing of the porch. Hiding there would be a short-term solution. If the intruder looks out the side window, there is no way he would miss seeing her.

The other end of the porch ends abruptly over the driveway. The house is raised, making it a twelve- or fifteen-foot drop either way.

A tremendous crash shakes the roof beneath Rose's feet. Already pounding, her heart feels as if it stops, then lurches back to life at double speed. The intruder must have upended the king-sized bed and hurled it against the wall.

Ultraviolence.

Rose is glad her cats aren't home. This would traumatize Laura Lei. She is also glad she isn't under that bed, exposed like a grub under a rock.

Even if Monster Man is of below-average intelligence, he might put the empty bed and the open window together. If he sees it. Blind and curtain are still closed. Rose hopes he will think she is out for the night.

A tinny rattle, then a muted crash, emanate from the window Rose oozed out of. Not a man for gently opening orifices. The intruder has ripped blind and curtain from the wall. Standing straight, Rose shimmies along, her back to the wall, until she runs out of roof.

No light streams through the denuded window. No fist or foot or piece of furniture smashes out the glass. The intruder must be as leery as Rose of attracting attention from neighbors.

A black-gloved hand, clutching a small flashlight, pokes out through the narrow opening. The beam probes the porch roof. Pushing her heels tight against the house, Rose makes herself as thin as she can.

The beam scrapes blue from the shingles, working closer to her toes. For Rose it holds the deadly fascination cobras are rumored to have for mongooses. Pressing her body so hard against the wall that the brick bites through the cotton of her tunic, she dares not blink or breathe.

The streak of light wavers, appears to lose interest, then is snatched away. Monster Man is not going to risk busting out the window. Rose lets her breath out in a silent sigh.

Heavy footfalls retreat. Muscles Rose didn't even know she had, let alone could clench, loosen. No helpless elderly lady to rape and terrorize, surely the intruder will take what he can, depart, maybe stop for a six-pack of Coors Light, then go home, watch some porn, and call it a night.

Loud crashes string her muscles back to rigidity. Rose imagines the Incredible Hulk on steroids rearranging furniture with all the finesse of a tornado. *Let the beast take his rage out on things,* she thinks. Things can be replaced. Abruptly, the furniture tossing ends. Rose listens for the sound of his footfalls leaving the room.

The shrieking of metal slices into her waiting ears. He has thrown the king-sized mattress and bedstead from where he'd upended it against the wall, clearing a path to the side window. Of course the window he chooses opens without a hitch. Rose remembers she never really liked this house. A pig-like grunt comes from the far side of the porch. He is coming out onto her porch roof.

Images flash through her mind. Squeezing back through the window she'd scraped out of, rabbiting down the stairs. Him grunting in pursuit. Boxes and blackness and locked doors; penlight stabbing her in the back shortly before his bulk slams into her.

No, Rose thinks, no stabbing and slamming. She'd rather risk falling and shattering her bones on the concrete.

Noiselessly, she creeps to where the roof ends above the driveway. Here the main roof swoops down until it meets the porch at a shared rain gutter. The roof is about a forty-five-degree angle and covered with asphalt shingles. If she slides off, there is nothing to break her fall.

Grabbing tightly to the edge of the steep-angled roof, her chest pressed against the shingles, Rose inches one foot out along the rain gutter, fighting the urge to look down. The gutter seems relatively stable. She doesn't weigh much, but she weighs more than a rain-soaked leaf.

Right hand splayed on the shingles like a starfish, the left white-knuckled on the edge, she works belly, chest, and one thigh onto the roof. Blowing out her breath, as if that will make her lighter, she gingerly lifts her remaining foot from the porch and drags her toes into the rain gutter. It holds her weight — sort of; she can feel it straining outward. Undoubtedly it is plastic. Whoever remodeled this house left no corner uncut.

Flattening her body against the slope of the roof, she inches away from the porch. The asphalt shingles sandpaper the skin on her cheek and palms. Her feet scuffle in the uncleaned gutter. Chunks of old leaves are bulldozed up and fall in hushed plops on the gravel below. Hoping the racket is louder to her ears than to those of the monster, she shuffles inch by inch until she is far enough away that a big man, with long arms, cannot reach out and grab her.

Rose is motionless and silent. In several seconds the noise from the monstrous intruder's egress through the window ceases. Rose prays his racket deafened him to hers.

Grating of rubber soles mincing heavily over shingles lets her know he is out and is coming around to the front. Rose wishes she'd experimented with bashing his brains out via the bed stand. She resists the urge to turn her face in the opposite direction. Some things have to be faced. Death is one of them.

The sound of steps stops. The light beam traces the edges of the porch roof. Rose breathes in through her nose and silently out through her mouth, willing her body to relax, to melt into the shingles, to become as thin and attached to the roof as wallpaper to plaster.

A sandy scuff of shoes lets her know Monster Man is moving away, going back the way he came. He thinks the house is unoccupied. Few people would believe a grown person — even one as motivated as Rose — could squeeze through that narrow window opening. Rose hadn't believed it herself until she'd done it.

That, or he believes the occupant has gotten off the roof somehow and is running for the police. Whatever he believes, he seems anxious to get offstage; the front of the house is spotlighted by the streetlamp.

144

More piggy grunts. He is back inside the bedroom. Rose can feel a slight shuddering of the house as he stomps through the bedroom and down the stairs. Under her feet the plastic guttering moves half an inch, cracking faintly.

An unmistakable crystal cacophony of breaking glass reaches her ears. For some reason, he has exited the house through the patio doors, then stopped to break out the glass. Why break the glass on his way out? He'd not needed to break it to get in.

Shoes on gravel. He has given up. He is leaving.

Rose lets out a sigh of relief and sends up a nondenominational prayer that she and the rain gutter have enough strength remaining to get her back to solid footing.

A sharp snap, like the breaking of a twig, is followed by the gutter moving outward. Rose slides down a few inches, fingernails raking the shingles. Metal straps holding the guttering to the eave groan and screech in protest.

The gravel crunching ceases abruptly.

Rose no longer breathes. She squeezes her eyes shut. Her muscles are reaching exhaustion, thighs twitching as if touched by a cattle prod, fingers losing sensation.

Silence from below.

And silence.

And such a long silence, Rose begins to hope the monster has slunk quietly away while she was busy being scared out of her mind.

"Huh!" whuffs up from below like the snort of an interested grizzly. Crunching recommences. The intruder is trotting back toward the rear of the house. He thumps up the wooden steps to the deck. Broken glass creaks in the metal slide as he yanks open the door.

The time for silence and hiding is at an end. As quickly as she dares, Rose shuffles one foot, then the other, in the failing gutter, moving herself farther from the porch roof. With each shift of weight the gutter wrenches away from the eave.

Rose fixes her eyes on the bedroom skylight where it bulges through the dark roof, a rectangular plastic bubble four feet long and fourteen inches wide. Rose knows this because the skylight was one of the few features of the house she had liked.

With a whine, the gutter separates from the eave, the loosed portion levering the rest free. Screws squeal as they pull from the wood. Rose uses the last of her footing to propel herself sideways over the skylight. It's not a big leap; still, it taxes Rose's depleted strength.

Spread-eagled on the plastic, hands firmly clamped over its upper edge, she gasps for breath. Sweat drenches her tunic, the wet fabric dragging on the plastic as she wriggles into a more secure position.

Face mashed against the skylight, she looks into the bedroom. The furniture is broken. On top of the pieces, the mattress leans against the closet doors in a tangle of sheets and blankets. Splinters of wood as long as her arm stick like knives from the ruined doorframe.

As she watches, a white beam of light pries apart the darkness, nosing through the debris. Following it, dimly silhouetted, is a great, lumpish, ape-like creature. Ape-like, it moves over the obstacles with great dexterity. At the side window, it straddles the sill, preparatory to ducking out onto the porch roof. Rose can see him clearly in the glow from the streetlight. Not his face — a ball cap's brim throws that into shadow — but his body. It is thick: Thick arms muscle out of a short-sleeved black T-shirt; legs like fire hydrants stump out of knee-length black shorts. His gut is a classic beer belly. He *oof*s as he bends over to get his head outside the window. On his feet are deck shoes. They offend Rose. A man ought not to set about murdering a person while wearing deck shoes. It is as if he doesn't take killing her seriously.

Rose doesn't have the upper body strength to remain on the skylight, splayed like a cat on a screen door. Her fingers are growing numb where they clutch the edging; they are losing their grip. Before the proverbial hit the fan, she remembers, she did three sets of ten men's push-ups every night after yoga. Now she doubts she could do five girl's push-ups.

She kicks off her shoes. Fixing the old, strong Rose firmly in her mind, she pulls up as hard as she can. Nice and sticky with sweat, feet and toes scramble monkey-like against the roof, helping her ascend. With a final surge, she gets her forearms onto the shelf where the skylight is seated into the roof.

No longer is she in danger of an imminent plunge to the ground.

She is in way more danger than that.

Light pierces her left eye. Monster Man is leaning around the edge of the roof, eyes hidden in the cap's shadow. He holds the flashlight in his left hand. In his right is a knife, a big knife. Probably he has watched *Crocodile Dundee* one too many times.

"I'll scream," Rose whispers.

He puts the flashlight into his pants pocket. Then he puts the knife in his teeth. Rose has seen that in cartoons, but didn't believe anyone actually did it.

Hands free, he throws himself upward onto the roof in a bouncing belly flop. One hand makes the ridge, then the other.

The sight of the knife pries the last ounce of adrenaline from Rose's glands. It gets her to the top of the skylight. From there she is able to straddle the ridge of the house. Weight off her arms and legs, for an instant she feels as if she could levitate into the stars.

Bending her knees and moving her heels toward the ridge, she clasps the opposing sides of the roof with her thighs until she is stable. Seven or eight feet away, limp as a flag on a windless day, Monster Man hangs from the ridge.

Emitting a porcine grunt, he moves his right hand six inches toward Rose. Then his left. If one counts one's life in six-inch increments, Rose has about fourteen remaining.

Craning her neck, she glances over her shoulder. The far end of the roof is shrouded in darkness, trees blocking the light from the next street. She could scoot back. To do what? Be pushed from the peak to the deck instead of from the gutter to the gravel?

Thirteen increments left. His arms are strong. He moves more quickly than she'd believed he could. Had it not been for his enormous gut, he would have gotten his feet up and straddled the ridge. Rose is grateful for beer and McDonald's.

Once he reaches the skylight, he will do as Rose did, and use it to climb up. Monster Man must not be allowed to gain the stability of the ridge.

This, then, is where Rose will make her stand.

Whatever that entails.

For a moment she is overwhelmed with helplessness, so much so, it dizzies her. To this hulk she is as a duckling to a bobcat. Everything about her is soft and harmless: canvas shoes, flowing harem pants, thin cotton tunic, wee bony fists, blunt bovine teeth, legs the monster could probably close one fist around.

Rose orders her mind back into the moment. *Be here. See here.*

Piggy oink by piggy oink, he works his bulk to less than five feet from her.

"Come any closer, and I really will scream," Rose whispers.

The brim of the ball cap lifts. Dark wet eyes glitter at her from the shadow. The lower part of his face registers as one huge knife, the hilt a black bar against his cheek.

Rose won't scream. He must have figured that out. Had she wanted to call down the attention of the neighbors, she would have been screaming her head off for the last five minutes. She guesses that is about the amount of time that has elapsed since she heard him in the downstairs living room. The rest of her life might not last much longer than that.

Why not scream? Hadn't she decided to go back to Longwood anyway?

She had.

The man with the slashing smile has changed her mind. Monster Man is not a burglar. Not a rapist. Monster Man is an assassin. He is here to kill Rose Dennis. Longwood no longer wants her back. Longwood knows that without the red capsules, her mind has returned. Longwood wants her dead.

Rose narrows her eyes and studies the knife wielder.

Would she rather die than face going back into the control of people who have an interest in maintaining her dementia?

Darn tootin' she would.

Barnacle eyes fixed on her, knife cutting an obscene silver grin in his face, the intruder humps his belly sideways. Four feet from her perch. If he gets a hand on the skylight, she is toast.

Oink. Hump.

Three feet.

"Who sent you?" she hisses. "Someone at Longwood?" A grunt and a hump and a black bar of shadow beneath the cap brim are her only answer. With the blade in his teeth, he can't talk. It would be like talking to the dentist when the drill is in one's mouth.

Rose steadies her breath and clears her mind. She suspects she is in no way spiritually prepared for the moment of death. In the bardo of transition, her slippery little drift of energy will attach itself to the first thing it sees, be it tomato worm, opossum, or paramecium.

Now she sees, really sees, the knife: the slight rise to a point on the back where it pushes into the man's cheek, the drop of sweat on the shiny blade, the delicate swoop of the serrations on its cutting edge, the haft wrapped in dark tape or leather, the strip neatly overlapping itself up to where it stops at the wider, thumb-shaped end.

Folding down over the ridgeline in an extreme Child's Pose that would impress her yoga instructor, Rose reaches out, grabs the haft, and jerks.

"Whoa!" she mutters as it comes free with a crack.

Monster Man is as surprised as she. "Hey!" he says stupidly. Recovering himself, he spits something at her. A solid speck stings her chin, then falls between her thighs, hitting the roof with a pathetic click.

He snarls. Half of one of his front teeth is broken off at a sharp angle.

Now she has pissed him off.

A nuclear brand of fear starts up her throat, cold enough to freeze her brain. Rose shivers, shaking it off.

Okay, Monster Man is mad.

So is she.

Vocalizing something very like the snarl of a large canine, he moves his gloved hands another foot toward her. The glittering dark eyes never leave her face.

Rose clutches the knife in her left hand, the blade pointing away from her. She passes it to her stronger hand, then wraps the other fist around it in a two-handed grip lest tremors or sweat loosen her hold. The roof is dark. The gloves are black. Rose's hands have little strength and no steadiness. She aims for the nearest sausage-sized finger. Tentatively, she stabs. The blade strikes something and sinks in a creepy quarter of an inch. Her stomach twists.

No sound, but fury fires the intruder's small eyes. Too quick for Rose to see, much less react, he lets go of the roof ridge. Clamping his hand around her left wrist, he pulls. Rose pulls back, but it is no contest.

Rose opens the fist she has gripped around her knife hand and lets the arm go limp. The sudden loss of opposing energy jolts him off balance. He nearly yanks Rose's arm out of its socket as he slips down the shingles. For a horrific moment she can see herself and the man and the knife cartwheeling off the roof together.

A curse and he steadies himself. No longer is he dragging her from her perch, but he still keeps a crushing grip on her wrist.

Knife in her right hand, Rose leans perilously far out over the ridgeline. Panicked, she stabs at his far hand as if she is tenderizing beef in one heck of a hurry.

Stab, stab, stab. Maybe the knife hits his fingers, maybe it hits the shingles. Delicate differences are lost to Rose. "Get off my roof!" she spits. Stab, stab. "Pig face." Now she is practically growling. Stab. "Dog vomit." Spittle flies from her lips. Stab.

The paw manacling her wrist opens. She laughs with freedom. Then he grabs. Black leather-covered fingers, like those of a bull ape, close over her thigh just above the knee.

With the squeak of a terrified rodent, Rose plunges the knife through the black hand and deep into the flesh of her thigh, pinning her and the monster together. That flash of the blade, like a giant tooth biting down, releases her last lost memory. Rose knows how Harley died; her beloved's god-awful tabloid marvel of an exit from this plane of existence. Hysterical laughter forces up from her belly. Tense muscles in her throat strangle it into a high-pitched giggle.

The man's eyes go wide, then narrow to mere slits, as if he sees her differently now that she's snickering.

Rose has frightened a hit man. That scares her quiet. Still, he flinches back, and his hand slides free of the glove skewered to her leg. Blood, dark as ink, splatters over her thigh. "You are one crazy bitch," he says as he tucks the injured hand to his chest and curls protectively around it.

This is a mistake. Rolling like a sow bug, he tumbles down the roof and over the edge.

Rose hears a sound like a giant sea lion, dropped from a helicopter, hitting the tarmac.

The glove remains, spiked to her leg by the oversized knife. Wide-eyed, she looks at the enormous blade protruding from her flesh.

"Don't you dare faint," she tells her body. "Not after all I've done for you."

CHAPTER 12

The sight of the knife protruding from her flesh breaks some inner dam and releases the pain. Quite a lot of it. In a sickening tide, it rushes through her belly to explode in her head. Vision swims; bile fills her throat. For a long moment Rose holds on to the ridge with both hands to keep from toppling off.

The internal shriek subsides to a thin scream. Rose takes a deep breath and listens. From below comes not a sound. Fervently she hopes the intruder is dead, head crushed like a melon, spine shattered, neck snapped.

"No," she murmurs. "Not dead." Dead would be rotten. Her karma would reek for a thousand incarnations. In relative truth, the man needed killing, but in absolute truth, there is no excuse. Worse would be the instant karma. Karma now. She'd have to drag the great lumpish intruder into the backyard, excavate a shallow grave with a serving spoon, then roll him in. She really would be a criminal, complete with a decomposing corpse buried in the backyard. Add that to assaulting a health worker, and Rose would be deemed criminally insane and locked up for a long, long time.

Groans percolate through the still night air, welcome to Rose's guilty ears. Grunts and foul language follow. Rose breathes a sigh of relief.

Right Concentration: She sends metta to the monster. *May you be well. May you be happy. May you be free of suffering, and the causes of suffering.*

May you leave and never come back.

From beneath the glove, blood runs in three small rivulets painting her thigh a bizarre shiny red-orange. The color is a trick of the streetlights. That, or during the previous weeks her body had been taken over by aliens with fluorescent orange ichor in their veins. Pain no longer loots and pillages her body but merely boils like molten lava in her left leg.

The intruder heaves into sight beyond the porch roof. Limping badly, his injured hand clasped to his belly, he crosses the street to a small dark-colored pickup. One-handed, he opens the door, then folds himself in. As

158

he drives off, Rose tries to guess the make of the car, get the license plate number. It is too far, too dark, her mind and vision too disturbed: squat dark man, squat dark truck. Not much to put in a police report.

Of course there will be no police report. Living outside the law brings a plethora of complications, she realizes.

The truck turns a corner and is gone from sight. Rose sits unmoving. Throughout the smashing glass, crashing furniture, stabbing, de-guttering, and falling bodies, not one single light came on in the neighboring houses. Either violent crime is more prevalent in Charlotte than she'd thought, or its citizens are uncommonly sound sleepers.

Good. It quashes Rose's temptation to cry for help.

She read somewhere that when impaled by a foreign object, one should not remove the object but leave it in situ for the ER doctors to deal with. That not being an option, Rose grasps the handle of the knife firmly, closes her eyes, and pulls straight up. Pain again threatens to unseat her. Liquid warmth pours over her leg.

Rose opens her eyes. Dangling from the knife, an inch above the dripping steel point, is the empty ape-skin glove, black and flaccid. Convulsively, she flings knife and glove from her. They hit the roof, then the ground, with a squishy thud and a clink.

She starts to cry, then stops. No point in crying when there is no strong shoulder to absorb the tears. There is nothing to be done but get on with saving herself. Trying to keep her squeaking and mewling to a minimum, she scootches, bumps, and inches along the interminable length of ridgeline. Each movement ignites a flare of agony. Rose tries embracing it. She fails. The seat and thighs of her thin rayon harem pants shred away as they drag over the rough shingles. Blood makes her hands and leg sticky.

Finally she is above the porch. She folds her good leg over the ridge and sits on the peak of the roof sidesaddle. Below is a ribbon of the concrete that she will hit if she slips. Arms trembling, she turns her body and lets herself slide until she is hanging belly-down on the roof, fingers clinging to the ridge. Forcing the bad leg out, she feels it drop over the edge of the main roof. With a heave, she rolls herself after it, and falls. The porch roof catches her. Such is the pain in her leg, the impact of landing is a non-event.

Walking is less agonizing than crawling. Rose gets to her feet. Using the wall to remain upright, she navigates around the corner to the side window and collapses through. For a time she lies gasping in the ruin of her bedroom.

Blood pastes the fabric of her trousers to her skin from knee to crotch, but there is no pumping or spurting. *Of course there isn't,* she thinks. Unless she is dead and doesn't realize it yet. That happens more than one might think, stubborn life forces unable to let go of the attachments of an incarnation. They wander around wondering why nothing works like it used to. Pain convinces Rose that she is not a ghost, not yet.

Running on the power of self-reliance, born of utter abandonment, she does not dissolve into the inviting embrace of self-pity. Crab-walking backward on heels, butt, and hands, she reaches the bathroom and peels off her clothes.

Trousers and tunic are ruined and filthy. The pajamas she'd pulled her clothes over have literally saved her skin. Belly, chest, and buttocks are unscathed. Thighs, hands, and forearms are red, rough, and stinging. She turns on the shower, then, too weak to stand, lowers her protesting body into the pathetic excuse for a bathtub.

Hot water washes the blood from her

hands and leg. The wound above her knee gapes like a little red mouth drooling pink. The cut is about an inch long and probably that deep. Had she still been a citizen of the so-called civilized world, she would get stitches.

She could sew it closed with cotton thread and a needle. The very idea makes her insides quiver.

Having dried herself as best she can, she closes the wound with four butterfly bandages. Half a roll of toilet paper wrapped around her leg and tied snugly with a scarf, knot over the wound, serves as a bandage, keeping the whole jury-rigged mess in place.

Body close to exhaustion but mind racing, Rose puts on a tank top and loose linen pants. The glove and the knife have got to be retrieved. They are evidence. Besides, she doesn't want some neighborhood cat getting hold of the mutilated glove and dropping it proudly at the feet of an unsuspecting householder.

Rose limps outside.

The two items are artistically displayed on the white gravel, spattered now with black splotches, a gold mine of criminal DNA. If the Charlotte police are anything like the New Orleans police, they don't cotton to all that *CSI* nonsense, just shoot suspects and work lucrative private security details.

Several feet from the knife lies the glove, her final stab has nearly severed the leather forefinger. What remains is attached only by the thinnest strip of black. Grimacing with distaste, she pinches it up. There is a lump in the dangling tip. A finger. Rose cut the intruder's index finger clear off; that's why his hand slipped free of the glove. A wave of revulsion rocks her. She doesn't drop the gory object. Evidence. One day she might need it, not to prove the intruder's guilt but to prove the entire incident was not a figment of an overheated delusion.

Glove in one hand, knife held gingerly in the other, Rose limps back through the shattered sliding glass door and into the kitchen. Trusting the neighbors to be as disinterested in illumination as they are in noise, she risks flipping on the lights.

Knife and glove laid on the counter, Rose contemplates her next move. She supposes she is in shock, supposes she's lost a lot of blood, supposes she has PTSD. All this is probably true, but her mind is running at high speed, the manic side of depression. A treat. She's suffered depression on and off for forty years, but never mania. If this is it, she is all for it.

Unable to bring herself to touch the glove

again, she holds the tip of the nearly severed part in a pair of hot-dog tongs. The kitchen scissors serve to slit the leather. A bloody lump, two inches long, is revealed. Meat clamped in the tongs, she holds it under running water. Pink liquid pours over the pile of pots and pans she'd made as an early warning device. They will have to be thrown away. There will be no eating out of them after this, even if they are sterilized.

The lump is rinsed clean. It surprises Rose that a severed digit still looks exactly like a finger. Some part of her expected it to be more scientific, less graphic. She lays it carefully on a paper towel.

Her painting supplies are in two of the big boxes in the living room. Rose cuts the packing tape and levers the easel free. Acrylic inks, brushes, and paint are in a large box Harley built for her. When opened, it sits on end like a slender steamer trunk, tubes of paint and ink hang neatly on cup hooks.

Leaving the rest, she carries the inks and a sketch pad back into the kitchen. Quinacridone violet tempts her, but black seems the most professional. Selecting a never-to-be-used-after-this salad plate, Rose pours several drops of the ink on it. Using the tines of a dinner fork, she spreads the ink into a thin, even coat. This done, she steels herself to the necessity of touching the artifact.

Holding her breath, as if the detached finger might have already begun to decompose and stink, she gingerly picks it up with thumb and forefinger, the nailed end pointing away from her hand. The intruder bit his nails to the quick.

"Gross," she whispers. Never has she touched anything that felt so dead: not rock, not wood, not hamburger, not chicken breast. This is one dead finger.

Holding it steady, Rose carefully rolls the finger in the ink, then onto the sketch pad. After ten or fifteen tries, she gets several excellent prints. Satisfied, she settles back on the stool she'd pulled up during her project and studies her work. She likes it. There is a visceral progression from the muddied early attempts to the cleanly defined whorls. Even the several drops of blood, quickly turning dark as they dry, add to the impact of the piece.

Rose has all but forgotten her medium. She is painting, or printing rather, with a severed human finger. Nausea nearly overcomes artistic license. Her lips in a moue of disgust, she sets the digit back on the paper towel, then folds the towel into a discreet opaque package.

The freezer? Flesh will be disfigured as the cells freeze and burst, destroying the print. Does she need both the finger and the prints to prove she isn't delusional?

The refrigerator? Not if she ever plans on eating the other half of the turkey-and-provolone sandwich.

The garbage disposal? Way too gross.

A compromise. Rose puts the towel-wrapped package into a ziplock bag and drops it into the produce drawer. The sketchbook is left open on the kitchen counter. Acrylic ink dries quickly, but she doesn't want to chance smearing any of the evidence. Evidence, she reminds herself as she glances at it before leaving the kitchen. Not art.

In the living room she returns to the box of painting supplies. The easel is set up in minutes, an eighteen-by-twenty-inch canvas in place. Black, white, Payne's gray, and ultramarine blue: Those will be all the colors she needs. She arranges the tubes of paint and several brushes on the top of a chest-high moving box marked DINING ROOM.

A quick trip to the kitchen for a roll of paper towels and half a pitcher of water, and she is ready to begin.

CHAPTER 13

"Gigi?"

The word penetrates the layers of Rose's mind. The sun is well up, morning. Mel, plastic bags in one hand, the ubiquitous cell phone in the other, is standing on the deck. Between them is the shattered sliding door.

"Gigi, what happened?"

The caution in her granddaughter's voice wakes Rose up to her surroundings. The entire top of the packing box has been used as her palette. Paintings are propped against various boxes. Two are on the couch, another, partially finished, on the easel. The floor and the sides of nearby boxes are splattered with black, white, blue, and shades in between. Paint streaks Rose's shoulders, the consequences of holding one brush in her teeth while using another, loaded with a different color.

Drawing herself out of the land of visions, the world from which she paints, Rose greets Mel in what she hopes is a normal and reassuring manner.

"Be careful of the broken glass," she says. "I've been painting."

"So I see," Mel replies, still with a distinct note of caution. *"Planet of the Apes?"*

For the first time since the painting trance took her, Rose looks critically at her work. A black hand, knuckles creased more like living skin than dead leather, clutches a knife the size a butcher might use for the serious work. Dark eyes, burning with sparks of blue, glare from beneath a cap brim, the shadow and the eyes melting together. Hunched and canted, a simian shape lurches through the spill of a street-light. A shadowy vehicle hints its existence in lines and planes. Seen from above, one thick leg extruding from a pair of black cargo shorts, another ape-like figure hunkers over, straddling a windowsill. All are in shades of night and terror.

"Bad day at the zoo?" Mel asks.

"Unclear perceptions," Rose says wearily. For identity purposes, her paintings are fairly worthless. "I had a gentleman caller last night. I perceived him as an animal. Now I've painted him that way. Doggone it!" Too tired to stand erect any longer, she walks to the couch and flops on it full length, her heels resting on one arm.

Mel steps through the doorframe.

"Careful," Rose says again. Most of the glass is in neat little squares, safety glass, but bits crammed into the frame could be sharp.

"Someone broke in?" Mel asks incredulously.

"No. Someone came in, with a key, I think, then broke the door on his way out to make it look like he'd broken in," Rose explains.

"How do you know?" Mel sounds as if she still does not trust Rose's reality, simian or otherwise.

"On his second visit he didn't leave the premises through the same door. I discovered the door broken but unlocked and open."

"Somebody really broke in while you were here?"

Rose can see Mel absorbing the idea.

"Gigi, that's awful!"

The genuine concern touches Rose. Oddly, it makes her leg and palms hurt. It makes her fatigue nearly unbearable. Mel cares. Rose is not going to let that weaken her. Mel does not need a grandmother who is any more of a burden than Rose already is.

"You know," Rose says, making herself sit up and look moderately perky, "it's not awful. It's pretty wonderful. Remember I said I thought people at Longwood were plotting my demise?"

"I remember," Mel says.

"Well, they were. They are. I am not crazy. QED." As the words come from her lips, Rose realizes they are true. A psychic weight lifts. She is not crazy, not delusional. They really are out to kill her. This is such an excellent revelation, she laughs.

"Gigi, would you mind walking me through QED step by step?" Mel asks warily.

Rose does, from first awakening to final unfinished painting. She shows Mel the wreck of the bedroom and her clothes, the blood spatters and smears on the skylight. Looking from below with the sun behind them, they look like mud. For the finale, pointing proudly at the open sketchbook, Rose boasts, "I got his fingerprint."

Mel is suitably impressed. She crosses the small kitchen to study the page of prints. "Wow!" she says, beaming at Rose. "How did you get him to give you fingerprints?"

Rose had left that part out as indelicate. "I . . . well, what happened was I accidentally ended up with his finger. Then I made the prints with that," she says.

Then that story has to be told in full.

"You want to see it?" Rose finishes.

"What kind of grandmother are you?" Mel asks. "Offering to show an impressionable child a cut-off finger!"

"You're way tougher than me," Rose replies.

"Of course I want to see it," Mel says. "Are you kidding? How often does a chance like this come along?"

Rose takes the plastic bag out of the lettuce drawer and dumps the towel-wrapped morsel onto the counter. With tongs and a fork, she peels the paper back.

"Jeez," Mel breathes. "It looks so much like a finger. I mean, you know, a *finger.*"

"Creepy, huh?"

"Wrap it back up."

Rose does, and drops the package back into the drawer.

"That'll be a big surprise for the cleaning lady," Mel says, after they've returned to the living room and are sprawled on the couch, the only usable area remaining in the house. "You don't think the break-in could be a coincidence?" she asks. "Guy thinks the house is empty. It's not. So he decides to kill the witness?"

"I didn't witness him until he came back

for me," Rose says. "That's the telling part. He was scot-free, run of the house to burgle at will. He takes nothing, then comes back for me."

"Pretty convincing," Mel admits.

"Don't forget, he broke the glass in the door on his way out, not in."

"So a key or a good lock picker," Mel says.

"And when I cut off his finger, he said, 'You *are* one crazy bitch,' not 'You are *one* crazy bitch.' That suggests to me that he was sent here by somebody who called me a crazy bitch. Now we're back to Longwood. Nobody else in this town knows me well enough to call me a crazy bitch."

"Grandma Nancy," Mel offers.

"Other than Grandma Nancy."

"Stella."

"Other than Grandma Nancy and Stella."

After a moment of quiet cogitation, Mel leaps up with a lithe grace Rose can barely remember. She gathers the paintings, eight finished, and props them against boxes where they can be easily viewed from the sofa. That done, she plops down next to Rose, her feet folded beneath her. "So that's our guy," she says. "He looks properly thuggish."

The two study the paintings for a while.

"Hispanic? Korean? Italian? Hawaiian?"

Mel suggests.

"Maybe." Rose stares at the paintings. There is more detail than she'd first thought. "Hispanic or Italian," she decides. "Very dark eyes, almost black." She looks at the piratical figure with the knife in its jaws. "Good straight teeth," she adds. "Or were. When I pulled the knife away, one of his incisors broke off."

"Ouch!" Mel says.

"It did make him a tad waspish," Rose says.

"Not tall but thick," Mel adds. "I'm guessing late twenties or thirty?"

"My guess, too."

"With these and the fingerprint, the cops should be able to find him, wouldn't you think?" Mel says.

"You'd think," Rose agrees. "But that doesn't make it so. Me, they'd nail in a heartbeat. A bird in the hand as it were. Maybe even a nice mention on the six o'clock news."

"Cynical," Mel sighs.

"I've lived too long in New Orleans," Rose excuses herself.

"His ears look really small and tight to his head," Mel observes. "Were they really like that?"

Rose looks more closely at the painting

Mel indicates. "Must have been. Why else would I have painted them that way?"

The doorbell rings and they both twitch.

"I'll get it," Mel says, unfolding herself and slipping effortlessly over the back of the sofa.

Rose wants to stop her, to tell her to be careful, but she doesn't. That seems too dramatic for a sunny suburban morning.

Mel is back. "FedEx," she says, tossing Rose the envelope.

"A credit card and an ATM card. Marion sent them overnight express."

"Wish I had a sister," Mel says.

"I wish you did, too." Rose opens the envelope. "There's something else." She upends the envelope. A plastic prescription bottle falls out. It's wrapped in a Post-it Note. "Antidepressants," Rose says, then reads the note: *I called my doctor and asked for a prescription. Not a problem. They hand these things out like candy. I'm surprised they don't have help-yourself bowls on pharmacy counters like they do dog treats at Petco.*

"Will you take them?" Mel asks.

"I guess," Rose concedes.

"Good. You'll need that money," Mel says seriously. "You can't stay here anymore."

Rose opens her mouth to protest, then closes it. Obviously she can't stay here. They

174

know where she is. They could try again.

"Why on earth would anybody bother to kill me?" she asks — not Mel, the powers that be.

"Drug deal gone bad, got crosswise to the mob, saw something you shouldn't, heard something you shouldn't, are an unwitting cog in some criminal enterprise." Mel lists the usual suspects.

"The last is the only one even vaguely possible, and it's a stretch," Rose says.

They sit in silence for a few moments.

"What comes next?" Mel asks.

"That's a good question." Rose sighs. "There isn't anything to grab on to. No suspect, clues, means, motive — the Sherlock Holmes stuff."

"Now that you've fingered the perp—"

"Very funny."

"Couldn't you call the police? They'd have to take you seriously, wouldn't they?"

Talk of calling the cops makes Rose uncomfortable. Breathing into the feeling, she tries to make sense of it. "They would believe I have a severed finger in my fridge," Rose says slowly. "They would see a lot of paintings of a mysterious dark man with a knife in his teeth, and a bunch of paint-smeared boxes. They would know I am dangerous, that I escaped from a mental institution —"

"Memory Care Unit," Mel corrects her.

"It will be the same to them," Rose declares. "They will probably be nice family men. They'll take me back to Longwood to make sure I'm taken care of."

"Tell them the people at Longwood are the ones who are trying to kill you," Mel insists. "Tell them you want to come to our house."

Rose shoots Mel a look.

"Right. They'd so listen to a dotty old lady who poisoned a nice nurse-lady. Never mind."

Silence settles around them. Then Mel asks, "Can you run the fingerprint somehow?"

"You wouldn't happen to have a friend whose mom or dad is a crooked cop, would you?" Rose asks hopefully.

"No cops," Mel says. "A couple of lawyers, I think."

"Unsavory?"

"Real estate and contract law. Or investment. Excruciatingly boring."

"Marion might be able to," Rose muses. "She can access the dark web — don't ask me what that is, but it has illegal items for sale, or so she tells me. Maybe a shady cop or disgruntled dispatcher runs license plates or prints on the sly and sells the information."

Mel fetches the sketch pad. Rose takes several pictures of the prints with her cell phone, taps in Marion's email address, then adds: *Can you find out whose these are? Story next time.*

"At least that's something," she says.

"Unless it's nothing." Mel sits down, her knees pulled up under her chin.

Rose says, "I think there are two separate areas of nothing/something. The first is what happened between the day your granddad died and the day your dad put me into Longwood. The second is what happened in Longwood from my incarceration up through the attempted murder last night."

"You don't think they are related? Like first you acted all crazy, and second you acted all crazy?" Mel asks.

"Then I got out and stopped acting crazy. That is key," Rose insists. "First and Second Crazy must be related. But coincidences do happen. Lightning strikes in the same place more often than people think. Let's say that First Crazy was caused by the shock and grief at losing Harley. Maybe throw in a few transient ischemic attacks, whatever. Then your dad gets me into this great facility. I start to get well. Then Second Crazy is induced for completely unrelated reasons."

"Sort of like walking down an alley and getting mugged," Mel says.

"Exactly. The alley didn't cause the mugging. Walking down it merely put the victim in the vicinity of an opportunistic mugger. Rather than wasting time on why I was in that particular alley, I think we should start with the mugger," Rose says.

"The opportunistic Longwood mugger."

"Yup."

"First you should get out of this house," Mel says. "Can you get a hotel with Great-Aunt Marion's credit card?"

"I could," Rose considers. "But credit cards are easily traced. Longwood undoubtedly has all Marion's contact information on a next-of-kin form. Marion would kill me if I exposed her in that way."

"Use the ATM and pay cash," Mel suggests.

"I'd have to be slumming to find a place that doesn't require ID."

"Why not stay at our house?" Mel offers.

That is unbearably tempting. The house is a trilevel, the guest quarters on the bottom floor, with a separate entrance. When she and Harley visited, they always stayed at Flynn's home. It is spacious, airy, homey, familiar. Mel is there. All things Rose positively aches for at the moment.

Prying her mind off the delights offered, "No," Rose says. "But thanks."

"Why not? It's perfect!" Mel exclaims. "If we're careful, Uncle Dan won't even know you're there. He's so laid-back, he hardly notices I'm there."

"It's not Dan. It's the murderers. If I'm ever going to get the Grandmother of the Year Award, Grandma can't be leading the Big Bad Wolf to Little Mel Riding Hood. Flynn is the man who put me in Longwood. You think if they don't find me here, they won't go straight to your house? The man whose finger I have in the freezer isn't the type to show mercy to the innocent."

"He'd have to deal with Uncle Daniel," Mel says.

"Dan is big and strong, but he's not a fighter. Violence takes nice people by surprise. The damage is done before we even figure out the bad guy is serious."

"True. Even a midget like Stella scares Uncle Daniel," Mel says.

"Stella scares everybody," Rose says unkindly.

Mel stands and picks up her backpack. "I've got school. Will you be okay? I can call in sick."

"I'll be fine. You get on with your day. I'll

work things out."

"Last period is honors study hall. I can ditch. I'll come over after."

"That should be way before bad-guy time," Rose says.

Rose washes down the cinnamon rolls Mel brought with a mug of tea. Fortified, she goes out the ruined door, across the weedy yard, to the garage. It is not so much a garage as a brick bunker, no windows, no side door, space enough for only one vehicle. Weathered garden gnomes stand in a line to one side of the door like Miss Havisham's bridesmaids. The door lifts, sliding along runners in the fashion of modern garage doors, but this is an early prototype. The hinged panels are of heavy wood — rotting in several places now — and must be hoisted with a chain-and-pulley system. Rose manages with a minimum of cursing.

Inside is a single vehicle, Harley's beloved mint-condition, cherry-red, 1949 Ford pickup truck. The truck takes up most of the space. An old croquet set, a couple of lawn chairs left behind by the previous owner, and the inflatable mattress they used before their furniture arrived are flattened against the walls.

Harley's toolbox is in the bed of the truck. Rose lugs it back to the house.

She spends the next hours building her fortress. The kitchen window is covered with cardboard that is nailed in place with strips of packing she scavenges. The windows she didn't nail shut during her pre-Longwood madness she nails shut now. She sweeps up broken glass and moves heavy boxes, building a wall to cover the shattered door.

While she works, she draws up two lists. One is of the supplies she needs Mel to procure. The other is of questions for Marion. Marion can do just about anything on the computer. Whether she will or not, Rose has yet to find out. Like many members of the Digitari, Marion is more than a little paranoid about being tracked across cyberspace by unfriendly individuals or agencies.

Rose needs Marion to feel safe.

She needs Mel to be safe.

That means keeping Mel out of the plan to a certain extent. Mel is not a girl for being kept out. She is smart and good at solving problems. She also has youth's confidence in her own immortality. Unlike most young people, Mel knows for a fact that grown-ups are fragile. Death can snatch them when one least expects it. Taken together, these two attributes place Rose's granddaughter in danger of unnecessary martyrdom.

When the bulwark of boxes guarding the broken door is complete, Rose finishes it by shoving the couch against the mass. On one side, she leaves a dog-door-sized space sufficient for her to squeeze in or out if she isn't concerned about dignity. This is camouflaged by a lightweight box. The upstairs bedroom she leaves as the intruder has redecorated it.

Downstairs, in the coat closet by the front door, she makes a nest to sleep in. Should a new monster be dispatched, he will have little choice but to break in via the front door. If Rose is awake, at the first sound, she'll run to the back of the house and slither out her dog door. If that option is unavailable, she will stay in her nest. With luck, the monster will thunder by the unassuming coat closet and toward the stairs. At that point Rose will quietly slip out the way he came in.

That is the theory, at any rate. And the story she'll spin for Mel.

Having rendered the house as unappealing and unoccupied-looking as she can make it, Rose calls Marion.

She tells her of the night's adventure.

"So," she finishes up, "we can clearly see that I am not crazy, and therefore we can

182

postulate that I am not demented. People were drugging me."

Marion takes a few seconds to digest the story, then says, "Good. Now I can quit humoring you and genuinely be on your side."

"Thank you," Rose says sincerely.

Marion gets down to business. "Here's what I have. All this is public access: Facebook, blogs, promos, profiles, chat rooms, tweets, YouTube. It is all out there for anybody to find."

Rose takes notes. Marion has gleaned a great deal of information: Longwood's shift hours, parking facilities, location of many cameras, senior management, layout of the Memory Care Unit, visiting hours, types of personnel used, both staff and private contractors. Rose is amazed at how much detailed information a dedicated computer genius can find lying around for the taking.

Marion reluctantly agrees to try to get the fingerprint run. "I am not a hacker," she tells Rose firmly. "I'm an explorer. Hacking is a whole different skill set. Besides, I don't want guys in black jumpsuits rappelling into my backyard from helicopters."

"Can you get Longwood's patient records?" Rose asks.

"Not without a password. I am not a

hacker."

That last is in case the call is monitored, Rose guesses.

They talk another hour and thirty minutes. At the end of that time, they have a plan.

CHAPTER 14

An *open-up-police*-style knock jerks Rose from a much-needed afternoon nap. For an instant, the paint-spattered, box-ridden chaos of the living room disorients her. Recovery is quick. Her mind is back to normal — or at least as good as it has ever been.

It is Mel, again carrying plastic sacks. As the girl brushes by into the house, Rose tells her, "I need your cell phone."

"Why don't you just ask for my eyeballs and liver while you're at it?" Mel says, mouth agape, so much like her mother, Rose wants to cry. "How long?"

"Not more than a few hours."

Mel gasps, appalled. "Huh! No," she says.

"Marion and I came up with a plan. It requires two phones."

Mel groans. "Oh boy, I can't wait. And whatever it is, I can do everything you're going to do. What kind of plan?"

Rose tells her.

"Can't Great-Aunt Marion just hack them or something?" Mel asks.

"Not a hacker," Rose says.

"This is totally insane."

"That has become my specialty," Rose says, hoping for a smile. She doesn't get one. "It should work," Rose insists. "It's not foolproof, but it's doable."

"That's what all this stuff is for? Why don't I just deliver it to Sing Sing and be done with it? I'm coming with you. To Longwood, not Sing Sing."

"That's not part of the plan."

"You'll screw up the electronic stuff. You're not all that tech-savvy, you know."

"Marion will be with me," Rose reminds her.

"Right. You're going to be Great-Aunt Marion's avatar. That is so not going to work."

"You thought it would when I told you a minute ago."

"That's because I thought I'd be with you."

Rose waits.

"Please," Mel begs. "It would be so much less scary if I were doing this stuff. You're going to get all freaked out about internet interactions, and then they'll grab you, and

186

that will be that." Mel is holding her phone behind her back protectively.

Rose knew keeping Mel out of their plan was going to be the hard part. What she hadn't foreseen was Mel's aversion to being without her electronics. To Rose, being off the grid is a holiday. For Mel, it seems closer to an amputation. Rose says nothing, waiting for Mel to work through the concept in her own time.

"Can't you just go get a burn phone?" Mel asks after a while.

"No. They don't have the bells and whistles," Rose says. Mel knows this.

The exchange of words is peculiarly familiar; Rose realizes it is like the few times she has tried to talk someone out of an addiction. Invariably an exercise in futility.

As they talk, Rose follows Mel back to the living room. When Mel sees the changes Rose has wrought, she ceases fretting over the coming separation from social media and looks around. "What's with the rearranging?" she asks.

Rose tells her, shows her the Rose-sized dog door with its camouflage, and the nest in the closet; explains her escape routes should an assassin come knocking.

Mel takes it all in without comment. When they are seated on the couch-become-retaining-wall, she says, "You do know how unbelievably weird this is, don't you? I mean, you really don't think this is a rational approach?"

Rose sighs deeply. "I do. And no, I don't," she admits.

"Why not just grab some cash and check in to a Motel 6?" Mel asks.

"I can't face it," Rose says. "I'd rather hunker down in a closet, with a doggie-door escape hatch, than spend a night in a soulless cheap motel. Let's hope the bad people waste their time checking out all Charlotte's fleabag motels."

"Yeah," Mel says, unconvinced. "Let's hope."

"Time for me to change and get ready to go," Rose says.

"I'm going with you. Just to the MCU," Mel insists.

"Promise you'll go home after you drop me off?

"Cross my heart." Mel crosses her heart. "And, for the record, I think this is deeply, deeply disturbing behavior."

"If you can think of another way, I'm all ears," Rose says.

"Just because I can't think of one doesn't mean there isn't one," Mel says.

Rose goes upstairs with half the bags Mel

brought. Izzy had a nice collection of wigs. When she'd lost her hair from the chemo, she'd made a game of them — not for her own sake, Rose knows, but to make the hair loss less traumatic for her then eleven-year-old daughter. Mel has brought a pixie cut in brunette and a jaw-length bob in the champagne-blond color that older women often choose to hide gray. From Izzy's dresser, Mel purloined a set of scrubs, the ubiquitous uniform of health care workers from janitors to brain surgeons.

The scrubs are comfortable and fit as well as scrubs do. Rose chooses the blond wig over the brown pixie. The bob's swinging sides obscure more of her face. Customarily Rose wears little makeup — lipstick and maybe a dash of blush. Tonight she puts on base, dusts the sides of her nose with a pale brown to make it appear narrower, lowlights her cheeks with a heavier blush, and lines and mascaras her eyes. The result is not remarkable, particularly in the South, where women often wear full makeup, but she no longer looks like the washed-out old crazy woman the people at Longwood know.

From the drawer of an overturned bed stand, she fishes out a pair of reading glasses with multicolored frames and hangs them around her neck on a beaded strap made for the purpose.

Studying herself in the mirror, she is satisfied. Gone is the vacant wraith that wandered Longwood's halls in Rose's skin. In its place is a middle-aged health care professional who takes pains with her appearance. The alterations, along with the fact that no one will be looking for her at Longwood, should be sufficient.

Pleased with herself, Rose goes back downstairs. Mel is on the couch making her fond farewells to her cell phone.

"What do you think?" Rose strikes a modeling pose.

Mel's face crumples the way it did when she was two, before she was old enough to keep her emotions from showing. Tears fill her lovely eyes.

Rose wants to shoot herself.

The wig, the scrubs: Rose is disguised as Mel's mom, Izzy, going to work during her chemo.

Rose rips the wig off and falls to her knees by the couch. "I am so sorry. What an idiot! I didn't think." Her voice grows thick with tears for Mel, and for herself for hurting Mel.

"It's okay," Mel says, sitting up and hugging Rose awkwardly around the head. "Just kind of . . . wham! For a minute. When

Mom was so sick, she even looked kind of old, her skin all loose like yours. Ghost time, you know?"

"I should have," Rose says miserably. "I got all caught up in the moment and forgot. Are you really okay?"

"Sure. For a half-orphan, I'm fab."

"Balderdash," Rose says.

"Balderdash?" Mel lifts an eyebrow.

Rose gets up, checks her knees for paint smears. "I used to swear like a regular person until you came along and spoiled everything."

"Mom wouldn't let you use foul language in front of the child?"

"Izzy wasn't like that," Rose answers, sitting beside Mel on the sofa. "She never made me do anything — or even told me not to do anything. When I'd do or say something too random, she had this way of dropping her jaw and making her eyes really wide, like she was so shocked, she didn't know whether to burst out laughing or run from the room. Then, because Izzy was Izzy, whatever out-of-line thing I was doing, I kind of sort of just didn't want to do it anymore."

"I remember that look," Mel says wistfully.

"I'm glad I'm wearing your mom's things

on this junket," Rose says. "It makes me feel less scared, more confident."

"I'm glad, too, I guess," Mel says. "Mom wouldn't have approved of what you're planning to do."

"Probably not," Rose agrees.

"Mom would have told you to call the police."

"Your mother was a woman who had great faith in the system. She knew how to work and play well with others. Your granddad was like that. It worked for them. Not me. How the real world works has always been a mystery to me."

They don't speak for a while. Mel goes back to her cell phone.

Finally, Rose rouses herself. "I guess this is it," she says. "Let's get me wired." Rose holds her hand out for Mel's iPhone.

"Wait," Mel says. "Let me make sure the ringer and vibrator are off. Dad usually calls around eight."

Dad calls. Of course he does. "Did you talk to him last night?" Rose asks.

"Every night," Mel replies without looking up.

"Did he mention Longwood? Me?"

"Nope. I haven't told him anything. You asked me not to, remember?"

Rose does remember. "Longwood should

have called him," she says slowly. She hadn't thought of that back in the fog-laced times.

"They must not have," Mel says.

"After that first aborted escape, Nancy came, and Stella," Rose recalls. "You'd think Longwood would have called Flynn. He's the man on all the paperwork."

"Maybe they did, and he called Grandma Nancy," Mel says.

That is possible, but Rose thinks it odd. If Flynn knew she'd gone missing and stayed missing, he would have said something to his daughter. No, Flynn would have flown home the instant he could get away.

Unless he wants her to go missing, die, and be written off without a murmur.

Now, *there* is some nasty food for thought.

"Cell phone," Rose says, putting that idea away. She holds out her hand. Mel hugs the phone to her chest.

"You won't answer it?"

"No."

"You won't read any texts?"

"No."

"Or look at the photo gallery?"

"Oooh, what's in the photo gallery?" Rose asks avidly. Mel is not amused. "Only kidding. No, I will not pry, peep, listen, or trespass in any way."

"And call me the second you get out," Mel insists.

"Can't."

"Oh! That's right. You can't call me because I don't have a phone. I can't call you. This so completely sucks."

"I'll come to your house as soon as I can," Rose promises.

"How will you know whether Uncle Daniel is there when you can't call me? This is not going to work."

Anxiety, a classic symptom when the addict fears losing her source.

"How about I come to the playhouse and hide there until you tell me the coast is clear?"

"How can I tell you when *I don't have a phone*!" Mel is almost shouting.

"I'll put a pillow in the window so you'll know I'm there. When Daniel is gone, you come get me. How does that sound?"

Mel clearly isn't impressed with the pillow idea. Rose watches as the girl tries to put together an argument against it.

At length, Mel blows out a long derisive breath. "Before cell phones, did you guys have to be all Hardy Boys and Nancy Drew all the time?"

"All the time," Rose says.

"Talk about early childhood mortification," Mel says, but she lets Rose pry the phone from her warm living hand.

CHAPTER 15

"Did you get the Kleenex box?" Rose asks.

"I had to go to three stores," Mel says as she leans over the arm of the sofa to retrieve a plastic bag. From it she takes a square box of tissues. The box is tan with an intricate black repeating pattern.

"Perfect," Rose says. "You are a girl in a million. Empty it out, but don't mess up the tissues."

While Mel busies herself with that, Rose goes to the pillaged art supplies box and digs around in its disheveled contents. Armed with a #12 X-Acto knife and a roll of packing tape, she returns to the couch.

"Okay, put it in," she tells Mel.

Her task of tissue deployment complete, Mel has picked up her cell phone again.

"Do I have to talk you down one more time?" Rose asks.

"I can quit anytime I want," Mel says. She puts her phone into the empty tissue box.

"Hold it snug against the side," Rose says. When Mel has the phone and box stabilized, Rose presses her fingertips along the cardboard until she feels an indentation. In that soft spot, she inserts the X-Acto knife. The tip of the blade clicks against a hard surface. "Got it on the first try," she crows. "You can take the phone out now."

Holding the box between her knees, Rose cuts a neat square about the size of the tip of her finger where she'd marked the cardboard with the blade. "Put it back in," she says, handing the tissue box to her granddaughter.

"Wait a sec," Mel says. "You are the one who is going to do this. Focus, Gigi. The phone will be on. You'll have to unlock the screen, okay? Push this. The numbers come up. What's my code?" Mel quizzes her.

"One zero four zero," Rose answers.

"Good. And don't think I'm not changing it the instant this is over. With all due respect. No offense meant."

"With all due respect. None taken," Rose says.

"Once it's unlocked, press this. That's home. Okay. Find the camera icon."

Rose finds it.

"Touch it."

Rose touches it.

"That's all there is to it." Mel's fingers are clamped around the device.

"Put it in the box," Rose insists.

"I am, I am," Mel protests. She puts the cell phone into the tissue box, the screen facing the interior, the back of the phone pressed against the side where Rose cut the small hole. Holding the box on its side, several inches above her knees, Mel jostles the phone around while peering in the oval cutout where the tissues are meant to come forth. "Got it. The lens is perfectly aligned with the hole," she says after a minute.

Rose leans over to look inside the box. On the screen of the phone a video of Mel's knees is running.

"Let me tape the cell in place, so the image doesn't get blocked." Rose plucks up the packing tape from where she's set it on the couch.

"That will leave my phone all sticky," Mel complains.

"Windex will take it off," Rose assures her.

After several attempts, Rose gets the phone taped securely to the side of the box, the camera lens aligned with the hole.

"Bluetooth," Mel says, fishing a heavily packaged item out of the plastic sack.

The earpiece is not a great fit. Rose's ears are small. Having pushed it in as far as it will go, she tapes it in place with pink cloth tape. In her early teens, that kind of tape was used to set pin-curls in front of the ears. The rest of the hair was rolled on juice cans to get the ideal bubble coif. Rose is surprised the stuff is still available.

Mel helps Rose get the wig back on straight. The hair covers the Bluetooth device and tape. But for a small pocket on the top, the scrubs offer nowhere to carry anything. During her raid on Izzy's closet, Mel has taken a small dark-green fanny pack made of ripstop fabric. "Mom used to wear it to work sometimes, so it should be okay to have it."

"Thank you, Mel. Thank you, Izzy. Here we go," she says. She turns on her phone, then calls Marion.

"It's me," Marion answers.

"Are you ready to do this?" Rose whispers.

"I suppose," Marion says.

"Don't whisper, Gigi," Mel advises. "Everybody walks around talking to their phones at the top of their lungs. Whispering will make you look suspicious."

"Got it," Rose whispers. She drops her own cell phone into the fanny pack and zips it closed. "Got it," she repeats firmly.

"Don't press your palm to your ear," Mel says. "Again, suspicious."

Rose lowers her hand. "Can you hear me now?" she asks Marion.

"Is that a joke?" Marion snaps.

"Not a joke," Rose replies.

"Well, don't ask it out loud."

Rose wonders how else she could ask it. "It's on," Rose says, turning the camera on. "Can you see anything?"

"Boxes and dark corners," Marion replies.

"Hi, Great-Aunt Marion." Grinning, Mel sticks her head in front of the hole in the tissue box.

"Yeah, okay, hi," Marion says. "Turn it off to save the battery. Turn it back on before you go in. This isn't going to be instantaneous."

Rose does as she is told. Marion has routed the whole process through one of her addresses in Croatia, or some off-the-wall little country, so the transmission from Mel's phone can't be tracked back to her.

Mel carefully replaces the tissues into the box while Rose runs upstairs. She returns with a good-sized shoulder bag, shell shaped and beachy. Reverently, Mel stows the tissue box containing her social life into the bag. Rose returns to the art supplies and drags out a clipboard. She tears a couple of blank pages from a sketchbook and snaps them under the clip.

"What was that click?" Marion demands.

"A clipboard," Rose tells her. "I thought I'd look more professional if I carried something."

"Okay," Marion says grudgingly.

"Will you stay with me while I do this?" Rose asks her sister.

"Do you promise if hospital security catches you, you will eat that phone before they can press redial?"

Marion really is paranoid.

Rose worries that she has good reasons for it.

CHAPTER 16

Regarding the ride with Rose to Longwood's MCU, Mel will not negotiate.
Shortly after seven P.M. Rose is deposited
half a block from the entrance. Sufficient
light remains in the evening sky to see
clearly. Rose does a quick search of the bush
where she'd discarded the cola nurse's keycard. Odds are against it working a second
time. Though Rose doesn't know how it is
done, she knows electronic keycards at
hotels are nullified if lost. Still, if it works,
life will be easier.

The card, on its snipped lanyard, is caught
in the spiky arms of the shrub a couple of
inches down. Rose retrieves it.

With Mel's assistance, Rose turned on the
camera during the ride from Applegarth to
Longwood. Taking her cell from the fanny
pack, she calls Marion.

"Here," Marion answers curtly.

"Are you ready?" Rose asks, resisting the

urge to press her palm against the ear device.

"As I'll ever be," Marion says. Her voice sounds hollow. She is on speakerphone.

"Dread Pirate Marion," Rose says, "prepare to board." Back straight, chin up. Eyes alert, she holds the clipboard in the crook of her arm and walks with what she hopes is casual purpose to the sliding glass doors of the MCU. She steps on the sensor mat and they slide open. Once inside, she lets them close, then tries the keycard on the black plastic reader. No luck. She drops it behind a potted ficus tree and walks into the foyer.

To her left is the dogleg of a hall, windowless, if she remembers correctly. A sign she hadn't noticed on her last trip reads SECURE COMMUNITY. Beneath it an arrow points in the direction of the lockdown ward.

To the right is a reception desk. A woman sits behind it playing solitaire on the computer. She glances up. Before Rose has the opportunity to use the lie she's rehearsed, the receptionist registers the scrubs and turns back to her game.

Heartened by this success, Rose loses no time ducking into the blind L-shaped hall. "I'm in," she says. "The keycard is a dud."

"Lose the purse," Marion says. "I'm blind."

"Right, right." Rose was so preoccupied with getting in, she's all but forgotten why she is doing it. She takes the tissue box out of the bag. She turns it until she can see the hole. "Hi," she says.

"Don't dick around," Marion growls. It isn't fair that Marion is having fits of nerves. She isn't within a thousand miles of the action. Rose should be the one allowed vapors. She puts the clipboard back in the purse. "Bless the ficus-tree epidemic," she says as she hides the beachy tote behind another potted tree gracing the bend in the hallway. "I'm putting —"

"I see it," Marion says.

"Okay. Good. I'm going to wait —"

"We've been over all this. Stop talking."

A shudder, like a horse ridding its coat of flies, runs over Rose. Placing her feet hip distance apart, she laces her fingers loosely in front of her abdomen. The box with the camera she anchors securely between her thumbs. Concentrating on her breath, she waits. Her monkey mind scampers madly up and down the hall, in and out of the lockdown unit, even out onto the greenway, snatching at fragments of memory, bits of speculation, images of capture, speeches of conquest.

Each time, she catches it gently and brings it back, only to have another monkey caper out and begin reinventing her wardrobe, predicting her future. The attempt at calm abiding is about as fun as a barrel full of monkeys would be in actuality, showing their fangs and slinging excrement.

Breathing, Rose perseveres.

A particularly nasty monkey is screeching that tonight schedules had changed, MCU patterns been reorganized, all is doomed, when Rose hears a soft tread on the hall carpet. She puts her back to the sound, and prepares to appear as if she's being surprised in midstep.

"Oh, hi!" she says, turning around half a second prematurely to face the candy striper. The girl doesn't act as if she notices anything off. "I was just coming to get you," Rose says somewhat breathlessly. "Here. Let me get that for you." She lifts the snack tray out of unresisting fingers. "There's been a bit of a disaster in the dining room." Rose grimaces. She is shooting for an *oh-yuck-somebody-tossed-their-cookies*, not an *oh-God-dead-bodies* look. "Find Linda, she'll tell you what to do." Surely there is at least one Linda on the premises.

"Linda?" the girl says, either confused or stupid.

"Brownish hair, cut so," Rose suggests, shrugging a shoulder in the general direction of her ear. "You'll find her." Rose turns and steps into the corner where she can see both back toward the reception area and the door into the lockdown unit. She mimes being in a predicament with both hands holding the tray, tissue box tucked awkwardly beneath her arm. "Buzz me in?"

The girl slaps her card onto the reader. The door slides open.

"Thanks, Lily," Rose says, reading the girl's name tag. "Go on now." Another smile, warm but dismissive.

Obediently, Lily leaves. Step one of the plan is complete. Rose's window of opportunity is open.

Hoping these early successes bode well for the mission, Rose walks into the SECURE COMMUNITY. Hearing the door slide shut behind her, she is hit with a wave of panic. Again she is trapped among the living dead with no way out. Until that moment, she hadn't understood how terrifying it would be. Her mind dulls, the lights waver, fog begins to form. For an awful moment she is afraid she will be sick. Or insane again. The tray of snacks trembles, a small quake rattling the juice boxes against each other.

Rose sets the tray down on a table at the end of the couch, taking time, letting the terror ebb. In her peripheral vision, she can see one nurse behind the desk, the other outside the high counter, leaning on it companionably. Presumably the night nurse come to relieve the day nurse. That, or maybe, since Rose poisoned Karen, they have taken to working in pairs.

With the cola-loving nurse in ICU, the night nurse will be new, will never have seen Rose. With a start, Rose realizes it is the day nurse, Shanika, at the computer. Shanika will leave before the residents are put to bed, unless the schedule has changed. Rose recalls that the day nurse saw her, as in saw Rose's humanity, through the cloud of dementia. A woman like that might not have much trouble penetrating makeup and a wig.

Keeping her face away from Shanika, Rose begins serving the snacks. "Hey," she says over her shoulder. "Lily had a mini-emergency in dining. Tonight you get me." There. Her explanation is delivered with only a slight quaver.

"Anything serious?" Shanika asks, moving from behind the desk.

"A spill," Rose says. She doesn't try to

change her voice. As a resident of the MCU, she had scarcely spoken. Besides, when she tried it in rehearsal, she sounded like a bad actor. As soon as Shanika leaves, Rose will commence her charade, luring the night nurse from the MCU with an imaginary summons from the man at the employee parking lot regarding "towing or something." People run when their vehicles are threatened.

Neither nurse pays her further attention. Taking her time, willing her pulse rate down, Rose removes the tissue box from beneath her arm and sets it on the table behind the snack tray. The last thing she wants is one of the residents grabbing tissues.

Even in dementia, people remain creatures of habit. Each citizen is in the same place they were when Rose jumped ship. The woman who sat atilt, like the Leaning Tower of Pisa, and her vacant-eyed companion are on the sofa where Rose last saw them. Both perk up at the advent of snacks. Rose feels a stirring of joy at having brought them a piece of life they still have the capacity to enjoy.

"Holy smoke," Marion breathes in Rose's ear. "Ghost of Christmas Yet to Come. Promise me you'll kill me and see that my cats get good homes."

Rose twitches so badly, the items on the tray start to cascade. She has forgotten Marion is with her. Collecting herself, she brightly says, "Okay!" and wraps Ms. Pisa's bird-boned hand around a box of apple juice.

"You don't have to sound so cheerful about the prospect," Marion says dryly. Rose surreptitiously turns the tissue box so the camera faces the nurses' desk.

"Have a good night," Shanika says. Her keycard smacks plastic; the doors shush open.

"The night nurse is logging in," Marion says.

"Yours will be better than mine," the night nurse answers Shanika.

Mid cracker-serving, Rose freezes. Ms. Pisa is reaching for the crackers, her mouth working like a baby bird's. Rose knows that voice. Glancing over at the snack tray, she sees it, a can of Diet Pepsi hiding amid the juice boxes.

Mechanically, she places a cheese-and-cracker pack into the expectant fingers. "It's the cola nurse," she whispers.

"The one you drugged?" Marion asks.

"Mmm-hmm."

"Not in ICU."

"Hunh-uh."

"She's back at work in record time," Marion says. "What do you bet she never was in ICU? Either that, or she has one hell of a constitution. She's coming," Marion warns.

Rose makes sure she is busy as Karen comes over to lift a couple of the boxed drinks from the tray.

"Lovely Lily!" the nurse says when she spies the diet cola. Two boxes of juice in one hand, she catches up her soda in the other.

"She is one big girl," Marion says.

Rose suppresses a giggle. Hysteria, she tells herself.

"So poor Lily got stuck with cleanup," Karen says amiably. She sets her soda on the nurses' desk and returns with the patients' juice boxes.

"Looks like." Rose keeps her chin down so the wig hair falls around her cheeks. "Here you go." Crackers are delivered to the vacant-eyed woman.

"My name is Karen," the cola nurse says. "Did Ms. Lopez borrow you from the hospital?"

"My supervisor doesn't mind," Rose says, hoping that is vague enough to be unchallengeable. She turns back to the tray. If Karen wants to shake hands or indulge in hospital gossip, Rose is doomed. With a stranger, she might be able to get away with it. With somebody who has likely bathed her, changed her, and fed her for weeks, she doubts the disguise will hold up for long.

Never has Rose felt so miserably, wretchedly three-dimensional, so hopelessly visible. If a red light began flashing FAKE, FAKE on her forehead, she could scarcely have felt any more obviously a fraud. Had she a keycard, she would make a run for it.

Fear turns into a cat and gets Rose's tongue. Words rattle in pieces behind her skull bone. None can be made whole. None can get down to her mouth. Silence grows until it becomes an active force whining in her mind like a guitar string ready to snap. Social awkwardness on steroids.

"Yeah," Karen says, reaching past Rose to collect two packets of snacks. "They trade us like they used to trade maids in Myers Park. 'If you're having the ladies in Tuesday, I can lend you my Tilly,' " Karen says in a high-pitched genteel drawl, and laughs. Rose manages a form of snicker.

"Stop that!" Marion says irritably. "No more trying to laugh. Get out of there. The woman will figure out you're you in a heartbeat. Keep your mouth closed. Don't look at her. This whole thing is off. Go. Go. Go!"

"Plan B," Rose whispers.

"There is no plan B," Marion fumes.

"I know," Rose snaps.

"Sounds like you've been lent out once too often," Karen comments.

"All finished?" Rose asks sweetly, snatching the snack and juice from the leaning woman's hands.

"Candy from a baby," Marion says. The old woman claws feebly in the direction of the stolen foodstuffs. Rose dumps them back on the tray.

"Ready for bed?" she coos, prying the poor thing away from her unfinished treat. Keeping the woman between herself and the cola nurse, Rose asks, "Which room?"

"Second on the left," Karen says. "Need help with toileting or teeth?"

"No thanks," Rose replies, nearly frog-marching the unfortunate lady out of the main room.

As she and her prisoner pass Rose's former room, she looks in. Nothing has been altered. Pictures are on the walls; the rocking chair with the decorative cushion is there. All Rose's personal items are in place. The bed even has a new floral-print coverlet much like the one she'd cannibalized for her escape ensemble. Longwood expects Rose to be returned. Or they want it to look as if they expect it, therefore not assumed dead, or as good as.

Rose deposits the old woman in bed untoileted, teeth unbrushed. Abusing the elderly can now be added to her rapidly growing criminal résumé.

"Let me know where the nurse is," Rose says softly.

"She's helping a little guy — looks like a mummy — out of a big brown chair," Marion reports. "Now she's headed in the direction you disappeared in."

"Thanks," Rose says. Her back to the door, she fusses with the bedcover until she hears Karen pass the room.

"Get out of there now," Marion says.

"Can't. No card. Besides, I have an idea," Rose murmurs.

"For God's sake," Marion hisses. "The nurse knows you! Ask her to buzz you out while she's busy."

"I can still make this work," Rose says.

"Don't expect any damned cakes with files baked in them from me," Marion grumbles. "I'll hang up. I'm not getting caught."

She doesn't hang up.

Hooray, Rose thinks. To the frail old lady she says, "Sorry."

"What did you say?" Marion demands as Rose whisks out of the bedroom.

In the social area, she grabs the tissue box, then runs to the nurses' station and sets it on top of a pile of files, the hole facing the computer screen.

"Oh Lord. You're going to do this, aren't you?"

"Yup. I do have a plan B. Half baked, but still . . ."

Marion groans. "Higher."

A manual for troubleshooting printer errors is tucked between the printer and the counter. Rose slips it beneath the tissue box.

"Left," Marion orders.

Rose turns the box to the left.

"Too much."

Rose rotates it back slowly.

"Good," Marion says. "Don't let her move me."

Not that Rose can do anything should the nurse choose to rearrange the desktop. Seating herself in the nurse's chair, Rose lays her fingers on the mouse.

Like an irate drill sergeant, Marion barks, "Upper right screen, scroll up. Up, damn it. There. See that box on the far right?"

Rose doesn't see it. The screen is a scramble of boxes. Karen will be headed back by now. "Where?" she whispers desperately.

"There. There. There," Marion insists.

The advice is not helpful. Past, future, fear: Rose breathes it out, breathes in the stillness of the moment.

Screen. Upper right. There it is: log out. Rose clicks on it.

"Jesus! How hard was that?" Marion hisses as Rose leaps from the chair.

"Good night, sleep tight —"

Rose hears the cheery chant from down the hall. "Got to go," she tells the tissue box.

"Where are you going? What are you going to do?" Marion demands.

"It's a surprise," Rose says, afraid Marion will abandon her if she figures out what she is going to attempt.

Chuck is the last remaining resident yet to be put to bed. In the short time since Rose last saw him, he has visibly diminished. No single dramatic event; he is just less corporeal, less substantial. Life force has leached from skin, hair, eyes, and muscles. He looks like an oak tree rotting back into the earth with the speed of time-lapse photography.

"Hi, Chuck," Rose says, laying her hand gently on his shoulder. A smile starts at the corners of his mouth. Opening his eyes, he sees the wig and the heavily made-up face. The smile fades.

"Where is this?" he asks piteously.

Rose's throat tightens with tears.

"What are you doing?" Marion asks irritably.

Rose ignores her.

"This is where you're going to sleep tonight," she tells Chuck. "Are you ready to go to bed?"

"Where is my good wife?" Chuck asks.

"You'll see her soon," Rose says, hoping he will, if not in dreams, then in his next incarnation.

Chuck makes no reply but allows Rose to guide him to his feet. As they go to his room, Karen meets them in the hall. "Night, Mr. Boster," Karen says. "I didn't catch your name," she says to Rose.

Name. Rose's mind goes blank. But for her own, and that of the nurse, no female names are available to her.

"Alice!" Marion shouts in her ear. "Mary, Peg, Carol, Kathy, Patty!"

"Alice Mary," Rose blurts out, then laughs. "I mean Mary Alice. Touch of dyslexia there. Come on, Chuck." She leads her unsuspecting accomplice farther down the hall. Whether Karen is satisfied, suspicious, still standing in the hall, or striding off to dial 911, Rose has no way of knowing.

Chuck wakes up a little at the sight of his room. He wanders away from Rose.

"Can you see the nurse?" Rose whispers to Marion.

"No. What — wait. She's sitting down at the computer. She's — damn it! She set something in front of the lens."

"Wait," Rose says to Marion. To Chuck, she says, "Be back in a sec." She darts from the room and down the short hallway. At the entrance to the room with the nurses' station, she slows and begins sneezing.

Hand in front of her mouth, she trots to the desk. Kachoo! Snort. "Got a snoot full of something." Kachoo! Sniffle. Rose grabs the tissue box and sets it atop the counter.

As she plucks tissues from the top, Marion shouts, "Left! Other left. More. Stop."

"Sorry about that," Rose says through a wad of tissue. "I'll finish Mr. Boster, then I'm out of here."

"Thanks for the help," Karen says, popping the top of the can of Diet Pepsi. She doesn't take her eyes off Rose while she does it. The cola-loving nurse is getting a bad vibe.

Wiping and sniffling, Rose hurries back to Chuck's room.

He is gone.

Before she can panic, the bathroom door

opens. He is wearing only his pajama bottoms. Toothpaste speckles his chin.

"Good man, Chuck," Rose says.

"The nurse is still staring after you," Marion tells her, and, "Who's Chuck?"

"Chuck is my good friend," Rose says, smiling at him. "Want me to find your pajama top?" Chuck says nothing. Rose finds it on the hook on the bathroom door along with a bathrobe like the one she'd butchered.

"She's reaching for the phone," Marion says.

"Darn!" Rose goes to the room's door and sticks her head out. "Karen, does Chuck get any meds before bed?"

"She's stopped reaching for the phone," Marion says. "She looks annoyed."

"I'll deal with it," Karen calls back.

"Now she looks totally pissed off," Marion says. "She's gulping Pepsi."

"Is she going for the phone again?" Rose asks.

"Wait. No. She is logging in."

"Hallelujah!" Rose whispers.

"She's going to patient records!" Marion shouts in Rose's ear.

Chuck is standing in front of his dresser. A picture frame made for an eight-by-ten photo holds only a snapshot. White tent in the background, a younger Chuck, forties or fifties, crouching beside a campfire, grins at the camera.

"Get the nurse to buzz you out," Marion commands. "We've pushed this as far as we can."

"Can you get what we need now?" Rose asks.

There is a moment's silence. Then Marion says, "I'm not a hacker. Maybe. Get out of there."

"One more thing," Rose says.

"Out!" Marion yells so loudly, it hurts Rose's ear.

Ignoring her sister, Rose steps into the bathroom. She removes the wig, wets her fingers, and fluffs up her hair. Looking more like herself, she returns to Chuck's bedside and lays the wig on the bed. His lamp is still on, but his eyes are closed. Rose takes his hand and holds it between hers.

He opens his eyes, sees her, and smiles.

"Hi, Chuck. I've missed you," Rose says, and is surprised to find she is telling the truth.

"You're the Rose," he says. Squeezing her hand, he lets out a long slow sigh.

"The nurse is back to staring down the hall," Marion warns. "I'm going to hang up if you don't get out now."

"Are you doing okay here?" Rose asks Chuck.

"Where is this?"

"She's getting up," Marion says. "Rose? Do you hear me? Get the hell out of there!"

"I'm in trouble, Chuck," Rose says gently. "The nurse wants to catch me. Please, could you yell or cry or anything to keep the nurse from getting me?"

Chuck closes his eyes. "My good wife loved roses."

"She's out of my sight," Marion says.

Rose jams the wig back on, then squeezes Chuck's hand. "Good night, my friend."

Karen is nearly to the room when she emerges into the hall. "Night," Rose says cheerily, and hurries past.

The big nurse stops. "Alice, Mary, Mary Alice, we need to talk."

CHAPTER 17

"We don't need to talk," Marion declares flatly. "Run."

Rose agrees with her sister. Unfortunately, there is no place to run to.

Karen turns and walks back down the hall to where Rose is halted in her tracks. Big, the woman is big. Huge. Rose resists the urge to fall on her knees, crying, *I did it, I did it. I poisoned your Pepsi, and robbed you, but I'm just a little old lady who didn't mean any harm. Please don't lock me up with the crazy people.*

"Sure," she says with a smile.

Karen plants meaty hands on sturdy hips, staring down at Rose. "First, I'd like to see —"

"Help!" comes a faint cry from Chuck's room.

In a flash, Rose is forgotten as Karen runs to her patient's room.

"Help!" Chuck calls again, louder this time.

Dashing into her old room, Rose promises herself that if she lives, and stays out of jail and the nuthouse, she will visit Chuck every week of his life. She jerks open the drawer of her bed stand. Latex gloves. She throws the box on the bed. Tissues. Another box tossed onto the bed. Sure enough, tucked behind them are six red capsules. The cleaning lady never gets this far.

Rose scoops the pills up and runs for the nurses' desk.

"Help me!" Chuck is bellowing. Karen can be heard muttering soothing nothings. "Fire!" Chuck yells.

Rose fumbles the first capsule open and dumps the tiny white beads into the Pepsi.

"Stop that!" Marion says, horrified. "Are you crazy?"

Rose dumps in the second capsule.

"I can't believe you are doing this again," Marion cries. "This is criminal. You are a criminal. You will be sent to prison. Ask for San Quentin so I can visit."

Hands shaking, Rose spills half of the third capsule, tiny beads scattering over the desk. The fourth goes in, and the fifth. Half of a red capsule falls to the carpet. No time to retrieve it; Rose kicks it under the desk.

"Fire!" Chuck yells again.

Karen murmurs.

"Chocolate!" Chuck cries.

Rose laughs. "A fan of the Smothers Brothers," she says.

"I get it," Marion says without a trace of amusement.

"Six," Rose says. She blows away the loose beads, then moves quickly around the wall into the activities room.

"Where did you go?" Marion asks.

"Hiding. With luck, she'll think Mary Alice slipped out and went home."

Chuck is no longer yelling.

Karen can be heard stomping down the hall, making every footfall count.

The lights are out in the activities room, but nowhere in the lockdown unit is it ever truly dark. Streetlight filters through the windows. Night-lights glow in at least one socket in every room. The hall and the nurses' station are brightly lit day and night.

The activities room is like, but not identical to, the room Rose remembers from when she was an inmate there. It is smaller, dimmer, the table a bit bigger. A sofa she hadn't noticed sits beneath the room's one window. The wall opposite the arch is covered with a bookcase. No closet, no drapes, nothing that can conceal a grown woman.

Not that Rose ever noticed Karen check the activities room, but the nurse has her radar on tonight. She obviously suspects Alice Mary Alice is not on the up-and-up.

In the dimmer half of the room, away from the arch and the window, chairs are neatly tucked under the big wooden table.

Quick and quiet, Rose pulls out the chair farthest from the light. She crawls under the table. In the shadowy forest of chair and table legs, she folds down, butt on her heels, nose between her knees, tucking herself into a stony heap no more than eighteen inches high and consuming less than three square feet of floor space. Grasping the horizontal brace on the displaced chair, she pulls it in as far as she can. Folding her elbows to her sides, hands over her face, she listens.

"Are you hidden?" Marion asks.

Rose dares not answer.

"Talk to me when you can," Marion says, then goes silent.

Footfalls halt. Her bottom and the soles of her feet toward the archway, face pressed against her thighs, Rose can see nothing. She feels — or imagines — a change in the quality of the dim light. The nurse's considerable bulk eclipsing the fluorescent spill from the adjoining room?

A distinct click, no imagining this time. Karen has turned on the light. Rose screws her eyes shut and holds her breath. *Woman found hiding under table in old folks' home. News at eleven.* Humiliating; even a closet or under a bed would have been less embarrassing. What possible excuse could explain being wadded up under the arts table in a secure hospital unit?

Playing at armadillo.

Chair yoga.

Looking for a contact lens.

Kissing her ass goodbye.

Click. The light goes off. Rose is sure of it. Karen expected the room to be empty. She scanned the clearly empty room and was satisfied. Still, Rose won't open her eyes until she's counted slowly to twenty.

She is considering making it a hundred when Marion says, "She's back at her desk. She's taking a long pull on her soda."

"Let me know when she's passed out," Rose whispers.

"How long does it take?"

"Not sure. Busy, then. Maybe an hour?" Rose can hold this pose without discomfort for a while, but in ten or fifteen minutes she will be distinctly miserable. In an hour she'll be crippled.

Time passes. Rose's left foot is falling asleep.

"Another big swig," Marion says encouragingly. "She's on Amazon looking at garbage can liners."

Om ah hum vajra guru padma siddhi hum. Rose silently chants a mantra to calm her mind. Nose between her knees, it is getting harder and harder to breathe. She allows herself to turn her head, resting her cheek on her thigh.

More silent chanting. Now her left leg from the knee down is asleep.

Two more swigs reported wirelessly by way of California. Karen has ordered a box of fifty kitchen can liners and a pair of thong panties.

"I think it's kicking in," Marion says finally. "She's still upright, still facing the computer, but she hasn't moved at all for six minutes. Not a finger."

Inch by inch, Rose pushes the chair out. The carpet keeps the scraping to a bare minimum, but to Rose's ears it is a shriek. "Does it look like she hears anything?" she whispers.

"Nope."

Carefully, dragging her dead limb between chair legs lest it bang into one, Rose crawls out. Free of the table, she massages feeling back into her leg and foot. While they tingle themselves to full power, she does a few Cat-Cows to loosen up her back. Hearing nothing from Marion or the nurse, she does a Down Dog to limber her legs.

"The computer timed out. Screen saver is up. Nurse most definitely zonked. Still upright, though," Marion says. "That's all I can tell."

Rose tiptoes to the arch and peeks around. Karen's broad shoulders are slumped. One arm hangs limply at her side, the unanimated hand looking peculiarly dead. The other arm is bent at the elbow, the hand presumably in her lap.

Rose slips back out of sight.

"She's swaying," Marion reports.

Rose begins to think this absurd shenanigan is actually going to work.

Again.

"Uh-oh, she's shaking out her hands," Marion says. "Rubbing her face."

Rose hears it before Marion reports, smacking of flesh on flesh.

"She's slapping herself, trying to wake up," Marion says. Then, "Reaching for the phone. She's fumbling for the receiver — she's got it!" shrills in Rose's ear.

Without stopping to consider ramifications or consequences, Rose zips around the wall. Grabbing the back of the nurse's office chair with both hands, she yanks it back. Wheels squeal their protest on the plastic chair mat.

The phone receiver drops, clattering against the desk.

"Holy mackerel!" Marion is shouting.

The beefy nurse turns sideways, reaching out for Rose, and toppling the chair in the process. Rose jumps back, but not far enough. One of Karen's long arms flaps to the floor like a landed tuna. Her fingers close around Rose's ankle.

Movement abruptly arrested, Rose loses her balance and falls hard on her rear end, wig flying, glasses smashing into her face on the end of their beaded chain.

The nurse stares at Rose. Her eyes are slits, the pupils nearly invisible, mere pinpricks of black in the pale blue eyes.

"You!" the nurse spits out the word.

CHAPTER 18

"I nearly lost my job over you," Karen mutters, eyes bleary, mouth barely moving.

"She's got me!" Rose cries out to Marion.

"You bet your ass I do," the nurse growls, pulling Rose in.

"What's happening? Damn it! I can't see!" Marion screams.

"Let me go," Rose begs. "I never meant to drug you. Okay, I did, but it's not what you think — oh, shoot — that's some grip you've got. How about I give you back your keycard? It doesn't work anymore, but — let go, doggone it — aaah. Let's discuss this like civil — yaaah!"

Rose babbles and screeches as quietly as panic will allow, her fingernails vainly trying to gain purchase on the tightly woven carpet.

Slow with drugs, but sure as the tide, the muscular Karen is reeling her in like a fish. Kicking desperately, Rose tries to get the nurse's hand loose from her ankle. Her soft-soled Toms are woefully inadequate against the iron-hard fingers. Karen's grip is so powerful, it cuts off the blood to Rose's foot. Years of changing bedpans and lifting old people have given her titanium muscles.

Karen drags. Rose slides. The nurse gets her other arm free from where it was pinned under her. A ham-sized hand joins its mate on Rose's ankle. Two-fisted, Karen jerks. Rose bumps half a foot closer.

"Whoa!" Rose yelps.

"What's happening?" Marion wails.

The cola nurse looks up, her face presenting a perfect target. Rose draws her free leg back to smash her foot into the woman's nose, break it, maybe take out a couple of her front teeth, bust her jaw, hit her in the throat, crush her esophagus. That will stop her.

Stop a nice health care professional, whom Rose has robbed and drugged.

Twice.

Karen is not a monster. Karen bought thong panties online. Rose can't smash her face or knock her teeth out. Straightening her cocked leg, she taps the nurse firmly but, she hopes, not painfully on the top of her head with the heel of her shoe.

In drugged confusion, the nurse grunts,

her single-minded attack momentarily derailed. The fingers around Rose's ankles loosen. Her shoe pops off, smacking Karen in the chin. The nurse makes an enraged animal sound and glares at the shoe as if it is a live thing come from nowhere to assault her.

Rose's bare foot slips through Karen's fingers.

The pinpointed pupils focus angrily back on Rose. "No you don't," the nurse slurs. She clenches her fists. They close on empty cloth.

The waistband of Rose's scrubs is down around her knees. Quick as an eel, Rose wriggles out of the scrubs. Her other shoe is lost in a trouser leg. Out of the pants, she crab-walks back until she hits the far side of the arch, nearly losing her underpants in the process.

Like a startled bear, the nurse snorts, "Ungh?" Then, bear-like, charges on all fours.

Squeaking, Marion shouting in her ear, Rose springs to her feet and retreats into the activities room.

Groaning and shaking her head from side to side as if to clear her vision, the nurse crashes into the side of the arch. Eyes narrowed, squinting into the dimness, she pulls herself to her feet. Head down and swaying, she stares around the room.

Rose wonders if Karen is seeing double, or really seeing at all. Then the eyes settle on her.

"You!" the nurse says. Her voice is thick and wet, it sounds like "Jew." Not bothering to move her feet — or incapable of moving them — the big woman dives at Rose.

Squawking, Rose clambers backward up onto the table and scoots to the far end.

Karen collapses over the back of a chair, chin striking the table, arms long across the wood, reaching for Rose's bare feet. Backing away, Rose feels her hand hit nothing, then falls, slamming her elbow against a wooden chair seat on the way down. Her back strikes the floor, knocking the wind from her lungs. For a moment, she lies there, naked legs tangled in fallen chairs.

A thud. The floor vibrates.

"Talk to me," Marion begs.

Rose can't. No breath. Then her lungs suck in. Breathing is truly a magnificent art, a miracle. Life or no life, all on an inhale.

Gathering her scattered limbs, Rose grasps the edge of the table and levers herself to her feet. Every part of her quivers, muscles shivering like water in a flimsy sack, breath shuddering in and out.

Beyond the table, she sees a foot and part of a leg.

"I thinks she's down," Rose gasps. The words creak out, a kid mocking the speech of a very old woman.

"About time," Marion says. "I can't take much more of this."

Neither can Rose. She isn't sure if she can even walk unassisted. Leaning on chair backs for support, she totters unsteadily around the activities table. In her mad scramble she'd knocked over the mugs. Pens are scattered across the surface and onto the floor.

The nurse is collapsed, head and shoulders beneath the table. Two chairs have fallen over. "She's definitely down," Rose says. For the first time since she'd been introduced to the MCU, she is glad it is small, separate from everything else, and, undoubtedly, well soundproofed.

"Let's get on with it," Marion says.

"Let me get my pants on," Rose says wearily.

"You don't have any pants on? Why aren't you wearing pants?"

"Tell you later." Rose retrieves the bottoms of her scrubs. One leg is inside out. Ignoring Marion's machine-gun questions — "What are you doing? What's this about your pants? Are you sure she's down?" — she turns the leg right side out, dons the pants and shoes, rights the office chair, and puts the phone receiver back in its cradle.

Marion sees her then. "Don't go AWOL again," she snaps. "Scared the hell out of me."

"Okay." Rose sits down in front of the computer.

A long intake of breath shushes in her ear; then Marion says, "One second. Okay. Here we are. The nurse's password is Quackers2! Capital *Q*, numeral two, exclamation point."

Rose types in the password.

"See the box Patient Files in the control bar?"

Rose finds it, clicks on it.

"The log-in is MCUsu6pm." She spells it out.

Rose is in the patient files. She clicks on her own name. Everything is there.

"Scroll through," Marion says. "I can slow the video down later for single pages."

Rose scrolls. Every patient in the secure unit for five years back, they'd decided. A lot of scrolling. Each second grates on Rose's nerves, sandpaper on a sunburn. The screen blurs. Rose puts on the reading glasses. They don't help.

Her free ear is attuned to the heap of

nurse meat in the activities room. This time she didn't check Karen's pulse. Didn't even take the time to see if the woman was breathing. The cola nurse survived the first drugging; she would just have to survive this time. Two massive doses in such a short time might wreck her liver or spleen or something. Rose hopes not, but she doesn't know what the drug/drugs is/are: opioid, narcotic, sedative, hallucinogen — probably not that. When she was on it, she hadn't seen anything interesting. Most likely mostly tranquilizers, downers of some sort. In college they'd called them "reds" for some reason. Rose does not know the chemicals used to make reds.

Seventeen bone-aching minutes later and they are done.

"Log out," Marion orders.

Rose's scrolling finger is cramped into a claw.

"Out," she says, and levers her body from the chair. After sitting still so long, she feels every blow her body suffered in the take-down of the big nurse.

"Now you get out," Marion says.

"Half a sec." Rose goes into the activities room. Karen is still unconscious. Or dead.

"I'm really sorry about this," Rose apologizes as she unclips the keycard from Karen's lanyard. She pats the nurse on the head. "Nothing personal."

"Are you out? Who are you talking to?"

"Almost. Nobody."

"Don't forget the camera. I'm hanging up. My head is about to explode. Call me when you're home. Wherever that is." And Marion is gone from Rose's ear. She feels both abandoned and free.

Rose walks down the hall to Chuck's room. At the door, she peeks in. He is asleep. She moves quietly to his bedside. Taking his hand, she says, "Thanks, Chuck. I owe you."

"My good wife loved roses," he murmurs.

Tissue box clamped under her arm, Rose presses the cola nurse's keycard to the pad. The door whooshes open. She's in the deserted reception area when she remembers she's left the beachy tote and clipboard behind the ficus tree. As she stops and turns there is a yip, like that of an overexcited Chihuahua.

The candy striper is standing in the wide doorway to the nonsecure area of the Memory Care Unit. Stark terror freezes Rose in her tracks; otherwise she would scream and jump into the air. As it is, her eyes go so wide, they hurt. Deer in the headlights. Automatically, her hand flies to secure the earpiece. Plastic touches her palm.

The wig is still on the floor behind her, forgotten in all the excitement.

The girl's hand shoots out and smacks into a flat round button the size of a woman's palm set into the doorframe. Long thin red lights start flashing near the ceiling. A silent alarm, so as not to frighten the patients.

The beachy tote with the clipboard, flashlight, and water bottle remains unretrieved behind the ficus tree. The girl turns and runs. Rose turns and runs. Her feet fly out from under her, and she falls hard, hip and elbow slamming into the floor. Fear overwhelms pain; she is on her feet in seconds. The tissue box tumbles nearly to the reception desk, blessedly empty at this hour.

Rose snatches up the box, then slams Karen's keycard onto the black plastic. The doors start to slide open. Then stop.

The doors begin to close.

Rose jams her shoulder and leg into the narrowing slot. Programmed not to mash human beings, the doors do not pinch her in two. Neither do they retreat politely to let her through. Muttering curses she hasn't used since Mel was a toddler, Rose shoves her body between the black rubber seals. She is grateful for the scrubs: no buttons, no belt, no buckles.

Her body is out. Before she can snatch her arm free, the doors close, trapping it at the wrist. Jerking, Rose abrades her skin. Blood makes the passage slippery. She takes a deep breath and pulls the last of her personage from the doors' hard rubbery lips.

Free, she runs toward the familiar dark welcome of the greenway. People will come after her. People with flashlights, then people with guns and badges. Or, worse, a nine-fingered man with a brand-new knife. Though this has been a night of encores, Rose doubts she will get away with hiding in the bushes until morning a second time.

Pain cuts into her side, forcing her to slow.

Feet pound on the sod behind her.

They've wasted no time.

CHAPTER 19

Digging deep for nonexistent reserves, Rose manages a painful burst of speed. Before the adventures in the MCU, she'd jogged five miles several times a week. But, then, it was jogging. On a treadmill. Twenty years, at least, have gone by since she's sprinted full out. Muscles in her thighs stretch and scream. There is the awful feeling of running in a nightmare, forcing legs through thick mud, lungs burning in short hot flares, sharp as razors in her throat.

Yelling, unidentifiable due to the breath rasping in her ears, drifts in her wake. Hounds baying in pursuit, no doubt.

Whirring and crashing; then a hand touches her back. Only a touch, but it might as well be the hammer of a wrecking ball. Already on the ragged edge, Rose goes down. Elbows and forearms slam into the grass, saving her from a broken nose and missing front teeth.

At least she'll look good for the mug shot.

A wheel spins beside her head; that, or her brain is spinning, catching bits of moonlight on the spokes and hurling them into the night.

"Gigi? Are you okay? You're fast for an old lady."

Rose tilts her chin up. "Grasshopper?" Then she vomits into the dry grass.

"Oh yuck. There was this hill when I tried out for track. Puke's Peak. Must run in the family." Mel helps Rose to her feet. Unsteadily, Rose watches as Mel picks up her bicycle.

"You look like an extra from *The Walking Dead*," Mel says sympathetically. "You should sit down and rest."

Rose shakes her head. "They saw me," she gasps, then coughs until she's sure her lungs will turn inside out like sticky pink balloons. "An alarm went off," she croaks.

"They don't know who they saw," Mel says. Then her face tightens. "Where's the wig?"

"Lost it in a fight."

"You were in an actual fight? As in scratching and clawing and punching?" Mel sounds aghast. Or awed.

"You should see the other guy," Rose chokes. "Same nurse as before. The one I drugged. Not in ICU."

"She saw you, as in saw Rose Dennis, for identification?" Mel asks.

"Exactly."

"Maybe she'll have drug-induced amnesia like you did," Mel offers.

"I was pretty memorable," Rose confesses. "She pulled my pants off, and I drugged her again — and some other things."

Mel whistles low. "Sheesh. Do you think they're after you?"

"Probably right behind me."

Mel is wearing a small backpack.

"Any chance there's water in that?" Rose asks.

"That's why I brought it. Just in case." Mel balances the bike against her hip, slips the backpack off, fishes out a water bottle, and hands it to Rose.

"You can't go back to the Applegarth house," Mel says as Rose drinks, walks, and drinks again. "That cat-door, closet hidey-hole is too lame."

"Lame," Rose concedes, recapping the bottle but hanging on to it.

"Our house?"

"Can't," Rose says. The moonlight, along with the light pollution from the city, makes the path easy to see. Rose urges Mel nearer the trees where they are less obvious.

"Sure you can. I gave Uncle Daniel permission to go to a friend's to watch the Panthers game."

"Not Daniel, the guy with the knife. Too dangerous before, way too dangerous now," Rose says. "If they don't find me, eventually he — they — are bound to check your house."

"Do you think you killed that nurse?" Mel asks. Both are whispering, walking as quickly as Rose can manage through the shadows at the edge of the greenway.

"I sure hope not," Rose says. "Murder, or at least accidental homicide. The nurse probably has three adorable children. Their fireman father will bring them to the courtroom every day so the jury can see their tearful little faces while they decide how long to put me away for."

"Not to mention what it would do to your karma."

Rose snorts. "That ship has sailed. I finally get a precious human birth and I fritter it away on a measly homicide."

"The drugs didn't kill her last time," Mel says.

"That's right." Rose is somewhat cheered. "They didn't even land her in ICU."

On the other side of the greenway is a dense growth of underbrush over a creek or ditch. Beyond it is the dead end of a street. Mosquitos, ticks, poison ivy — all the toxins of nature are probably represented in that wet, dark cut, but it will hide Rose until she is sure she can get clear — or the indigenous critters drain her of all of her blood.

She walks with Mel another couple hundred yards to where the hobbit gate is hidden in the rhododendrons. "Here's where I get off," Rose tells Mel. "I'm getting no nearer your house than this. Be sure and set all the locks, and don't answer the door unless you know who it is."

"I won't take candy from strangers, either," Mel says. "I've got an idea. Can I have my phone?"

Rose has not let go of the tissue box. The cardboard is crushed, corners smashed, one seam bursting with white tissues. She gives it to Mel. Mel rips out the phone, hands Rose back the cardboard and paper, and then begins tapping the cell phone with her thumbs.

"It's nearly dead," she accuses.

"You act like it's a kitten," Rose grumbles.

"Will you be okay here alone for a while?" Mel asks.

"I was going to hide out in the ditch back there a ways until the coast was clear, then go the Motel 6 route," Rose says. She can't hide a shudder.

"I've got a better plan. Go inside the gate. Nobody can see you there, and you won't get eaten by bugs and snakes. I'll be back in a while."

"Going to keep me in suspense?" Rose asks.

"I've got to see if the plan can work before I get your hopes up," Mel replies. She dumps the bike, takes Rose's arm, and escorts her into the shadows of the bushes. Rose winces as she reaches for the gate's handle, the raw flesh on her wrist pulling, the blood oozing on the damaged skin.

"Are you hurt?" Mel asks.

The concern in her voice is a balm. "The only thing that really hurts is trying to avoid the pain," Rose says. Inside the gate, she sinks down on the grass and leans back against the fence. Sitting is wonderful. "I'm going to breathe it in and embrace it."

"Really?" Mel asks dubiously.

"Yup."

"Does it work?"

"Every now and then."

A moment's hesitation; then Mel says, "All right. I won't be long." And she is gone, back onto the greenway, the gate closing quietly behind her.

Head back against the rough boards, Rose

breathes in the pain, trying to embrace it. There is a lot to get her metaphysical arms around. Her hip feels as if she partially dislocated it when she fell in the foyer of the MCU during her mad dash to freedom. Her wrist stings and burns. Both elbows ache from her fall from the table in the activities room, then her dive to the sod when Mel came up on her.

Trying to rise above the tumultuous demands from her body that she drown herself in a hot tub and a bottle of wine, she lets the night settle into the pores of her skin, breathes serene darkness as far into her lungs as they will allow without making her start hacking again. Sipping water, she observes waves of terror and violence breaking inside her, chilling her breastbone, prickling her scalp, tightening her throat.

Adventure costs more than it used to. Or maybe the price is just paid in a different currency.

Karma is. Is. That is fact.

This night Rose has created a mountain of the stuff, broken it into a million pebbles, and thrown them into a million ponds. Reverberations trembling through her, the nurse, Mel, Chuck, the candy striper. Like the red light flashing from the silent alarm, waves will go out and out, touching more lives: Daniel, Flynn, Marion.

In every city and town, on every continent, others are also mindlessly dumping avalanches of rock into billions of ponds. Rose can feel the waves gathering into a tsunami, a global panic attack.

The First Noble Truth: There is suffering.

As far as Rose can see, the storm of suffering she has been blown into, and is madly contributing to, is nowhere near over.

Would it stop if she went back to the Longwood MCU and let whatever they were doing to her be done? In the plus column, they would stop sending knifemen after her. Mel would no longer be drawn into night ops to save poor Gigi's wrinkled old posterior.

Of course, Rose would be drugged to the gills and "probably wouldn't last out the week."

Would the world be better or worse off if she went gently into her next life as a vole or a banana slug? Mel would mourn, bless her, but she'd be alive to do it.

Or not.

Rose isn't the only sentient being setting potentially deadly forces in action. Maybe she can stop her part of the ride, but Longwood will continue to do whatever it is they are doing, racking up a karmic debt that makes hers seem paltry by comparison.

Rose is not important enough to be drugged and murdered for her own sake. There is a profit motive somewhere, either to an individual or the institution. If it is profitable to hasten one little old lady into that good night, it will be ever so much more profitable to hasten a dozen, or a score.

Follow the money. Everybody says that. Rose can't fathom where the money is, let alone track it. To Longwood, she is worth seven grand a month on the hoof, if she is alive, but Longwood has a waiting line. What with the baby boomers beginning to lose their collective marbles, dementia care is a seller's market.

If Longwood doesn't profit from the demise of the elderly, then it is an individual or individuals using Longwood. The profit must be significant to be worth the risk. But then, how great a risk is offing demented elders? Probably not a lot. Loved ones would drop a tear and breathe a huge sigh of relief, the body would be interred or cremated, and room would open up for the next victim.

Caring for the aged is harder than caring for little kids. Children will stop wetting the bed, begin speaking in full sentences, become more help around the house. With the old it is the opposite. Rose's mother died of complications from dementia in Rose's living room. Hospice had given Rose all the morphine she needed. No one did a post-mortem, no police came, no autopsy was suggested. Hospice didn't ask for the unused morphine to be returned. If Rose had wanted to off her mother, she could have, no questions asked.

People grow old, they sicken, they die. Sometimes assisted living becomes assisted dying. Rose accepts that. Accepting what is doesn't mean giving the nod to ongoing evil. Even the Buddha, if the stories were true, killed a man during one of his incarnations: A pirate was set on murdering five hundred people. In his great kindness, the Buddha slew the pirate, taking on the karma of one murder to save the pirate from the unutterably bad karma of five hundred murders.

Not that, in all honesty, Rose gives a flip about the next lives of whoever is intent on ruining hers. Compassion is all well and good — Rose is a hundred percent in favor of it — but it has been a heck of a night. Besides, after all the effort she and Mel and Marion have gone to getting hold of the files, it would be a shame not to even look at them.

She won't go back to Longwood.

Nor will she sit here uselessly waiting for Mel to return. Muscles are starting to set up, concretized by trauma and neglect. Either she gets up now, or she'll have to be hoisted with a forklift, all in a chunk like the statue of Jeff Davis. Gingerly, she makes it to her feet. She tries a Warrior Pose to get the energy flowing. Too much pain to breathe in and embrace at that given moment; she settles for shuffling up the grassy knoll.

Her invasion of Longwood's turf will undoubtedly inspire another attempt to get her back in the MCU, or quiet her in a more permanent fashion. Finding Applegarth untenanted, they will come here. She will take first watch. At present, watching is all she can fathom doing with any degree of success.

Next to the fence, beneath a stand of enormous hostas, a few yards short of the crest of the slope, she lies down on her stomach. Lizard-like, she works her way through the thick leaves until she can see over the top of the hill. Chin on hands, she surveils the house and part of the street beyond. If she sees danger coming she can at least trot back to the greenway and warn her granddaughter. Given the trouble Rose has exposed the girl to, this is a pitiful scrap of protection. When the best one can do is pitiful, that is what one does.

Prone on the cool grass, sheltered by night and sweet foliage, Rose relaxes for the first time she can remember. Pain pours forth into the earth, and with it the last of the strength she's been clinging to with her fingernails. She's lost her husband. She's been locked away in an Alzheimer's ward. She's had the flu. She's been in a brawl with a big nurse. She has slithered beneath a planting of hostas like a cottonmouth, to watch for a person who might come to kill her. Drugs she doesn't even know the names of still enjoy half-lives in her tissues. Prescriptions she's been on for years have been scrubbed from her system by time and illness. Her brain floats in a chemical soup concocted by evil toddlers in a devil's pharmacy.

Swathed in the surreal, her mind drifts away from her body. This is the moment she is in. Every moment is a once-in-a-lifetime event.

This one is a doozy.

Incrementally, she evanesces until she is one with the cosmos. That, or she dozes off for a bit. The faintest crunching brings her back. Lights off, a small dark pickup truck is gliding around the corner. Directly across the street, it swerves to the curb. The engine is turned off. No one gets out. Her friend from the rooftop has been sent to watch her granddaughter's house.

Astral body, etheric body, and physical body crash back together.

This moment is primitive: predator and prey.

Rose is exceedingly tired of landing on the wrong side of that equation. She inches backward. Dead leaves and grass tailings push up the legs of her scrubs. Long pointed hosta leaves quiver as she slides under them, their tips mimicking brown recluse spiders crawling down her neck.

She hears the truck door open, then, very softly, close again, a quiet thump and a click. Parting the night-silvered leaves, she watches as a man gets out of the vehicle. But for a bandage around his right hand creating a splash of white, the intruder is unchanged: black ball cap, T-shirt, cargo shorts, deck shoes with no socks. Considering the rates Longwood charges, one would have thought they could afford a new, undamaged thug.

He wears no gloves, and he isn't carrying a knife. Does that mean he is here merely to case the joint, as the saying goes? See if this is where Rose has gone to ground after fleeing the MCU and, perhaps, Applegarth?

The man pauses for a minute, looking both ways, then makes a beeline for Rose. Her spectral self leaps to its feet and flees. Her corporeal self does not. There is no way he can see her. He must just be heading for the darkest, blindest side of the house, as she had done. Rose eases backward until she can no longer see him. Whipping around like a frightened snake, she continues down the slope crawling on her belly. The knoll isn't high enough to eclipse an upright human being.

She is less than an alligator-length from the hobbit gate when she is hit with a gust of laughter. This horror is followed by the joyous sound of young voices outside the gate. Mel is back. The gate bangs open, and a pale oval flashes as Mel lifts her face, catching the light.

Chuff, chuff, chuff, train sounds, as if an engine huffs uphill. Rose staggers to her feet. Resting has been a mistake. She can hardly stand, let alone run. The knifeman's round head appears from the street side of the slope, dark moon rising. He is coming fast, his deck shoes eating up the distance.

"Go!" Rose shouts. Mel flinches, startled, then, suddenly as if she's a magician's assistant, is whisked from view, gate still agape. Vision narrows until all that Rose can see is that black rectangle in the dark wall of fence. Sucking breath in choking gasps, legs turned to jelly, she propels herself through the gate.

Mel is coming toward her through the dark tunnel of shrubs.

"No!" Rose wants to yell, but only manages a strangled whisper. She yanks the gate closed behind her. "He's coming," she breathes as she drops to hands and knees. Flailing in the darkness, hands clawing through the duff. Her fingers close around a sad excuse for a stick, a foot long and no bigger around than a broom handle. On her knees, Rose shoves the stick through the hobbit gate's handle, letting it protrude on both sides in a makeshift crossbar. Bracing her spine against the gate, Rose digs her heels into the ground, a human barricade.

"I'll hold the gate," she gasps. "You go."

Mel grabs her arm.

"Go!" Rose pleads. "I can't run anymore."

"C'mon," Mel urges.

Fighting her granddaughter is only putting the girl in greater peril. Rose forces her protesting body away from the gate and, Mel pulling her arm, stumbles forward.

The knifeman crashes into the gate.

Rose and Mel squawk simultaneously. Then Mel is snatched out of the bushes, Rose along with her, losing her footing and falling to her knees. The hobbit door rattles as the thug tries to pull it open or push it out. The stick will break before the door, Rose knows. When Harley built a thing, it stayed built.

The thug yelps, then curses. Rose hopes he is right-handed, hopes he jammed the bloody stump of his severed finger into the metal as he tried to force the gate. Hopes the pain will slow him. It can't slow him enough. Not long enough for Rose to find her feet, let alone walk.

Hands catch her. She is lifted up. Mel on one side, a boy on the other.

"Come on."

"Don't hurt her."

"Get her on."

"Hold on, Gigi."

Chatter boxes Rose's ears as she tries to help them and fails. Then she is astride the back of a bicycle. "Hold on to me," the boy says. "Keep your feet up."

Mel races away on her bike. The bike Rose is on lurches forward. Rose lifts her feet, legs out straight, and clings to the boy's waist.

A loud cracking sound brings her head

around. The knifeman hurtles out of the bushes, stops, turns his head in Rose's direction. All he will see is the back of her disappearing into the moonlight on a bicycle. Rose thinks of E.T. silhouetted against the full moon on a bike, and wild irrepressible laughter bursts from her aching lungs.

From behind she hears: "Crazy bitch!"

CHAPTER 20

"You're in an igloo?" Marion sounds annoyed, as if Rose is enough trouble without dragging housing into it.

Rose lounges back on a bed of animal "skins" of thick soft acrylic, a zebra and a tiger. A polyester wolf skin, complete with stuffed head, lies in front of a flap that, when open, shows a neatly trimmed yard.

"A teepee," Rose corrects. It is a real teepee with poles and canvas walls. The walls are decorated with boyish paintings: stick-figure Indians, stick-figure buffalo, stick-figure cowboys on stick-figure horses. Rose loves it. She's slept eleven hours straight and feels downright festive.

A cause for happiness.

"Mel's pal Royal has it pitched in his backyard. He was careful to inform me that he personally was much too old for it. His little brother, a mere lad of ten, is now the chief of the neighborhood tribe. The brother is at camp for a couple of weeks. Mom and Dad took the opportunity for a grown-up getaway. Royal, fourteen and a rising freshman, was left to guard the home front under the watchful eyes, and deaf ears, of Grandma. I am the criminal in residence for the nonce."

Rose stretches her right arm out. Her wrist is bandaged and wrapped in gauze. The scrapes on her elbows have been cleansed, treated with Neosporin, and patched with bandages. All is done as prettily as a Christmas box from Lord & Taylor.

Mel and Royal took first aid in seventh grade. On their homecoming the previous night, while Grandma watched a rerun of *Dexter* at top volume abovestairs, Rose was smuggled into the basement.

Peroxide, secrecy, bandages, and cold pizza and grape juice by candlelight in the life-sized teepee have changed Rose's perception of the night from a bad, geriatric acid trip to a delightful camp-out, missing nothing but s'mores.

For years Rose has read various texts affirming that life is but a dream, all phenomena essentially empty, devoid of a separate individual existence. Before she'd fallen asleep, there had been a second or two when she almost understood those concepts.

"What's with this Royal person?" Marion asks.

"Thomas Hardy's coincidental meetings on the heath are nothing compared with Charlotte's greenway. As it happens, Royal, Mel's friend, is the kid that gave me water the first time I broke out of the MCU."

"Then turned you in to the men with the butterfly nets," Marion reminds her.

"True," Rose admits. "But he did it in a kindly way, and with exquisite manners. Kids today!" Rose huffs. "They are way smarter, and more sophisticated, than we were at their age."

"We were the last of the feral children." Marion sighs. "Allowed to run free."

"Little savages," Rose agrees. "Mel is like a young Hillary Clinton — but universally lovable. You should have seen the way she took over, got help, transported the victim, opened the field hospital, found shelter and food. Mind-blowing."

There is a flat silence from Marion's side of the ether.

"What?" Rose demands.

"You promised me," Marion says.

"I promised you what?"

"That you wouldn't go gaga over the grandchild."

"I didn't!" Rose protests. "Not for years."

"You called her a human larva. You insisted she wasn't even your grandchild. She was Harley's."

"That was a relative truth. The absolute truth is that any child who falls asleep in your lap is your grandchild."

"You are confusing kids with cats," Marion says with asperity. "Admit it."

"Admit what?"

"You're gaga."

"I will not dignify that with a response," Rose says.

"Harumph." Marion tires of the subject. "I haven't gotten every page of the MCU patient files stopped and sorted yet. Maybe tomorrow. I did run into a piece of luck while I was exploring."

Rose waits while Marion fiddles with her computer. There is nothing to hear, but Rose has listened to that particular brand of nothing so many times over the years, she can practically tell if Marion is on iPad, laptop, or PC.

"You're on speaker," Marion tells her. "Can you still hear me?"

"Loud and clear."

"There are several services on the web that analyze print art — for a fee."

The images that Rose had made using the severed finger, photographed and emailed to Marion; the connection takes Rose a second.

"Got pen and paper?" Marion asks.

Rose sits up and looks around. "I'm in a teepee," she says. She sees an Indian-chieftain-style headdress and half a glass of leftover grape juice. Could quill and ink be that easy?

"Can't you text me or email me?" Rose asks.

Silence, spiced with paranoia, pours out of the earpiece of Rose's phone. Once upon a time speaking aloud or, worse yet, writing a secret down was the height of indiscretion. Now they provided the only hope of genuine security.

"Hang on," Rose tells her sister. She plucks a feather from the headdress. It is an actual feather, not plastic. She cuts the quill at an angle with a Buck-knife-look-alike that is dull enough for a ten-year-old suburban Indian to play with, then dips it in the Welch's. Dragging aside the wolf pelt, she tries it on the white canvas of the teepee floor.

Not great. Not easy, but doable.

"Shoot," she says to her sister.

"Edward 'Eddie' Martinez. Twenty-nine, male, Hispanic. Jailed twice. For assault at age seventeen. For assault and battery at twenty-two. Served six years. Paroled January of this year. Address 1477 Palmetto Drive, Charlotte, North Carolina."

Rose scratches the information laboriously onto the canvas.

"Do you want his parole officer's contact information?" Marion asks.

"Why not." Rose scratches that down as well.

"You owe me four hundred twenty-seven dollars. Pay me on PayPal," Marion says. "And, interesting note, the night nurse is not now, and never was, in ICU. The first time you dosed her, she was just sent home. This time nobody is admitting anything happened."

"Did you poke and explore?"

"Nope. Went old school. Called the nurses' landline in the MCU this morning. They deal with old people; they expect us to call on the landline. Asked for Karen. Nice lady says, 'Karen's not here.' I say, 'Eek, eek, she told me to call her at work! (Dither) Is anything wrong? (Natter) Did she have an accident? OMG! OMG!' (Shortness of breath) 'No, ma'am, just a little tummy ache a day or so back. She's been back on duty since.' "

"Either Longwood or the news station made up the story about Karen being in the

261

ICU. A lie is suspicious," Rose says.

"No ICU, no news, local or otherwise, about your adventure of last night."

Rose thinks about this for a while. The candy striper saw her. The silent alarm went off; the door tried to close Rose in the unit. The night nurse should be in ICU — or at least home nursing a massive hangover. "What do you bet she didn't tell her boss the whole truth?"

Rose suggests. "The candy striper probably thought I'd just walked in; she didn't know I'd been to the lockdown. Karen doesn't know why I was there, that I stole the files. I bet she woke up around four A.M. with a terrific headache, got scared, and never told a soul."

"Afraid she'd get fired. I'd fire her. I'm hanging up now," Marion says.

And she does.

Pacing in a teepee is not particularly satisfying, but Rose is managing it. Mel and Royal sit on the floor cross-legged amid the clutter of items Rose asked Mel to bring. They watch her, heads following as if viewing a truncated tennis game.

"We've got the knifeman's information, but what do we do with it?" Mel muses.

"Give it to the police," Royal says. Royal

is a sensible boy. Rose likes him. During the medical triage and powwow the previous night, Rose learned his dad is an honest-to-gosh Secret Service agent working for Homeland Security. She suspects Royal of having inherited right-wing law-and-order tendencies. That might not serve her in the present crisis.

"No police," she says, stepping over the wolf's head. "They'll bundle me off to some psych-evaluation institution and keep me there until I rot."

"Gigi thinks women of a certain age are not given proper credence," Mel says. It is a direct quote from one of Rose's tirades.

"Old people are like sheep," Rose grumbles. "Everybody wants to fleece us."

"That's because you're so helpless and fluffy," Mel says.

"I refuse to be fluffy," Rose fumes. "Since guns are legal, there should at least be a law that you can only buy them if your Medicare supplement covers the expense."

"Do you want me to get you a gun, Mrs. Dennis?" Royal asks. He sounds absolutely sincere.

Mel drops her jaw. A gesture identical to her mother's, Rose notes with a stab of pain.

"You know where and how to buy a gun?" Mel asks incredulously.

"No," Royal says. "But I could lend her one of Dad's."

This strikes Rose as hilarious, but she doesn't laugh lest she offend. She knows nothing about the workings of the fourteen-year-old male mind. Or any male mind, for that matter. She was forty before she realized that when she asked a man what he was thinking and he said, "Nothing," he wasn't lying.

"No guns," Rose says.

"She only poisons people," Mel tells Royal in a stage whisper.

"Only when there is no other recourse," Rose defends herself.

"Mr. Martinez was probably the hired help," Royal says. *Mr.* Martinez — Rose does so admire his manners. "The police could find out who hired him."

Such faith the boy has.

"I can find out who hired him," Rose says.

"How?" Mel asks.

"I'm going to ask him."

The kids exchange a look.

"Um . . . won't he just kill you, Mrs. Dennis?" Royal ventures.

"Like meet him at midnight in a haunted house, and the next day your body is found floating facedown by the docks?" Mel asks.

"I don't think there are any docks in

Charlotte," Royal says.

"You know what I mean."

"Sort of," Rose says. "But better, and without the floating-facedown part." She stops pacing and folds down to their eye level. "I'm going to follow him. When he goes someplace where he can't murder me — or at least not without it being labor intensive — I'll ask him who he's working for."

"Have you run this by Great-Aunt Marion?" Mel asks.

"Nope. I won't until it's over," Rose says. "She'd try and talk me out of it."

"And we won't because we're just crazy kids?" Mel asks, affronted.

"No. Because Marion is my older sister," Rose explains. "For the last sixty-eight years it has been her job to talk me out of harebrained schemes. You guys won't try and talk me out of it because you have too much respect for your elders."

"So true, Gigi Rinpoche," Mel says, bowing.

"Thank you, Grasshopper." Rose bows back.

Royal starts to get up, then settles back down. He starts to speak, then doesn't. After a longing glance at the teepee flap, he blurts out, "We're underage. At worst we'll get six months in juvie."

By eleven o'clock Rose is on stakeout. 1477 Palmetto is half of a dilapidated duplex in a deteriorating neighborhood. What had been a two-way street when the homes were built has become a four-lane highway. Zoning has gone by the wayside. Between forlorn little houses and duplexes built in the twenties and thirties are commercial ventures: Pay Day Loans, Latrina's Lounge, comic-books shop, vape shop. Rose's chosen lurking spot is a red leatherette booth at the Arby's across from Eddie Martinez's address.

He is home, she guesses. The pickup parked on the weedy lawn is the one she's seen him in twice before.

Shortly after eleven thirty he emerges. Wearing pajama bottoms and a muscle shirt, he sits in a battered overstuffed armchair on the dilapidated porch, drinks from a coffee mug, and smokes a cigarette.

Near one o'clock, he comes back out in shorts and the muscle shirt to move his truck and mow the tiny front yard with an old push mower.

Rose gets another cup of coffee. She'd thought the life of a hired assassin would be more interesting.

At one forty-seven, he again comes out.

266

From a shed behind the duplex, he loads a mower and two five-gallon plastic buckets containing tools into the back of his truck.

Rose has Lyft up on her phone. She's loaded in the Arby's address and a bogus destination. They won't let events progress without all the boxes filled. On her screen she can see a minuscule car orbiting the area three minutes from the Arby's. Rose requests a pickup.

For the next three hours Rose surveils Eddie Martinez mowing lawns, clipping hedges, pulling weeds, watering plants, and, inevitably, donning a gas-powered leaf blower that makes as much noise as a diesel truck clawing its way up a steep incline and harassing the leaves.

At each stop, Rose skulks. In residential areas it is harder to find cover, but she makes use of a park, a playground, and a couple of big friendly trees. To pass the time, she texts. An article she'd read said the average high school student texted fifty times a day. Even with time on her hands, Rose doesn't come close to that. Meditation is more entertaining than texting, and the point of meditation is to do absolutely nothing as long as possible.

Tailing a person via Uber and Lyft proves amazingly efficacious. As soon as she sees

Eddie loading his equipment into his truck, she calls for a pickup. The drivers seem delighted to enter into the cloak-and-dagger aspect. Rose suspects her harmless fluffiness puts them at ease. Always a different car and a different driver. Sometimes Rose sits in front, sometimes in back. And, too, Eddie Martinez seems oblivious to the fact that he might be the stalked, not the stalker, for a change.

Five thirty finds Rose back in her booth at the Arby's across the street from the duplex. She drinks a cup of coffee while he washes his truck with loving care, stroking the hood dry with a chamois cloth.

She calls Mel. "Hit men are really boring."

"You haven't talked to him?"

"He was always more or less alone — no witnesses — and surrounded with sharp objects. Besides, I promised I'd call you before I made contact," Rose says.

Mel, and now Royal, are well and truly in Rose's perilous pickle. More than once she's considered playing the authoritarian, insisting Mel keep clear. She hasn't done it. Mostly because it won't work. Rose is the younger of two sisters. She's never had children. Never wanted children. Never even babysat children. Marion didn't have children, so no little nephews or nieces to dandle. When Mel came along, Rose had no concept of how to be a mother, much less a grandmother. So she just played with the kid. The two of them had been co-conspirators Mel's whole life. Thirteen and sixty-eight, yet on some plane they are equals. Mel won't blindly obey Rose any more than Marion will.

Reap what you sow, Rose thinks, not regretting a moment of the sowing.

"Are you coming home? I mean to the teepee?" Mel asks.

"I'm going to hang out awhile longer," Rose says. "See if he goes out. If he seems settled in for the night, we'll try again tomorrow."

An hour later Eddie emerges from the duplex a changed man. He wears chino pants, creased and clean, a short-sleeved, button-front plaid shirt, and shined cordovan penny loafers. His thick short hair is plastered to his skull with water or hair cream, a part as straight as a ruler's edge dividing the dark cap.

Rose requests a Lyft that is four minutes out. Antsy, she leaves Arby's and hovers on the sidewalk, a fat telephone pole between herself and her quarry.

As Eddie is backing out, seat belt fastened,

hair checked in the rearview mirror, a silver Prius driven by Brian pulls up to the curb. Rose hops in the front passenger seat.

"Follow that truck," she says.

"You got it," Brian replies with a rakish grin. Evidently he's grown up on the same movies and TV shows as Rose. He is a striking-looking man, midsixties, all lean angles and raw bones, wavy gray hair nearly to his shoulders.

"Trick is to stay back, but not too far back," he says.

Rose raises an eyebrow.

"Mansplain?" Brian asks. He has what Rose always thinks of as Paul Newman–blue eyes.

"What are we following him for?"

"The usual," Rose replies.

"Cheating boyfriend?"

Rose snorts.

"Hey," Brian says. "Times they are a-changed."

"Not cheating on me," Rose says. "On my husband. That's our pool boy."

Brian laughs. "Okay, don't tell me. Secret squirrel. The plot thickens." He pulls out, the Prius not making a sound, and falls in behind Eddie's truck.

In an old neighborhood of small houses with nicely kept yards, the pickup truck parks under a live oak. Eddie gets out.

"Drive past," Rose says. In the side-view mirror she sees Eddie smooth his hair, then knock on the door. "Go around the block, then park."

"Ten-four."

Eddie isn't long. Brian has just parked the Prius when he comes out of the house accompanied by an attractive woman, dressed with a Hispanic flair for figure-hugging clothes and neon-bright colors. Holding her hand is a little girl of four or five wearing pink leggings under a short purple dress, and sparkly shoes. Curling black hair falls to her waist. It is kept off her face by a plastic diamond princess tiara.

"Any cuter and she'd be a puppy," Brian says.

"Grandchildren?" Rose asks.

"Guilty," Brian replies. "The youngest is about the age of the princess." He nods at the little girl Eddie is buckling into the center of the bench seat in his truck.

"Any pictures?" Rose asks to be polite.

"Not that far gone," Brian says, and smiles. One of his front teeth has a chip in it, adding to the roguishness. "They any relation to you?"

"We are all one," Rose intones sententiously.

"Namaste that," Brian says.

He eases the Prius away, trailing a block or so behind Eddie and the woman and child.

In a mile or two the neighborhood changes from working poor to rising trendy, with bars and restaurants that are still home to the locals but in a few years will probably be teeming with noisy thirty-somethings and well-to-do college kids.

Eddie drives into a parking lot next to a yellow stucco building. VINCENZO'S FINE ITALIAN FOOD is painted in script on a hanging sign bordered with ironwork in the shape of a grapevine.

"Drive by?" Brian asks.

"Please. Let me off around the next corner."

As ordered, Brian rounds the corner, then pulls the Prius to the curb. "Do you want me to wait?" he asks as Rose opens the door.

"No, thanks. I might be a while."

"No charge," he says.

Rose smiles and closes the car door. Then she calls Mel. "I think this is it. He's on a date, a woman with a little girl." She gives Mel the name and address of the restaurant.

"On our way," Mel says. "Where shall we meet you?"

"I'll text. You promise you won't come in?"

Mel sighs gustily. "Not unless we hear gunshots."

"Especially not then," Rose pleads.

"Okay, but if you bleed to death with two qualified first responders across the street you'll only have yourself to blame."

"I can live with that," Rose says.

"No pun intended," Mel says.

"That was not a pun." Rose puts the cell phone into the front zipper pocket of the backpack Mel lent her. For a moment she dithers. In the morning this had seemed like a brilliant idea. After a long tiring day, aching and weary and seriously in the mood for a good stiff drink and a hot bath, it seems like . . .

Like the only viable idea.

Either she gives up and lives in terror every minute of every day, or she soldiers on. Rose slips the backpack over her shoulder, turns the corner, and walks purposefully toward Vincenzo's, whistling the theme song from *The Bridge on the River Kwai* under her breath.

CHAPTER 21

Before reaching the restaurant, Rose leaves the sidewalk to walk through the parking lot. She notes down Eddie's license plate number, then continues to the back of Vincenzo's. She's never known a restaurant not to have a back door, usually opening out of the kitchen into a garbage collection area, but she isn't taking any chances.

There is a back door.

In the front of the building, on the sidewalk, are six tables arranged inside a low cast-iron fence. Two young women, both on cell phones, occupy one of them.

Rose pushes open the door to the restaurant. Vincenzo's is cut in half by a six-foothigh partition that separates the bar from the dining area. The bar side is dimly lit, the bar long and of polished wood. About a third of the stools are occupied. The dining side, an almost equally narrow space, is packed with tables covered in white cloths.

Wicker-covered-wine-bottles-become-candle-holders and mason jars full of pencil-thin breadsticks serve as centerpieces.

Four tables are occupied. Eddie, the woman, and the little girl are seated at the back, near where the partition ends, giving access to the bar, kitchen, and restrooms. Eddie sits with his back to the door.

He must feel safe at Vincenzo's. Rose hopes to change that.

She wends her way through the crowd of tables until she is standing next to Eddie's chair. Ignoring her, he continues to study the menu. His date notices Rose is not a waitress, and smiles the way people do when they are not sure whether or not there is going to be a problem.

"Hi," Rose says with an answering smile. "I'm Rose Dennis, a friend of Eddie's."

Eddie lifts his gaze from the menu, then does a classic double take. Rose's smile widens. "Hi, Eddie, it's good to see you taking a little time for yourself." Eddie doesn't move or speak. In the tradition of Medusa, Rose's face has apparently turned him to stone.

Rose focuses her smile on his date. "You must be . . ."

The woman's smile warms, comfortable now, deciding Rose isn't going to report that their truck has been towed, or her escort is under arrest for attempted murder. "I'm Tania," she says. Turning to Eddie, she punches him none too lightly on the biceps. "Eddie!"

Eddie takes on a sheepish aspect. Sheepish. Rose is amazed. In none of her paintings of his face had she recorded a whiff of sheepishness.

"Yeah, uh, Miss —"

"Dennis, Rose Dennis. You worked on my roof." Eddie's features flatten like a soufflé in an earthquake. His mouth works as if he's trying to clean peanut butter off his back teeth. Rose gives Tania a little shrug. "I think it's all coming back to him."

"Yeah," Eddie says woodenly. "Ms., uh, Dennis. This is, uh . . ." His face goes blank. Tania punches him again. "Tania Edgars, my fiancée" is knocked out of him.

"How do you do," Tania says as Rose says, "Pleased to meet you."

Eddie's face is functioning, but his voice has again abandoned him.

Tania rolls her eyes theatrically. They are lovely eyes. "And this is my daughter, Amy."

"Your Majesty," Rose says with a bow. Amy touches her tiara and giggles. "May I borrow Eddie for a minute?" she asks Tania. "I promise not to keep him long."

Eddie makes a noise somewhere between a choke and a growl. His lips thin. "Be right back," he mutters. Rose gives him an encouraging smile and ushers him around the partition to the bar.

She climbs on a stool. From her perch, she can see Amy and part of Tania seated in the dining area. Eddie puts himself four-square between her and the table he's just vacated.

"What are you doing here?" he hisses. "Can't you see this is a family place?"

Rose is taken aback by the vehemence. Amy waves shyly at her from the table.

"You leave Amy alone," Eddie says in a menacing whisper.

"Why? Because there was only one thing wrong with the Dennis woman — she was *alive*?" Rose waves back at the little girl. "Just who tried to murder whom?"

"Stay the fuck away." Eddie starts to turn back toward the table.

"Edward 'Eddie' Martinez. 1477 Palmetto. Arrested at seventeen for assault. Arrested again at twenty-two for assault and battery. Paroled this January. Parole officer, Carol Thompson."

Eddie pivots, steps closer to Rose's stool. She tenses, waiting for a beefy hand to smash her to the floor. Nothing happens.

"How do you know all that?" Eddie's eyes dart up and down the bar as if one of the stools holds a pigeon.

"I ran your fingerprint," Rose says.

"How'd you get —" He breaks off and stares hard at Rose. "You didn't . . ."

"I did."

Eddie looks like he might lose his breadsticks. "That's gross."

For a while neither speaks. Finally Eddie ends the silence. "I want it back."

"You want what back?"

"My finger. I want it back."

Rose laughs. "What would you do, have it bronzed? It's too late to get it reattached."

"It's mine. I want it."

Rose worked hard for that finger. It is evidence. It is more than that. It is art. "Well, you can't have it."

"Why not? It's my fu—"

Rose looks pointedly over his shoulder to where Amy is building a fort with breadsticks and flatware.

Eddie drops his voice and leans in menacingly. "It's my effing finger."

"I need it for DNA evidence," Rose says.

"Bullshit. You don't need a whole finger." Eddie is getting increasingly agitated. Rose's interview is in danger of going off the rails.

She lowers her eyes, refusing to meet his

glare. "You can't have it because it's gone," she murmurs.

"Gone?" He slaps the bar with the wrong hand and grunts as the pain registers. "What did you do? Throw it in the garbage? You threw my fu— my effing finger in the garbage!"

"No," Rose manages, her voice cracking slightly. "I ate it."

Eddie slumps onto the stool next to Rose, their knees almost touching. "You are shitting me." He starts to slap the bar again, then thinks better of it. "You really ate it?"

Rose nods guiltily. "I'd read the whole Donner Party story, then there were those guys in the plane crash in the Andes and . . . you know. I kind of wondered what we taste like. It's not like I wanted to eat a whole person or anything. I'm not a cannibal."

Eddie is slowly shaking his head from side to side like an old dog who has lost his sense of smell. "Jesus effing Christ." He fixes his eyes on the bar. "What did it taste like?"

"Finger food," Rose says.

He looks at her, eyes narrowing.

"I have your information, your DNA, your fingerprint, and the knife. This would be strike three, Eddie. Next time you go away for life." Rose doesn't know if North Carolina has the three strikes rule or not, but it sounds good.

Eyes black and hard as chips of obsidian, he shoves his face close to Rose's. "How about I just kill you the rest of the way," he says.

"Information. My death. Safety deposit box. Do I have to spell it out?"

Eddie's eyes go from fiery to blank. "Uh. Yeah. Spell it out."

"I have all the evidence you kindly left at my home, along with a complete statement of what transpired. If anything happens to me, or to anybody even slightly related to me, all that evidence will be sent to the police, your parole officer, and the newspapers."

Eddie gapes as if he can't believe what he is hearing; then he lowers his gaze to the bar.

"Can I help you?" A bartender has glided over.

"Gimme a draft," Eddie says.

"I'm fine." Rose waves him away.

"You'd really do that, wouldn't you?" Eddie asks. He looks angry and lost and miserable. "You'd wreck my life. They said you were one crazy bitch."

"That's what I'm here for, Eddie. Not to ruin your life. To find out who 'they' are. Who hired you?" The bartender is back with the draft beer. "To call on me that night?"

"How the fu— the eff— would I know?"

That he wouldn't know hadn't occurred to Rose. She thinks about it for a moment. "How did they contact you?"

"Email." Eddie takes a long draft of the beer, then wipes the foam off his lip with the cocktail napkin.

"Who emailed you?"

"It's not like that." Eddie runs his fingers through his hair, ruining the part and leaving hair stuck up on his crown like chick's fluff.

"What is it like?" Rose asks patiently. Eddie doesn't seem to be stonewalling; he seems to be trying to think. Rose guesses thinking is not his long suit.

"You know, like Angie's List, Craigslist, shit like that."

Rose nods.

"This is a site like that. Most of it is regular stuff. I get my lawn jobs there. But if there's a particular need, somebody there contacts somebody, and it gets set up. All secure and untraceable. I found out about the site when I was in the clink."

Rose wishes she'd ordered a drink. She puts her elbows on the bar. "I hate it that everything is in cyberspace. Sometimes I think I need a cyberspace suit to keep from exploding into a billion pieces."

"Tell me about it." Eddie sighs. "First time I went away — back then — at least you knew your client. Now it's all digital."

Inwardly Rose curses Al Gore for inventing the internet. There is no way she could unravel that skein of cybertrails. She doubts even Marion could.

"You never met with an actual person?" Rose asks.

"Nobody."

"How did they pay you?"

Eddie's face twists into a pained expression. "What difference does it make?"

"The difference between life in prison and going home with Tania and Amy," Rose says.

"So now I'm your bitch?"

"Pretty much. How did they pay you?"

Eddie drains his beer. "I needed a truck for my business," he says. "Tania won't marry a guy with no work. She says she's had enough of criminals and deadbeats."

Rose punches him in the arm, much harder than Tania had. "You were going to murder me for a used truck?" she explodes. "You couldn't have at least asked for a new one?"

"Keep your voice down," Eddie whispers.

"Tania's tired of criminals. You're a criminal," Rose says, the low cost of her life making her vindictive.

"I am not!" Eddie rejoins. "That was one last job, just to get my business going. I don't do crime no more."

"Where did you get the truck? You had to pick it up, or have it delivered." There had to be contact at some point in the exchange.

"I picked it up at Goodman's Used Cars. The paperwork and everything was all done. I had to get insurance. That was it."

Rose takes out her notebook and writes down *Goodman's Used Cars.* She puts the notebook away. Looking hard at Eddie, she says, "Eddie, you are a two-bit crook. Don't tell me you graduated from that to murder for a lousy used truck."

Eddie fidgets. He glances over his shoulder at Tania and Amy. He takes a deep pull on his beer. Finally, he says sullenly, "My mom's not from here, if you get my drift. The email said somebody would call ICE on her. This isn't exactly a sanctuary city."

"Oh, gosh." Rose thinks about this. "Your mom is an illegal alien?"

"Mom never did an illegal thing in her life," Eddie says sharply.

"You didn't kill me, though. What happened to Mom?"

"She's in detention. You happy?" Eddie finishes his beer in one long swallow.

Rose isn't happy. She is not happy at all. But that is blood under the bridge. "Okay. I'm sorry. Now that they can't hold Mom hostage, what happens if you don't kill me?"

"I don't know. I guess they repo the truck. Or come after me. Or Tania. Or Amy." He glances at the two girls he wants to become his family, then back at Rose. She can feel him struggling with life in prison on the one hand and life as a victim on the other.

Before he can come to his own conclusions, Rose says, "Don't even think about it, Eddie. You don't kill me, maybe they come after you, maybe they don't. They're not going to want the exposure of going near Tania or Amy. Citizens don't like people who kill young women and children. And, face it, you're not a high-end employee. They can undoubtedly write off the cost of a used truck and never even feel the bite. So you don't kill me, you will probably be okay.

"You do kill me, and nothing will ever be okay again. You will go to prison, Tania will marry a fabulous man and have a beautiful family, watch them grow up, have kids of their own, and all that time you'll be folding other men's boxer shorts and eating off plastic trays. And," Rose says, dropping her voice for the coup de grâce, "you know as well as I do what's coming down the road. Within a year or so all prisons will be non-smoking."

"Shit," Eddic says.

Rose watches him as he uses his cocktail napkin to wipe his mouth. "Eddie, would you really have murdered me?"

Eddie's eyes narrow and he looks at her shrewdly. The muscles of his face relax, and he lets out a gust of beer-scented breath. "Sure." He sucks in his lower lip, then releases it with a small pop. "I don't know. Then? Probably not. Now? I'm warming up to the idea."

Rose pats him on the knee. She sets the backpack on the bar and unzips it. Using Marion's ATM, she'd withdrawn five hundred dollars. Counting out five crisp twenties, she says, "This is for telling me about Goodman's. There will be another hundred for anything you think of that helps." Rose tucks the remainder of the cash into the backpack and zips it shut. She's nervous about flashing the cash but wants Eddie to know viscerally that there is more where his came from.

Shouldering the backpack, she stands. "Remember, Eddie, dead I am worth a life sentence. Alive I am worth one hundred dollars a clue."

"How do I get hold of you?" Eddie asks sullenly, but he folds the hundred dollars into a money clip and stuffs it in his front pocket.

Rose writes her email address and phone number on his cocktail napkin. "Call or email. We'll meet and talk face-to-face, like real people." She steps around him and walks toward the restrooms. She doesn't glance back.

Once in the relative safety of the ladies' room, she locks the door and slumps down on the commode.

The adrenaline that kept her going during the interaction with Eddie Martinez evaporates like rain on the desert. Fatigue joins gravity. Rose barely has the strength to lift her arms. Laboriously, she fumbles the iPhone from the pack and texts Mel. *Where are you?*

At a table outside.

Of course. Rose wishes the kids were in a bunker ten miles away. Sighing, she heaves herself up and commences her metamorphosis. In the backpack are a wig — short and dark — a lightweight microfiber cardigan in teal blue, and a Whole Foods tote bag. Rose dons wig and cardigan, then dumps the backpack into the tote.

She leaves Vincenzo's via the back door.

Mel and Royal are at one of the tables farthest from the door of the restaurant. An empty chair, its back to the entrance, awaits Rose. The girls on their cell phones are still on their cell phones, ignoring the food in front of them. A man has taken the table next to Mel and Royal. An open *New York Times,* a paper, an actual paper made of paper, hides most of him. A couple with a whining infant fusses at a table next to the phone girls.

Rose slides into the waiting chair and drops the tote to the ground.

"Well?" Mel asks.

"I think it went okay. Who knows?" Rose says. She is too tired to be a leader or a grown-up. "What are we doing now?"

"We're going to wait, watch him come out, so we can see what he looks like," Mel says.

"For identification purposes," Royal adds.

A waitress appears with menus.

"Pinot grigio?" Rose asks hopefully. The woman writes it down as if a glass of wine is merely a beverage and not a heavenly reward.

"Diet Coke," Mel says. Rose sniffs. "Regular Coke," Mel says with exaggerated patience. To Royal she explains, "Gigi thinks diet drinks make you fat."

"They do," Rose says. "How do you think they stay in business? If they worked, everybody would get thin and quit buying them. It's all a marketing ploy."

"Zero calories. How does it make people fat?" Royal asks.

"You can bet that is a very carefully guarded trade secret," Rose tells him. "Ask your dad to poke his nose in the files if he ever gets detailed to a diet drink production plant. Scientific proof would be great. All I've got for now is a hint from the Akashic records."

"The what?" Royal flips his bangs from his eyes with the side of his hand. Fifty years later, and in a landlocked city, the surfer look still rocks.

"The Akashic records are kind of like a psychic Google," Mel says. "Gigi doesn't really believe in it.

Rose laughs. "Mel is my interpreter."

"All the great Rinpoches travel with an interpreter," Mel says.

Rose is finishing her bread bowl of corn chowder, and working on her second glass of wine, when the phone in her tote chimes. Mel nods. She has her cell in her hand.

Rose takes out the phone. *Little girl in pink leggings,* Mel's text reads. *Curvy lady in or-*

ange. Then: *Dude with bandaged hand.*

Heads down, eyes glued to devices; a family dinner out. Not suspicious.

I thought he'd be bigger, Mel texts.

Rose refuses to rise to the bait.

Looking up and down the street. Not at us, Mel texts.

Rose resists the urge to glance over her shoulder.

Leaving.

A couple of seconds later Eddie, Tania, and Amy walk past Rose's table toward the parking lot. They don't spare a glance at the diners.

"Last place he'd look," Mel says smugly.

"Hide in plain sight," Rose says.

Having signaled for the check, Rose downs the last of the wine in a single gulp.

"Need a lift?" The man at the table next to them folds down his paper.

"What are you doing here?" Rose demands. It's her Lyft driver, Brian of the blue eyes and enticing smile.

"Backup," Brian says, and winks.

"How did you know it was me?"

"Little chipmunk ears. Unmistakable."

CHAPTER 22

The following morning Royal lets Rose into the basement for a quick shower while Grandma listens to the news at top volume upstairs. When Rose finishes, she finds Mel has bicycled over to the teepee, laden with fresh clothes from Izzy's closet. Applegarth, they decided, was too dangerous to risk a supply run.

Rose's taste in clothes falls somewhere between flamboyant and Barnum & Bailey. In Izzy's fitted slacks and tailored shirts, she feels as if she's wearing a costume, disguising herself as a real person. It is for the best. Izzy's excellent taste and conservative fashion bent blend nicely into the Charlotte habitat.

Mel is dressed like a bright middle school girl: skirt, camp shirt, and sandals.

"It isn't Saturday or anything, is it?" Rose asks, frowning.

"Uncle Daniel called school and told

them I was sick," Mel says. "All I have to do is say I have 'female problems' and Uncle Dan can't get out of the house fast enough."

"Poor Uncle Daniel," Rose says.

"Such a tool," Mel agrees. "So I go to the TV station and do my 'student project' — cunningly finding out who told the news people the nurse was in ICU, and you were dangerous, et cetera, while you go to Goodman's Used Cars to see who bought the truck for Eddie," she confirms as they leave the confines of the tent.

Since Marion is still wading through years of patient files — and none too pleased about it — Goodman's is the only avenue Rose can think to pursue.

"Unless you can think of anything better to do," Rose says.

As they round the corner of Royal's house, crossing from backyard to front, Mel throws out an arm to stop Rose.

A woman with shoulder-length blond hair swinging, crisp white linen suit gleaming like Sir Lancelot's armor, is folding her long slim legs into a red Lexus.

"Who was that?" Rose asks when the car is out of sight. The woman absolutely reeks of power.

"Royal's grandma," Mel tells her.

That isn't quite how Rose pictured deaf

old Granny. "I feel like I should vote for her or something."

"She used to be with this big-deal law firm. Since she retired, she does pro bono work for undocumented immigrants."

"How does that work with the Secret Service son?" Rose asks.

"They don't talk politics at the dinner table, if that's what you mean," Mel replies.

"Here's my silver Honda, driven by" — Rose checks her phone — "Belva. Good luck. Text when you're done. We can meet you back here and swap war stories."

"Sure. You can tell me what a 'gipper' is."

Goodman's Used Cars is on the south side of Charlotte, where the city peters out in a drizzle of unglamorous commercial enterprises. Like many other car sales lots Rose has seen, Goodman's has enough pennants flying, it could've been signaling the Coast Guard.

Rose waves her driver away and wanders down between the rows of cars under a star-studded sign — literally, yellow plywood stars the size of garbage can lids — wondering where she should begin. Surely, close by will be a slightly balding, middle-aged man, with too many teeth, wearing a cheap suit.

Seeming to materialize out of the chrome

and metal, a guy twenty-five or forty, lean and tanned — skin weathered rather than aged — appears, leaning on the cab of a Toyota Camry a row from where Rose meanders. He wears a straw cowboy hat, rolled up on the sides and dark from years of sweat. A black T-shirt, worn loose over plaid shorts, reads WIDE SPREAD PANIC. His long thin feet are encased in leather sandals, probably Mexican made. Chestnut-brown hair waves to his shoulders.

Tilting his head back to shade his eyes, he smiles at Rose. "I saw a midnight blue Miata convertible on the other side of the lot that would look real good on you."

Rose knows this man. He is the guy girlfriends warned her about, but she never listened. He is the man with a wicked streak, who seems to have all the time in the world for little ol' you. He sees the devil in a woman and winks at her.

At twenty-two, Rose couldn't resist him.

At sixty-eight, why bother?

She smiles back. They share a psychic wink.

"Unfortunately, I'm just looking for a car salesman," she says.

"Carter Goodman at your service." He sweeps the hat off and bows. When he stands, he flourishes his hand and, like magic, a business card appears between his fingers. Rose takes it.

Used car salesmen have changed a lot in the last forty years, Rose thinks.

"Now I wish I was here to buy a car," she confesses. "I'm on an information-seeking mission."

"If the information regards cars, music, or philosophy, I'm your man."

"Cars," Rose says.

"Any one in particular?"

"A black 2005 Chevrolet Silverado," Rose says. "A man named Martinez picked it up a week or so back."

"Right. Good vehicle for the money."

Though she dreads the answer, Rose has to ask. "How much did it cost?"

"Sold for three thousand nine hundred and ninety-five dollars," Carter says. "Sweet deal. Had less than seventy-five thousand miles on it."

Less than four grand. Rose's life is valued at less than five figures.

"Do you remember the details of all the cars you sell?" she asks.

"Sure. I've got one of those memories that lasers facts in stone."

"What a drag," Rose says.

"What's special about that particular truck?" Carter asks. "I can probably find one like it for you."

Rose wonders how much she should tell him. Her father always told her and Marion to "tell the truth, the whole truth, nothing but the truth, and damned little of that."

"I'm just curious who the previous owner was," she says.

"Now, that, I don't know. The truck was an internet sale. People get deals on the net. The vehicles are delivered to my lot for pickup. That way the buyers and sellers get a safe transfer, a buddy of mine gets first crack at selling them auto insurance, and maybe next time they don't go to the net, they remember what a swell company Goodman's is, and they come to me."

"Maintaining the flow of kindness," Rose says.

He smiles, his teeth very white against the tanned cheeks. "And, of course, there's the hundred-dollar fee I charge for the service."

"No paperwork?" Rose queries.

"There's always paperwork," Carter says. "Cars leave a paper trail a cross-eyed termite could follow all the way back to Detroit. Want to take a look? See if we can find the origin story of your previously owned Silverado?"

"That would be great," Rose says. Sunshine. Used cars. Nice man. Questions answered. Help freely offered. This is what sanity looks like. Commuting at night, by bicycle express, to teepees, and having drinks with hit men — that is the aberration. Of course, Rose knows there are people who live and die in the shadow of lies, betrayals, violence, and crime.

It has to be exhausting.

People should love one another right now.

Buy the world a Coke and keep it company.

The Age of Aquarius was way too short as far as Rose is concerned.

Carter's office, though the traditional glass-walled fishbowl, is as refreshing as he. A cheap Mexican rug lights up the floor. A Boston fern on the sill softens the square of the window overlooking the lot. Two acrylic paintings, one of a truck in the desert, broken down, hood open, and one of a fog-shrouded winter beach, a classic VW Bug up to its doors in the tide, do the same favor for the walls.

"History of my life," Carter says.

"You did these?" Rose is impressed.

"I did. Good looks and talent. You don't find guys like me hanging on trees." Turning to a filing cabinet, he opens the top drawer. "Let's see what we got here on your Silverado."

Rose studies the truck painting, admiring the way Carter has managed the rust and dust on the metallic curves of the hood. "Do you do your own framing?" Both pictures have frames made from car parts. The frame of the truck painting looks as if it had once been a grille.

"That I do," Carter says. "Here we go." He lifts out several sheets of paper stapled together at the corner.

"No computer?" Rose asks, taking the leather sling chair opposite the desk.

"Can't do business without it." Sitting down, he brushes a pile of shiny brochures off a paper-thin laptop. "However, car dealers still cling to hard copy, signatures, pink slips. Probably will for at least a couple of years. Okay, here we go." He peruses the pages one at a time. "Local guy, Gastonia — not too far from here, next county over. We've moved a couple of cars for him. Name is Jack Gaines. Good mechanic on older models — less computer control. Fixes them up, then sells them on the internet. Does great bodywork.

"Are you in the market for a vintage?" He flashes a grin at Rose. "That's what we call vehicles not quite old enough to be marketed as antiques. I've got a couple of other trucks I could show you."

"Not today."

"What's special about this truck?"

"I think it might have been used in the commission of a crime," she says.

"You don't smell like a cop."

"More a Miss Marple."

"Nah. Chris Cagney." He scans the second page. "Says here it was bought by an Edward Martinez. Paid by PayPal. Need Martinez's address?" Carter starts to pass the pages to Rose. His eye catches on the second page, and his hand stops in midoffer. Rose reaches for the document, but he takes it back. Holding the pages upright, he taps the bottom edge on the desk to align the pages. Given they are stapled together, the gesture strikes Rose as not only unnecessary but self-conscious, too.

"That's all I got," Carter says. "You might be able to track Jack down — Gastonia's a small town. Oh, sorry." He grimaces as he takes his cell phone from his pocket. Glancing at the screen, he says, "I've got to take this. Sorry. Good luck."

Rose hadn't heard his phone chime, nor the buzz of a vibrator. Maybe newer phones sent a tingle directly to the owner's cerebral cortex. In this instance, however, Rose guesses she is being politely thrown out on her ear.

Nodding thanks, she stands and leaves the office. Carter shows her his back, speaking heartily into the phone, the rectangle of plastic held to his car by his shoulder as he replaces the Martinez file in the cabinet.

Rose doesn't turn right and leave the building but left and into a room marked TOILET — IF YOU NEED IT, USE IT, a small rebellion against North Carolina's infamous bathroom law.

Keeping the door open the merest crack, she watches Carter Goodman. He turns around to check the hall and the front showroom. Phone in hand, punching buttons as he walks, he leaves the building. Moments later, Rose sees him pacing between rows of midsized sedans, phone to his ear.

Keeping an eye on him, she sneaks back into his office. He reaches the end of the row and turns back, walking directly toward the office window, free arm gesticulating, showing every evidence of having a heated conversation. Rose drops to her hands and knees. Crawling over to the Boston fern in the window, she squints through the fronds, eyes barely above the sill. When he reaches the end of the row, no more than twenty feet from Rose's eyeballs, he turns again and paces the other way.

Rose pops up, feeling a bit like a prop in a

game of Whac-A-Mole, and scurries to the file cabinet. The drawer is still open, the Martinez file not completely slid back into its folder. Rose plucks it out. In a quick scan she sees nothing Carter hasn't already told her, but clearly something in these sheets of paper set him off.

Feeling every inch a rat and a rotten citizen, she stuffs the file in her purse, then slinks surreptitiously from Goodman's used car lot.

CHAPTER 23

Searching for individuals who matched Rose's patient profile, Marion had worked through three years of the files Rose videoed at the MCU. She searched by date of entry, diagnosis, primary care doctor, length of stay, date of death — any venue that might produce a pattern or a repeated name.

In the previous three years five people, including Rose, were placed in the MCU with a diagnosis of rapid-onset dementia. Of those five, Rose and three others were diagnosed with both rapid-onset and early-onset dementia. The others were Camilla Reynolds, James Madding, and Charles Boster — Chuck.

Reynolds and Madding are deceased. Three months after becoming a resident of the MCU, Reynolds, a seventy-three-year-old white female, broke a femur in a fall and died of heart failure six days later. She was survived by her son, who sold his home in Charlotte shortly after his mother's death and moved to parts unknown. Madding, a sixty-nine-year-old white male, suffocated after a chunk of meat became lodged in his throat seven weeks after placement in the MCU. He was survived by a younger brother, who sold the family home in Charlotte and moved to Aspen, Colorado, two months after James Madding died.

Chuck Boster, seventy-one, white male, is still living. But for Rose, he is the most recent inductee, incarcerated in the Memory Care Unit forty-three days before Flynn put Rose there. If victims are being put in the MCU for sinister purposes, Chuck fits the criteria for "not lasting the week." Chuck is top priority. Not only is he alive, but he also has a wife living in Charlotte. Even if Rose could locate Reynolds's son, or Madding's brother, travel by air is out of the question. She is a fugitive from the law.

More than that, Chuck is her friend. Through her drug fog and his severe dementia — or drug-induced confusion — they connected. They shared comfort and compassion under difficult circumstances. Given the state of her mind when in the Memory Care Unit, Rose marvels at the effort and concentration it must have taken Chuck to yell "Help!" and "Fire!" when she'd needed a distraction.

Madding seven weeks, Reynolds three months — if death is the goal, why not kill the victims the day they arrive? Because, to use Andre the Uber driver's word, it would look "hinky."

. . . these things can happen too fast and too often. We need to be careful of our special needs patients . . . Wanda said that, Rose remembers. The deaths must be spaced out, made to look natural.

"What are you thinking?" Mel asks. Mel, flopped on the faux animal skins, is watching as Rose does her best to apply makeup using a palm-sized piece of mirror the "Indians" use to signal one another when they are in residence.

"About how long it takes the world to cease caring about an old, demented person."

"Like a day and a half," Mel says heartlessly. "I talked to Dad last night," she says. "Nothing. Nobody called to tell him his stepmother broke in, iced a nurse, and escaped. Again.

"Also I called Longwood and asked for an Adele Bonniface, supposedly the assistant communications director who called the TV station about your great escape."

"And?" Rose says, putting on her lipstick — Izzy's lipstick. It is deep red with cobalt undertones. The effect is that of an instant tooth whitening. Most satisfactory.

"They'd never heard of her. No such department, no such position, no such person."

Once Rose would have been shocked that a news service would broadcast unverified information. Those halcyon days were as gone as the eight-track tape player.

"Fake news," Mel says. She has come of age during the rise and realization of fake news. Like most kids her age, Mel has little interest in what is happening in the adult world. Rose likes that about kids. They have the rest of their lives to suffer anxiety attacks about unverified rumors of flesh-eating bacteria in Outer Slabovia.

"If Longwood was innocent, they would have informed Flynn. The MCU must be where the deed is done, where I was drugged," Rose says. "We need to find out who inside the MCU is participating, who is providing the victims, and why. Longwood is not doing the Angel of Mercy thing, offing pathetic oldsters. Victims are being provided by the criteria of early onset, rapid onset. We need to find out what value we — the aforementioned victims — have dead that we don't have alive. Hopefully Barbara Boster will shed light on that."

"You should call first," Mel says. "Nobody drops by like in the olden days. Not ever. You call first, even if you're sitting in a car at the curb in front of their house."

"She's probably deaf and doesn't answer her cell phone," Rose replies. "If she even has one."

"You are such an ageist!" Mel tells her.

Rose is affronted. Some of her best friends are old people. "I'm still not going to call. Barbara Boster might refuse to see us —"

"Or won't be home. Or will be in the bathroom and not hear the doorbell," Mel interjects.

"That could happen, but the element of the sudden unknown is a powerful thing. In art, theater, dance, life, when people are presented with the sudden unknown they wake up for a second or two. Occasionally for long enough you can be in the moment with them, see who they really are."

"Yeah. Then they chase you onto the roof with a knife in their teeth or spike your OJ."

"There's that," Rose concedes. "I'm not going to call. Don't want to ruin the surprise."

Mel rolls her eyes.

Rose is wearing a tea-length watermelon-colored linen sheath dress and black ballet-style flats from Izzy's wardrobe. Mel is disguised as her granddaughter in skinny jeans, with artful damage at the knees, and a floaty lime-green top longer in back than in front.

"Knock, knock." Royal's voice comes from beyond the entrance of the teepee.

"Enter at your own risk," Mel calls.

Royal pokes his head through the flap. "Grandma's gone," he reports.

"Thank you, Royal." After having laid eyes on Grandma, Rose has become more careful of attracting her notice.

"Sure I can't come? I could be your other grandchild, the smarter, better-looking one," Royal says with a grin.

Mel chucks a pillow at him.

"I will do my best to include you in any dangerous, unsavory, or illegal actions we take in the future," Rose promises.

"Think about it. Old ladies love me," Royal says.

"Gigi is so onto you," Mel returns scornfully.

"Doesn't matter. They can't help themselves. No disrespect, Mrs. Dennis," he adds, remembering his manners. He sits next to Mel. "I could hang out nearby, cell phone at the ready," he suggests.

"I think both Mel and I could outrun Chuck's wife, if it comes to that," Rose says.

"Gigi thinks other old people are genuinely old, and she's merely faux old, still has the strength of ten men and can leap tall buildings in a single bound," Mel confides to her friend.

"Barbara Boster probably is old!" Rose protests. "Chuck is seventy-one."

"So that would make his wife, what? Maybe seventy or sixty-nine?" Mel says. "And you are?"

Rose sighs. "Point taken. I will work on my predilection for ageism."

"We don't have a clue what we're doing," Mel whispers to Royal.

"I heard that," Rose says. "I have the ears of a bat. We do know. We are going to the Boster house. We will be open and mindful of the composition. We will observe hues, tones, and nuances, and note those that cause disharmony."

"Gigi is a painter," Mel explains to Royal.

"You said," he reminds her.

Mel gestures to a stick buffalo figure with mutant reindeer horns. "She really likes your work."

"I was six!" Royal protests.

"No," Mel says. "Seriously. She really does. Don't you find that . . . disturbing?"

"Show Royal the purloined letters," Rose says. "See if he sees anything we missed."

Mel crawls over to where the papers on the sale of Eddie Martinez's truck lie. She tosses them fluttering in Royal's direction. He snatches them out of the air and scans them. "Mr. Martinez's address."

"Check," Mel says. "Gigi already knew, but the used car guy told her, and about Jack Gaines and PayPal, all that stuff."

"Maybe Mr. Gaines could tell you the buyer's name, but on the internet, it could be anybody saying they are somebody else."

"We thought of that," Mel says. "Anything else. I mean, like you or I have ever bought a car, but we're extremely intelligent and sophisticated for our age."

"I never should have told you that," Rose says, angling the signal mirror, trying to see if her hair is sticking up in a duck's tail on the top of her head.

" 'T. Brevard.' Maybe a seller or buyer in Brevard," Royal suggests, handing the pages back to Mel.

"That's the town a couple of hours from here in the mountains I told you about," Mel says to her grandmother.

" 'T. Brevard' is in script," Rose says. "A handwritten note. That made it stand out for me. An item Carter — the used car sales

308

guy — could have noticed scanning the page on the fly, as it were. If you can think of how one might chase that wild goose, Royal, please join the hunt." Rose glances at the screen of the cell phone on the cushion between her and Mel. "Two minutes. Gray Volvo. Sharon driving. Once more unto the breach."

"Gigi likes being abstruse and recondite," Mel says to Royal. "See ya."

Given the cost of Longwood, Rose guesses Charles Franklin Boster is well-off. How well she is beginning to grasp as Sharon of the gray Volvo drives them past mansion after mansion in Eastover.

"I hope she doesn't live in a gated community," Rose worries. "That could louse up our nifty surprise."

"It's not gated," Sharon says. "Some homeowners have been trying to get that passed, but there are too many public thoroughfares to get it by city government."

"Good to know," Rose says.

"This is it." Sharon eases the Volvo into a wide curved driveway. In the half moon of earth between the street and the house, screening it, is a stand of ornamental bamboo at least forty feet high. An answering arc of startlingly white marble steps runs down from outsized double doors with gold-tone — or maybe solid gold for all Rose knows — handles in their middles.

The house is all of brick, painted gleaming white, with white shutters and white trim. There are three stories and a White House–themed circular balcony over the front door. Rose prices it at three or four million, and five thousand square feet minimum.

"Mr. Got Rocks," Rose says, unhooking her seat belt.

"And money," Mel returns.

"Don't forget your flowers," Sharon reminds them.

To ensure Mrs. Boster's goodwill, Rose — technically Marion, since it was her ATM card — has sprung for a dozen soft pink roses, the petals edged with crimson.

Mel precedes her up the steps, past the urns planted with ferns and trailing vincas. She stops just short of the welcome mat, an incongruous thing of rough brown straw-like material. The mat is decorated with fat, childish yellow daisies, and the words WELCOME Y'ALL in lawn-green capitals.

Rose scuffs a toe over the Y'ALL. "That lowers the intimidation factor a few percentiles. See a doorbell?"

Mel finds the button and presses it. Inside,

bells toll in mimicry of Big Ben.

They wait.

Rose sticks her arms out like the wings of a chicken so she won't sweat on the linen dress.

"Probably had to send the butler in from the pool area or the tennis courts," Mel says.

A butler wouldn't surprise Rose, but when the door is finally dragged open, it is by a barefoot man in khaki shorts and a button-down short-sleeved shirt, worn untucked. He looks to be in his early forties; his sandy hair is receding, and a paunch is beginning to punch out the shirt.

He doesn't speak or invite them in, just waits, probably for them to start their sales pitch or fund-raising speech so he will have grounds to tell them to bugger off.

"I'm here to see Mrs. Boster," Rose states coolly.

The man blinks. Though he is bland and harmless-looking, there is a touch of the lizard in that slow blink.

"Hey, Barb!" he shouts. "Someone here to see you." The man takes the flowers from Rose's hands and trails them down by his side the way he might hold a baseball bat he hasn't decided whether or not to use.

"To see me?" A female voice filters down a long hallway, followed by the hush of soft-soled shoes on thick carpet. A woman in her midthirties, with jaw-length soft auburn hair, drifts into view over the doorman's shoulder. She wears white shorts and an aqua tank top that shows an abundance of décolletage. This bounty, as well as the woman's face — a pleasant face with wide-set brown eyes — is deeply tanned and lightly freckled.

"I'm Barbara Boster," she says in an oddly hopeful tone.

"My name is Rose Moore." Rose was once told that Moore was one of the commonest names in America, more so than Smith or Jones, but without the fishy alias overtones. "This is my granddaughter. My husband is a friend of Chuck's."

"How nice! What's your husband's name?" Barbara asks.

"Peter, Pete."

"Peter Moore." Mrs. Boster thinks hard enough that a tiny crease appears between her eyes. "I never heard of him, but it could have been before my time." Rose guesses there are about forty years of Chuck's life that are before his wife's time.

"Come in, y'all come in," she says with a sudden smile, as sweet as a child's. "We're lettin' all the AC out standin' here."

Mel and Rose follow her into an entryway

carpeted in rich violet and lined with beautifully framed and matted botanical prints. It smells new. The prints are lovely, Lilian Snelling's work, but mass-produced, the art not worth one-fiftieth the cost of the frames.

"Aren't they pretty?" Barbara has stopped at the end of the hall and turned back, catching Rose studying one.

"They are," Rose says. "I love her detail and the vibrancy of the colors."

"Yeah," Barbara says. "I thought they went real well with the new carpet."

Rose winces internally, though they do go nicely with the carpet.

"This has all got to be repainted." Barbara waves at the walls and the arched ceiling eleven or more feet overhead. That's when Rose notices the prints are shadowed by a slight discoloration where larger pictures formerly hung.

"New artwork?" Rose asks.

"There used to be all these pictures of the inside of caves that Chuck took. Chuck was a good photographer. They made me sad — that and all dark wood flooring. Coming in the front door was like going underground. I like it light and airy."

"You've done a beautiful job transforming it," Rose comments.

"It's gettin' there." Barbara begins walking again, Mel and Rose trailing in her wake. Behind them Rose hears the door whump shut, the sound like an air lock sealing.

The hall spills out into an enormous sunken living room that was built when formal rooms were in vogue. Now it is a cross between a great room and an entertainment center. The grand old fireplace, with its carved wooden mantel, serves as a base for a television easily seventy-five inches wide. On the screen, black football players are standing around while white men talk to each other. Rose wonders if it is Sunday. Or if football is all day, every day now.

"Have a seat," Barbara says. The couch yawns white and sleek and enormous. Sitting on it is rather like being swallowed by Moby-Dick. The TV whines nasally in sports-speak. "Can I get you anything? A beer or a pop?"

"A beer would be great," Rose says. It is ten thirty in the morning, and, on the whole, Rose isn't a day drinker — or a beer drinker — but this seems like a brewski kind of moment.

"Coke okay for you?" Barbara asks Mel.

"Yes. Thank you," Mel says politely.

"Diet or regular?"

"Regular," Mel says.

"You go, girl." Barbara smiles at Mel, then leaves the room.

The doorman has followed them in. He sits in a white leather-covered chair wide enough that Mel and Rose could have sat side by side never touching. Rose and Mel perch on Moby's lower lip, both on their best behavior. The roses are dropped to the floor like a cast-off newspaper.

"So your husband and Chuck were pals back in the day," he says. "Oh. Sorry." He stands and crosses the three yards of carpeting, hand outstretched. "I'm Derek, Barb's big brother. Helping her get squared away." He shakes first Rose's hand, then Mel's. His grip is dry and warm, but too firm for delicate bones.

Barbara returns with a tray bearing three cans of Coors Light and a Coke, all unopened. Rose is relieved. After Longwood, she is leery of beverages of unknown provenance.

They all pop their tops. Rose has never tasted Coors Light. Turns out there isn't much to taste, but it is cold and wet, so she swallows it gratefully.

"So how did your husband know Chuck?" Barbara asks, sitting gracefully on the end of the couch and tucking her legs under her.

"He isn't here," Derek says. He has returned to his vast chair and sits on the edge as though unwilling to commit to its embrace, beer can resting on his knee.

"Yes, I know," Rose says. "My husband has dementia. I'm considering Longwood. When we went to see about it, Pete recognized Chuck. They hadn't kept in touch — we moved to New Orleans about thirty years ago — but he knew him on sight."

"Did Chuck recognize him?" Derek asks.

"No," Rose replies. "The incident was stressful for Pete. I think it scared him. Pete knows he has memory issues, but not how bad they are. I can't keep him home much longer, so . . ." Rose lets the sentence drift off, looking hopefully at Barbara and her brother. Derek takes a long pull on his beer. Barbara fiddles with her necklace, running a tiny gold cross back and forth along the chain.

"It seems like a nice place," Barbara ventures. "I mean, they've got hot and cold running doctors, and it costs a bundle. The people seemed real nice."

"Has your husband been there long?" Rose asks.

"A couple of months, I guess." Barbara wipes a swath of silky hair back from her face. "Chuckie was a lot older than me, so I kind of knew I'd be a widow for a long time."

Rose feels a stab of alarm. "Has Mr. Boster died?"

"Oh. No. But the docs don't think he's got much time. There's kinds of dementia that go on for years, and kinds that are quick. Chuck's got the quick kind."

Might not last out the week. The words trickle in through a hospital room door in Rose's mind.

"A blessing, I guess," Barbara is saying. "I mean, who wants to live babbling and drooling? Chuck got pretty lost there at the end. Couldn't even find his way to the bathroom. I'd find him outside or standing in front of the door not knowing where he was." Her face softens in lines of sadness. "Poor old guy. I wish I could go see him."

"Seeing you upsets him," Derek says firmly. Barb sighs.

"How did you find out about Longwood?" Rose asks.

Barbara bites her lower lip, her teeth making drag marks in the lipstick.

"Didn't you get a brochure, an ad in the mail?" Derek nudges his sister's memory.

"That's right," Barbara says. "I forgot. Real nice brochure. Chuck was getting where I was afraid he'd fall in the pool or

317

get out and get lost, so we checked it out."

"Excuse me," Mel interjects. "Could I use your bathroom?"

"Sure, hon," Barbara says. "Down that hall on your right."

Mel, smiling with embarrassment, edges out of the room.

"So no individual person recommended the facility to you?" Rose presses.

Dogs bark. Derek lifts his fanny to fish his cell phone out of his rear pocket. For a moment they all wait while he pokes at the screen. "Robocall," he says, and wriggles farther over the edge of the chair, elbows on his knees, beer held between them in both hands. "Barb told you. A brochure. What's this really about?"

His voice, never warm, has grown hard and cold. Has Rose pushed too hard? Hit a nerve? Or is he merely overprotective of his sister?

"I'm sorry if I seem to be a nosy Parker." Rose flutters her hands in helpless confusion. "It's just . . . Well, I'm so scared of making the wrong decision. What if I put Pete in a place where they — you know, you hear so much about elder abuse. Then there was that awful thing in Louisiana. Fire ants! This poor woman was stung to death by fire ants. Fire ants in her bed!"

"That's just awful!" Barbara exclaims. "Ugh!"

Derek slips awkwardly from the blancmange of a chair. "No worries, Mrs. Moore. No fire ants at Longwood. It's a classy setup in every way. If you go online — do you use a computer?"

"I took a class once through AARP," Rose says vaguely. This story is sure to get a rise out of Marion.

"You get your granddaughter to Google Longwood. That's all we can tell you. Good luck." His eyes stray to the football game over the fireplace.

Once again Rose is being dismissed.

Mel materializes at the top of the shallow steps into the sunken room.

"We'd best be going," Rose says.

"But you only just got here!" Barbara cries. "You haven't even finished your drinks."

"Not everybody can sit around all day and polish their nails," Derek snaps. He picks up the abandoned roses, evidently intending to throw them out along with Rose and Mel.

"What's with the roses?" Barbara eyes the drooping blooms. "They make me think of cheating husbands."

Rose thanks Barbara for the beer and her

time. "Y'all come back, now," Barbara says, sounding as if she hopes they will.

Derek herds them to the double doors. When they are outside he reseals the air lock. The click of a lock falling into place officially ends the visit.

"So much for Chuck's wife loving roses," Rose muses.

"Bronze Suzuki driven by Thomas. Four minutes," Mel says. As they round the stand of bamboo, she adds, "Checked out the upstairs. Brother Derek's clothes are in the master bedroom."

"They could be Chuck's. Maybe, like your dad, Barbara can't bring herself to get rid of them."

"Nuh-uh. Not like in the closet. Dirty tighty-whities on the bathroom floor, stinky gym socks in the hamper."

"One begins to suspect Barbara is not Chuck's *good* wife," Rose says.

CHAPTER 24

"We have to get Chuck out of Longwood," Rose says.

Royal's grandma is on a date, so the teepee tribe is enjoying the AC in the living room.

"Longwood didn't abuse you," Mel says. "Shouldn't he be okay there?"

"Remember when I told you about the women in the hall saying I wouldn't last out the week, and we thought I was crazy? I wasn't. Early-rapid-onset patients don't have a very impressive life span in the Memory Care Unit. Even Barbara — in her own Elly May Clampett kind of way — knew that."

"I was surprised at how nice she was," Mel says.

"Me, too." Rose is on the floor stretching as they talk, easing tense muscles, and doing spinal twists to release built-up toxins. There is a veritable mother lode of them.

"At the end, Barbara said there were two kinds of dementia, the slow kind and the quick kind, and Chuck has the quick kind. What do you want to bet Derek's 'robocall' was a text from the evil overlord to be on the lookout for nosy white-haired ladies and precocious teenaged girls?"

"He did change from a passive-aggressive creep to an aggressive-aggressive creep after the call," Mel notes.

"Derek is the not-brother?" Royal asks.

"Right. He of the dirty underpants," Mel clarifies. Royal and Mel are on the couch, one on each end, their feet crossing in the middle. Each has a cell phone in hand and plays with it when the conversation flags.

"Weeks after Chuck is put in the MCU, Derek is in bed with the wife, who, we assume, is about to become a wealthy widow. Derek dominates Barbara; that was obvious. He must have come into their lives in an intimate way — maybe a personal trainer, or a private chef. The kind of job that gave him access to the house and the wife in an ongoing way."

"Maybe they remodeled the kitchen," Mel says. "The guy Dad hired practically moved in with us for six months."

"Then Derek got hold of the drugs that make people demented, and administered them to Chuck," Rose goes on. "When Chuck got bad, bingo, bango, bongo, he's carted off to Memory Care where they can finish the job."

"Isn't that kind of dramatic?" Royal says. "No offense meant, Mrs. Dennis."

"None taken." Rose rolls through to Sphinx Pose, relishing the stretch in the small of her back. *Release your buttocks.* Her yoga teacher's voice intrudes into her mind. Rose releases her buttocks. "Life is dramatic," she says. "No matter how weird what you think up is, there are people out there actually doing it."

"I noticed Derek got antsy when you pushed him on exactly who recommended Longwood. He sure wanted Barbara to remember the brochure," Mel says.

"Didn't you say your dad heard about Longwood through a brochure?" Rose asks.

"Yup. Uncle Daniel showed it to him. Because you're my grandmother, and Dad is all about including me in adult decisions now that I'm men-stru-ating —"

Chanting, "TMI, TMI!" Royal drops his phone so he can put his fingers in his ears. Mel kicks him, and he laughs.

"So I actually read the brochure, and went to their website. Very professional. Lots of five-star reviews. Doctors and cooks got awards for things," Mel finishes.

On her back, Rose hugs her knees tightly to her chest and rocks in tiny circles, massaging her sacrum. "The brochures are coincidental, ubiquitous, or certain recipients are targeted. If we were targeted, there has to be a person inside the target's home, or in her circle of friends, who knows there is a demented person, and has enough clout to make a case for Longwood when the brochure arrives. In Chuck's case, it appears Derek is that inside person."

"So if Chuck was demented, why not put him at Longwood?" Royal asks logically.

"Maybe he wasn't demented," Rose says. She stretches out long and relaxed in savasana, Corpse's Pose. "I wasn't."

"Yes you were," Mel says.

"You were kind of out of it when I found you," Royal adds.

"That's because they were drugging me!" Why doesn't anyone seem to get that?

"Barbara said Chuck was demented before. And I know for a fact you were demented before Dad found Longwood," Mel says.

Rose enjoys being a corpse for a minute or two. "Because we were drugged at home, in our houses, before Longwood. Drugged by the inside person," she suddenly realizes.

"Not just Chuck; me, too."

A long silence ticks by.

"Who do you think the inside person was in your case?" Mel's voice is very carefully bland.

Rose quits breathing.

Flynn, Mel's dad. He's the one who took her to the doctors who deemed her demented. The one who chose Longwood. Flynn drove her to the front door and walked her in.

Mental fog, physical danger, and a general ignorance of which direction the next blow is coming from, and who is behind it, have kept suspicions of her stepson on a subconscious level, a level where Rose experienced an aversion to calling him, letting him know what she was up to. The aversion has not been fully or logically addressed. Until now. Now Rose knows part of her suspects Mel's dad of getting her out of the way after his father died.

Possibly Longwood did phone him about her attempted escape, had been phoning him all along, keeping him apprised of her movements. Maybe Flynn is conveniently out of town for nine days so the window of opportunity for the unfortunate demise of his father's second wife will be wide open and Flynn will have an alibi. Flynn could have purchased a used truck and had it delivered to Goodman's.

Rose stays on her back, eyes closed.

"You think it is Daddy, don't you?" Mel asks in a small flat voice.

Daddy. Mel hasn't called Flynn Daddy in several years. Except when the child's heart in her teenaged breast is wounded.

Is Rose accusing Harley's son, Izzy's husband, Mel's father, of conspiring to murder her? What possible reason could Flynn have for wanting her dead? Is Nancy, Harley's ex, right? After Harley died, in her grief, did Rose lean too hard on Mel, become a burden on a family already touched by tragedy?

That might be motive enough to get Flynn to tell her to go home, but not to kill her.

Money.

Rose hasn't been able to follow the money. Now she realizes she is the money. She is worth twelve million, give or take a million. Her paintings bring in a lot of money, and Harley had a genius for investing. Between them, they'd done very well for themselves.

Or for their heirs.

Daniel? Daniel stands to gain as much as his brother, and Daniel is underemployed, making little more than minimum wage, where Flynn brings in between one hundred fifty and two hundred fifty thousand a year. Rose doesn't know Daniel as well as she does Flynn, but he strikes her as the sort of guy whose idea of an evil deed is blowing dandelion fluff in the direction of his neighbor's lawn.

On Harley's death all the money comes to Rose. When Rose dies, the bulk is to be divided between Harley's sons, Daniel and Flynn.

Why kill her? Why not just wait until she kicks the bucket naturally?

Because, alive, she can change the will.

She can't see either Daniel or Flynn plotting and scheming to kill her for money. Of course, because she cannot see a thing doesn't mean it isn't there.

As a young woman, Rose had been a devotee of the god Science, embracing the concept that if a phenomenon could not be replicated in a lab with a couple of rats, it did not exist. Then she began noticing that the moment a scientist "discovered" a phenomenon — germs, black holes, the internet, cell phones, subatomic particles — it was instantly transmuted from magic to Science.

It stood to reason that millions more phenomena that Science closed its collective eyes to existed as well.

To be inclusive, Rose long ago decided to believe in all things she could not see.

Can she believe that under the kind and civilized demeanor of Flynn or Daniel — or Flynn and Daniel — there lurk greed-frenzied monsters that will send their step-mother on to a better life before she can leave all those lovely millions to a shelter for homeless mother cats? Picturing it is rather like picturing the Hardy Boys mugging Anne of Green Gables.

Who else? Lying on Royal's floor, eyes closed, Rose thinks. Marion would never leave her home and cats, not even to kill someone for a small fortune. Rose is safe on that front.

Camilla Reynolds and James Madding, the MCU's early-rapid-onset dead, have to have been well-to-do to be lodged at Long-wood. Had the sudden moves of their near-est and dearest after their timely expirations been because they were heirs by way of chicanery? Is that the deal? Invalidate, incarcerate, then dispose of? Marion might be able to find out if there were substantial inheritances involved.

If not Daniel or Flynn, then who?

Rose's eyes pop open.

Nancy Dennis. Harley's ex was never a big fan of Rose's, though Rose was not the other woman. She wasn't even the next woman. There was that nasty email telling her to stay away from Flynn and Mel. Can that have been to isolate Rose, make her distrustful of those who might help her?

Rose can remarry. There may be new stepchildren, new grandchildren. Foreseeably, Rose can change the will, leave the money to them. Does Nancy want to guarantee all the money goes to her sons?

Again Rose hugs her knees into her chest, then rocks until she is upright and in a half lotus. She despises this line of thought. Nameless, faceless suspects are interesting. Suspicion of those close to her is torture.

In the teepee, her whereabouts are known only to one family member, Mel; if Rose cannot trust her with her life, life isn't worth having. She is safe enough for the moment. When she gets time, she will make an appointment with her estate lawyer and change the will, cut everyone out, then spread the word. That should keep family from killing her. They'd want her alive so she could change it back in their favor. Unless they decided to off her out of revenge.

For today, tonight, tomorrow, she needs to figure out how to get Chuck out of Longwood and stashed somewhere safe until the drugs wear off and he can fend for himself.

And if he doesn't, if he dies because of her interference?

Kidnapping and murder have much longer jail sentences than assault and breaking and entering, even for a first offender.

"I'm going to the teepee to meditate," Rose announces.

"Om," Mel replies, not looking up from her cell phone.

CHAPTER 25

Sitting in a half lotus, on an acrylic zebra skin, Rose lets her gaze soften. Her mind itches to count the time since her awakening in the Memory Care Unit and her final escape. Days? A week? Breathing in, she relaxes, not into the numbers but into the need for numbers, the need to calculate the half-life of drugs, withdrawal, fear, and stress.

There is the suffering of suffering.

The suffering of change.

The suffering of self.

Letting concepts drift free, her mind opens beyond the battered, poisoned gray matter of her brain. Rose lets go, and lets go again, settling into still radiance, inherent energy, and the thoughts and emotions rising and dissolving.

Then she is dissolving. Water pouring from her closed eyes as grief, deep and warm and eternal, fills her, stretching in every direction; grief she's not had time nor mind for, the magnificent presence that was Harley Dennis, her husband of fifteen years, her boyfriend, her roommate, her partner in crime. The man who rescued her and loved her, who found her foolishness and eccentricity delightful. The hardworking, levelheaded, Presbyterian CEO who had always wanted to marry an artist and, when he was sixty-five, did so.

What a grand whirl it had been.

Rose cries for herself, and for all sentient beings who never know what true love feels like. She cries for the dogs they raised, the cats they served, the wealth of joy they created together.

Heartbroken happiness emanates from her as she floats in a vast sparkling sea of grief.

From a distant shore an irritating noise bores through to ears she's forgotten she has. It stops. She breathes, settles. The noise augers in again.

The iridescent sea vanishes. Tears stop. Rose opens her eyes to the walls of the teepee, eerily glowing gray from the light on the screen of her cell phone. The plastic rectangle buzzes like a grasshopper in a paper bag.

A good and righteous Buddhist would not break meditation for worldly affairs, but then a good Buddhist wouldn't be mired in karma up to her eyeballs. Knowing she postpones enlightenment for at least a lifetime, Rose picks it up. Black letters spell out UNAVAILABLE on the tiny screen.

"Hello?" Rose answers warily.

"You've been stirring up a hornet's nest," a man snarls into the phone as if trying to keep his anger at a respectable decibel level.

"Who, may I ask, is calling?"

"It's me. Eddie. Who do you think? Other than me and my mother rotting in detention, how many people's lives have you screwed up?"

"Everybody's who tried to murder me," Rose replies acidly.

"Yeah, well . . . I thought we were past all that. Since you cut my finger off, I'd call us even."

Rose does not think half a digit balances the scales when pitted against a life, but she forgoes comment.

"You know where SouthPark Mall is?" Eddie asks.

"I can find it."

"We gotta talk. There's a Chick-fil-A. Meet me there in half an hour."

A fast food outlet in a mall; that seems safe enough. Besides, Rose is hungry. Concern over Chuck's impending doom, if, in fact, his doom is impending, has kept her too distracted to bother with lunch.

"I can do that," she says.

"Do it, then. Thirty minutes." Eddie cuts contact.

Stirred up a hornet's nest.

It had to be her and Mel's visit to the Boster mansion. Derek must have called and reported it. Barbara could have done it as well, but Rose's money is on Derek. A woman didn't live for sixty-odd years without learning how to read the signs of dominance and abuse.

Not everybody can sit around all day polishing their nails. Derek had said that. The subtext is *you do nothing of value; your life is empty of worth.* Rose suspects Barbara is either innocent of betraying her husband — other than in the biblical sense — or has been coerced into it. Derek, the not-brother, must have wormed his way into the Bosters' life, then begun seducing Chuck's much, much younger wife, possibly in the guise of taking care of her when Chuck started going round the bend.

As she puts on her shoes, she tries to connect the dots: Drugged in her own home until demented. Put in a respected local facility for which Flynn conveniently got a flyer at the appropriate time. Dementiainducing drugs continued inside the MCU.

Unwittingly? The prescription sent along with Rose?

Unlikely. The first thing responsible doctors do in elder care is review medications. But possible, the switched drugs smuggled in in the original prescription bottle. Still, that would only be good until the prescription needed to be refilled.

Three connected dots: drugged at home by criminal #1; incarcerated, drugged at the MCU by criminal #2. Chuck's dots might be the same. Both Rose and Chuck have money; an heir — or heirs — might be tempted to kill them before they squandered their fortunes or changed their wills.

How did criminal #1 and criminal #2 get together? Not once, but judging by Marion's findings, three or four times in so many years. Rose suspects a criminal #3 who serves as matchmaker for #s 1 and 2.

She isn't going to solve that equation tonight. She doubts she will solve it until Chuck is rescued, and his mind sufficiently restored that they can compare notes.

Or he dies a horrible death because some crazy old bat decided to take him off his meds and out of reach of medical help.

"Not thinking that," Rose says to herself.

■ ■ ■ ■

Rose locates SouthPark Mall on Google Maps. After a heated discussion, she elicits promises from Mel and Royal that they won't follow her. Though Eddie has his softer side — as evidenced by Tania and Amy — she does not want him to see Mel, or even know Mel exists. Rose has not forgotten the Eddie who came down the ridgeline with a knife in his teeth.

The mall is busy enough that Rose feels safe. Guards stand around the way mall guards do. She mentally takes note of their whereabouts. The one loitering between LensCrafters and the Disney Store is closest. He doesn't look much younger than she, and not in as good shape.

Ageism. Mel was right. Rose banishes the judgment.

Hunched over, elbows on knees, Eddie is waiting on a park-style bench outside the Chick-fil-A. He is sporting the black ball cap, cargo shorts, T-shirt, and deck shoes. Rose wonders if he is on a job, and if that job is her. She waits until he notices her; then, while he watches, she goes over to the security guard by LensCrafters. Eddie flinches as if he is thinking of bolting. Rose pats the air reassuringly. He settles back down.

"Excuse me, Officer." His name tag reads WARREN VAN FLEET. "Warren, may I call you Warren?" Rose hopes her moment of television fame has not made her face a household name. "Could you help me?"

"That's what we're here for. And Warren is fine," he says. He has a nice voice, deep with a hint of a southern drawl. Up close he is bigger than Rose had thought. There is a bit of lard, but under it she can see muscle.

"I don't want to be a pest," she says sweetly.

"Never a pest. Truth is, I'd be glad for a purpose. It'll take my mind off my feet." He smiles a tired smile, but one with warmth and endurance. Rose guesses he is the kind of guy who will work until the day he dies regardless of financial need.

"I'm meeting with that man on the bench, at least I think it's him, the one in the black ball cap." She points. Eddie squirms like a six-year-old who has to go to the toilet. "I'm thinking of hiring him to do my yard work. I wanted to meet him in a public place. I'm sure he's a wonderful young man and wouldn't hurt a fly, but, you see, I lost my husband recently . . ."

"That's a shame," Warren says sympathetically. "How did he die?"

Rose suppresses a giggle. Fortunately it comes out sounding like a sob. "I don't want to go into that."

"Of course you don't, of course you don't. Trust a Van Fleet to stick his foot in his mouth. What can I do for you?"

"Dealing with all these new things . . . I've been having a lot of anxiety issues. Scared of my own shadow." Rose smiles apologetically. "That's why I'm interviewing a lawn man in a mall, for heaven's sake. If you could just kind of keep an eye on things? I'd feel a lot more secure knowing you were watching out for me. Sorry to be such a silly old thing."

"No apology necessary. Glad to do it. You need me, just whistle."

"Just put my lips together and blow?" Rose can't resist.

His eyes widen, then crinkle into a grin. "You got it, lady."

"What was that about?" Eddie growls as Rose sits down primly on the end of the bench.

Eddie is pale under the swarthy skin, leaving an unhealthy grayish tinge around his mouth and nose. In contrast, his cheeks are ruddy. Scared, Rose surmises, scared and angry. Not a good combination.

A moment passes while Eddie glares from beneath the brim of his ball cap.

When it becomes clear Rose is not going to be intimidated, he says, "You turn me in to that mall cop? You did, and you got a dead mall cop on your conscience."

"If I turn you in, it won't be to a mall cop, or in a crowd of innocent bystanders, and I will be as far away from the incident as I can get. I was just saying hello. Warren is a friend of mine."

"I thought you were new here, didn't have any friends." His eyes travel from Rose's face to a bowling bag between his feet.

"I bond quickly," Rose says. "What's in the bag, Eddie?" Given its round shape and sturdy handles, Rose can't help but picture a severed head. It is precisely the sort of vehicle severed heads would be delivered in.

"You want to see it?" Eddie asks dangerously. "You want me to take it out and show it to you?"

"A verbal description will be sufficient," Rose manages. She is surer than ever it is a severed head, but can't fathom whose. The cola nurse? Chuck? The thought of Chuck Boster and his "good" wife's love of roses makes her eyes sting. "Let me see it." The words stick in her throat, producing a croak.

Eddie shoves the bag in her direction with

the side of his foot. "I wouldn't open it too wide if I were you," he warns. "Wouldn't want your cop pal peeking in."

No trail of blood smears the pale tile floor where the bag has slid. Fluorescent lights and black fabric make it impossible to tell if any bodily liquids stain the bag. Rose doesn't smell anything. She's read that blood smells like copper tastes. Or vice versa.

Not wanting to touch it, she bends in half and gingerly unzips the curved top flap. It falls inside, hanging down into the greater darkness.

"Take a good look," Eddie needles her maliciously. "You're the one got all this started."

"Am not." If her fingers touch hair, or anything squishy, she is going to scream. Then Warren will forget all about Bogey and Bacall and arrest both her and Eddie.

Pinching the flap between the tip of her thumb and forefinger, Rose peels it back.

"You happy now?" Eddie prods.

Rose shoots him a nasty look. "God, Eddie, you had me scared to death." Giddy with relief, she laughs. "This is nothing but a gun. Not even a fancy semiautomatic, a plain old cowboy wheel gun. A gun! Talk about sudden-onset impermanence."

"Keep your voice down," he hisses. "It's not just a gun. Read the note."

"It came with a gift card?"

Eddie puffs up, grows red in the face. For a second Rose thinks he might hit her, or explode like a cartoon character and fill the air with Eddie confetti.

She gives Warren a little wave. He smiles and waves back. Eddie seethes less conspicuously. "It's in the bag. A Post-it Note. Yellow." He buries his face in his hands.

"You've got a smaller bandage," Rose notices. "Is your finger — I mean stump — healing up okay?"

"Just read the frigging note," Eddie mumbles thickly.

The Post-it has partially adhered to the butt of the pistol. Rose plucks it free and reads it aloud. " 'Finish the job or next time we won't put this where you will be the first to find it.' You're supposed to shoot me?" Rose asks.

"Keep it down!" Eddie growls. "I've never even shot a gun."

"I could teach you."

Eddie looks up hopefully. "You'd do that?"

"No!" Rose exclaims. "Because of the whole John the Baptist thing, I was so relieved you hadn't been chopping off heads and carting them to malls in bowling bags that I suffered an inappropriate burst of generosity. I'm over it now. Of course I won't teach you to shoot. You shouldn't even be allowed to use a butter knife. You're a criminal. Don't let me forget that."

She glances at the note again. "What do they mean they'll 'put it where you won't be the first to find it next time'? If you don't use this one to shoot me, they keep delivering bigger and better guns?"

"I'm a convicted felon," Eddie explains with exaggerated patience. "It's illegal for me to have a firearm. If I don't deliver on this job, they'll hide a gun where I won't find it, then the cops get an anonymous tip, and it's a one-way trip back to Central for me. Now do you get it?"

"I'm keeping up," Rose says. She puts the note back in with the gun, then zips the bag shut.

For a long time they sit on the bench, neither speaking. Finally, Rose says, "You are between a serious rock and a hard place. You kill me, you go to jail for a long time. You don't kill me, same thing happens."

"God damn." Eddie blows out a sigh. "All the counselors and shit they make you talk to in the clink, even the other prisoners, they all tell you not to do that one last job. It's the one that hangs you." He sounds like he is about to cry.

Rose picks up the bowling bag and sets it on the bench between them. She takes out her cell and pokes the buttons. "There, now you shooting me is on my To Publish list if anything happens to me."

"That's just great," Eddie says. For several minutes, Rose watches the shoppers. Eddie watches the floor between his feet.

"You know, Eddie, this is that whole wicked web karma," Rose says. "You've pretty much hit bottom. First they'll repo your truck. Then you can't work. No work, no Tania. Then a gun, prison. You are right royally screwed."

"Rub my nose in it," Eddie says.

"Just thinking out loud," Rose replies.

"Yeah, well, don't."

"I might be able to get you out of this mess," Rose says pensively.

"I bet. You've done such a good job with that so far."

"What other choice do you have?" Rose asks.

"Since I met you? None."

Rose punches him in the shoulder.

"What was that for?" he nearly whines.

"You are not the victim here, Eddie. Get your mind around that."

"Okay. So. What do I have to do?"

Rose smiles and pats the bowling bag. "Just one last job," she says.

CHAPTER 26

Given the vast number of things Rose has to regret, the great gouts of bad karma lapping at her heels like an incipient tsunami, the worst is lying to Mel. Honesty bonds them. From the moment they met, Mel twenty minutes old, Rose fifty-four years, Rose swore she would not only tell Melanie the truth but would also protect and defend the child's truth as it changed and evolved.

Tonight Rose has smashed that oath all to hell, no shading, no omissions; an outright, premeditated lie. Like all liars, Rose justifies her action as necessary. She and Eddie are setting out to break serious go-to-jail laws. Eddie, Rose refuses to feel responsible for. Once a man tries to kill a woman, all bets are off.

If things go wrong tonight, even their status as minors would not save Mel and Royal from the justice system. Knowing they would insist on helping anyway, Rose has chosen to tell them she is going out to dinner and a movie with Brian, the Lyft driver, who waited for her outside Vincenzo's.

They seem to take it in stride that a recently widowed, recently drugged, in-the-midst-of-crisis woman is interested in a date with a cute boy. When she leaves, they are smirking, pleased with themselves. Cell phones in hands, the two are flopped on the couch, more or less watching TV.

Eddie, in his truck, picks Rose up four blocks from the house.

"You did good with the scary," she comments as she buckles herself in. Eddie grunts. Instead of his usual deck shoes and cargo shorts, he is wearing black Levi's, heavy motorcycle boots, a long-sleeved black pullover, and black leather gloves. The empty index finger of the right glove sticks straight out where he holds on to the steering wheel. Rose considers telling him she didn't really eat his finger, and he can have it back if all goes well, but she doesn't.

Rose is neither scary nor disguised. She wears gray slacks and a pink oxford shirt borrowed from Izzy's closet. On her feet are pink-and-gray Nike running shoes. In a Harris Teeter tote she carries cardboard signs she's made, and a brick.

"Got something to cover your head?" she asks.

"Got it." Eddie is clearly not enjoying the prospect of their evening out.

"Mud on the license plate?"

"Yeah. For all the good it will do."

Rose heard mud was one way criminals made their vehicles less identifiable to law enforcement. She, too, doubts its efficaciousness, but stealing or switching plates adds a new level of lawlessness to an already damning pile.

"My contact" — Rose hopes to keep Marion's name and existence as deep a secret as she does Mel's — "has rented a house near Brevard in a development called Connestee Falls. It's yours for three weeks. Private, lots of trees, lots of seasonal folks and renters coming and going. You should be safe there."

Eddie grunts again.

"It's got a pool, a golf course, a gym, and pickle ball courts," she adds enticingly.

"What's pickle ball?"

Rose doesn't know. "It's fun," she says. "My contact also assured me that the nurse I've worked with previously is on duty tonight."

It is Karen's dedication to duty — or her aversion to admitting the extent of her dereliction of duty — that put this idea in Rose's head. The plan hinges on Karen working the night nurse's station. Even so, the cola-loving nurse and the handmade placards are the weakest point in Rose's plan. If Karen is not sufficiently in hate with Rose, this whole house of cards will come crashing down. Should that happen, Eddie might get away, but Rose probably won't see the outside of a prison cell for the foreseeable future.

Negative thoughts.

Rose lets them go and takes an envelope out of the tote. "This has directions to the house. It's on Ugugu Lane. I don't know if that's the right pronunciation. There's also a thousand dollars in cash. That should keep you in food and whatever else Chuck might need for a week or two."

"This Chuck guy, he's crazy," Eddie says. "I should keep the gun." Eddie is wound so tight, he crouches in the seat like a hunchbacked troll and clutches the steering wheel close to his chest.

"Not crazy. Drugged. Totally malleable. He'll be out of it for a day or two; then he'll start to get better." Rose so very much hopes this is true. "Chuck is a gentle soul. I keep the gun."

As she speaks, she unzips Eddie's bowling

bag, takes out the revolver, and replaces it with the envelope containing the cash and directions. They drive beneath a streetlamp, and Eddie's eyes flicker to the money.

"Don't even think about it," Rose warns. "Or —"

"I know, I know, Armageddon," Eddie grumbles.

Before she can suppress it, a look of surprise flits across her face.

Eddie snorts. "Yeah. I know some big words, too. Catholic family. Armageddon. Excommunication. Damnation. What part of that isn't on the menu for tonight?"

Rose can't answer that.

At eight thirty P.M. they are unobtrusively lurking in the red-tipped photinia eight paces from the sliding glass doors of the MCU, Rose with her tote bag of placards, brick, and gun, Eddie with a crumpled grocery sack containing, Rose assumes, the rest of his disguise.

"Just relax. Act like you belong here. Be cool, but not overconfident," Rose advises.

"Not babble like a crazy old lady doddering in the bushes with a gun in her purse?" Eddie whispers.

"I do not dodder," Rose grumbles, but she takes the hint and stops talking.

They watch the doors. At eight thirty-seven a young woman in a black skirt, red-checked blouse, and red kitten heels, eyes glued to her cell phone, steps on the mat. The doors slide open. The receptionist is going home for the night.

"I'll keep the door open. When she's gone, you come," Rose reminds Eddie of the plan, if what she has in mind can be dignified with the word "plan."

As the receptionist steps out, Rose steps in, murmuring a pleasant "Good night."

"Good night," the woman echoes, her eyes never leaving the tiny screen.

Before the doors slide closed, Rose jams the brick between them. No alarms, at least none she can see or hear, go off.

Eddie emerges from behind the hedge. He walks quickly to the doors. On his head is an orange wig. He muscles the doors far enough apart for him to squeeze through. Rose sees his face and gasps. "Jeez! I didn't mean that scary."

He is wearing a Donald Trump mask.

Under the empty-eyed gaze of the gross and terrible Trump, horror Rose has kept at bay slams into her. Like a Greek tragedy, her every action inevitable and disastrous, foreknowledge no defense. Oedipus is going to sleep with his mother. He is going to kill his father. It will not end well. She is doomed and there isn't a doggone thing she can do about it.

Bugger that.

She is saving a friend's life when no one else will. Chuck is not demented. He'd yelled "Help!" and "Chocolate!" One could fight through a drug haze if the need was great enough. No one could fight through dementia. Too much structural damage. Rose doesn't know if that is true or not, but it soothes her.

Not doomed. Not predestined.

She has two choices: She can abandon Chuck and eventually rejoin him when her luck runs out, or she can do this.

"Let's do this," she says.

Inhaling to make herself bigger, she leads Eddie into the truncated hallway connecting the reception area with the lockdown unit. Eddie, in his scary mask and spike-studded boots, she plants beside the ficus tree in the dogleg of the short hall where he can't be seen from the reception area or the nurses' desk in lockdown.

Rose slips up to the sliding glass door, Harris Teeter tote in hand.

Karen is on duty.

Karen is alone.

So far, so good.

Rose takes the placards from the bag, then

raps lightly on the glass to get the nurse's attention.

Karen's eyes flash from boredom to shock. "You!" Her lips form the word. As she reaches toward the phone to call security, Rose smacks the first placard against the glass. It reads:

YOU STUPID BITCH

The nurse's face hardens into a mask of fury. Blurred fury. About her eyes and features there is the fogginess of drugs not yet cleared from her system.

Rose drops the card and presses the second sign to the glass.

NOT ONCE BUT <u>TWICE</u>!! HA HA HA

Karen's face turns dark red. She flies up out of her chair as if it is an ejector seat. Rose can hardly believe it. This is working. She doesn't dare breathe as she lets the sign fall and puts the third in its place.

SHIT FOR BRAINS

Karen storms from behind the desk, rage in her every movement. Stalking toward the door, she appears huge, murderous. Rose is surprised that the big woman does not paw the ground and snort steam like the bulls in cartoons. Involuntarily, Rose flinches back as Karen whacks her plastic ID against the security door's reader.

The door swooshes open.

To activate Eddie's part in the scheme, Rose was to yell "Now!" But the nurse is preceded by such a wave of hatred, Rose manages only an "Eek!"

A hand, strong from years of handling dead weight, closes on a fistful of Rose's blouse. Buttons pop, hitting the wall with tiny snicks. Dangling from the nurse's fist, Rose scrabbles madly in the tote. There is only a single item in it, but she can't find the wretched thing what with the Goddess of War flipping her back and forth like a rag doll.

Eddie finally gets the message and comes pounding menacingly from behind the ficus tree, his boots whomping on the tile.

Rose gets hold of the revolver and drags it out, the tote flopping from her arm by one trapped handle. "Freeze!" she pipes. Karen doesn't loosen her hold or notice the gun. She only has eyes for Eddie and his mask. Rose is jerked back and forth as the nurse sways on her feet.

Eddie looms.

Karen's fingers loose. Rose staggers back a couple of steps. Steadying the revolver in both hands, she aims at the nurse's center mass.

Mouth angular and wild like one of the horses Rose remembers from *Guernica* in the Museum of Modern Art, Karen sucks in air through her nostrils.

"Not a peep," Rose warns. "You know what I'm capable of. You know I'm not a poster child for sanity." The woman doesn't look as impressed as Rose would like, but she doesn't say anything either.

"Back," Rose orders. The woman doesn't move. Eddie makes a sound like the howl of a basso profundo ghost. Karen steps back, hands held partway up, more in a warding gesture than one of surrender. She backs into the unit, Rose and Eddie following. The door slides shut behind them.

"Sit on the sofa," Rose commands. Karen sits. It occurs to Rose that she should have said "floor" or, better yet, "Spread-eagle, hands behind your head," but it is too late to change tactics.

Karen opens her mouth to speak.

"Not a peep!" Rose repeats and thumbs the hammer back. There is a satisfying metallic click. "Third room on your right," she reminds Eddie. The Trump mask nods, eerily appropriate for a criminal enterprise.

"What in God's name do you want?" Karen whispers. She sounds near tears. "You come back and back like herpes. For what?"

"You're peeping," Rose says, trying to sound dangerous.

Eddie reappears half dragging a confused, pajama-clad Chuck. Chuck's hair is standing on end like a rooster's comb. His face is blank of affect, but for points of fear in his pale eyes.

"Don't —" Karen starts.

Eddie growls and whuffs. He is under strict orders not to speak, not to do anything that will make him one iota more identifiable than he has to be. The muted roar is effective. Karen subsides. "Toss me your badge," Rose orders her captive. For a second she thinks the nurse is going to refuse. Rose shoves the revolver a bit closer.

The nurse unclips the badge and throws it at Rose's feet. Eddie grabs it up, opens the door, then drops the badge inside so Rose can use it. From the corner of her eye, Rose sees him hustling Chuck down the hall. A minute later, she hears the pickup roar to life. In two hours they should be safely hidden in the mountains of North Carolina, as anonymous as any tourists fleeing the heat of the lowlands.

Rose has done it. She has rescued Chuck. If she hasn't accidentally murdered him.

She waits another minute. Karen is thinking, gearing up; Rose can read resolution, stocked by cresting anger and druggy logic, writ plain on her broad face. Any second now, she is going to blow her top. Without taking her eyes off Karen, Rose backs to the sliding glass door, retrieves the badge, and presses it to the black plastic reader.

"This is going to cost me my job." The nurse spits out the words in a stream like foul-tasting liquid.

"You didn't tell them about last time?" Rose asks.

"They would have fired me. I need this job. I've got a kid."

Rose feels bad about that. "Okay," she decides. "You'll be a hero." She steps outside the door. "You single-handedly disarmed me and saved the other residents from fates worse than death." As the door whooshes shut, she tosses the pistol into the lockdown unit.

Neat as a Hollywood stuntman, Karen hurls herself from the couch and snatches the gun from the floor. From a prone position, she shoots six times.

Click. Click. Click. Click. Click. Click.

Rose shrugs, mouthing, "Sorry." Then turns and runs, hoping to reach the greenway before the modern equivalents of hounds of hell are loosed.

CHAPTER 27

Alternately walking and jogging, Rose follows the greenway the two and a half miles back to Royal's house. There, she ducks through the flap of the teepee and collapses on the wolf skin, using its head as a pillow. Sweat sticks her clothes to her body and burns between her breasts as if acidic poison oozes from her skin.

A fan would be nice, but the teepee has no electricity. Marinating in her own toxic waste, she stares at the apex of the tent where a smoke hole that has never known smoke exposes a fragment of light-polluted sky, streetlamps turning a high thin overcast a pale orange.

The end of the world would be pale orange, Rose thinks; *the last ding-dong of doom would ring out from the speaker of a cell phone.* This night she has held a fellow human being at gunpoint. Drugging Karen — twice — and wrestling with her on the

MCU's floor hadn't left Rose as . . . what? Changed? Drained? Battered?

Because of the gun, the evil triumvirate of guilt, aversion, and fear is tainted with the nearly imperceptible scent of smug self-satisfaction. What is it about human beings that so loves violence? Gladiators, football, war, hunting, cockfighting, books and television and movies filled with bombs, guns, and gigantic beasts of various origins all wreaking the most horrific havoc: people love it.

A piece of Rose loves it: John Wayne, Sigourney Weaver, Melissa McCarthy, the Wild West, and WWII. Heroics; that is what Rose can't resist. Not the violence, she tells herself, but overcoming evil with good. Sacrificing self for others.

Maybe.

Then maybe human beings are hardwired to beat their wives, burn witches, lynch African Americans, guillotine royals, waterboard Muslims, and shove guns in medical health workers' faces, to get their own way. A nasty bit of business on her part, she has to admit that. This is a dastardly deed even an adorable little old lady won't get away with. The MCU people might not bother to mention that the gun wasn't loaded. Not that it matters.

Chase, capture, trial, sentencing — all that frightens Rose. Worse is going to be Mel's disappointment, perhaps even condemnation. Gigi has not only held a nice lady at gunpoint, but she's also lied about the fact that she was going to do it. Not only that, but Rose is going to go right on lying to her granddaughter, at least by omission. Mel can know nothing about the night's events, or where Chuck has disappeared to. On some not-too-distant day, Rose will be processed through the legal system. She does not want Mel to be subpoenaed and forced to participate in getting Gigi locked behind bars.

Rose sends out a heartfelt sigh. She has screwed things up, but she doesn't know what else she could have done; nor does she have a clue as to how to go about unscrewing them.

Karma, she decides. This whole saga has to be her working out an outrageously weird previous lifetime. That is the only thing that can explain why a moderately pleasant Buddhist painter finds herself lying in a pool of sweat in an urban teepee staring at a tangerine sky.

Forcing herself upright, Rose takes off Izzy's ruined blouse, uses it to mop up the worst of the perspiration, then replaces it with one of the old T-shirts Royal has contributed to the cause. The slacks come off, to be replaced by a pair of plaid boxer shorts Flynn has unwittingly donated.

Rose turns to her electronics.

Doctors' care is provided by a pool from the Longwood hospital, rotating in as needed and as their schedules permit. Food in the MCU is the same as is prepared and served in the main dining hall. Nothing promising from those arenas.

Marion has also processed the staff of the lockdown unit. There are eight nurses and four orderlies staffing the seven-bed unit. Rose reads down the names: Karen Black — the cola-loving nurse — Shanika Sanders, and six names Rose doesn't connect with. Their shifts hadn't coincided with the handful of lucid hours she'd enjoyed while incarcerated. The orderlies, all male, are Jason Farber, Kenan Bowls, Sean Powell, and Anthony Brevard.

Rose lifts her gaze from the screen. Anthony. Tony. T. Brevard.

Rummaging through her few piles by the light of the computer screen, she ferrets out the papers on Eddie's truck. On the third page is the handwritten notation: T. Brevard. This is the note that turned off Goodman's genial flow of information and sent him gesticulating out amongst the Buicks, cell phone to his ear.

She crawls over to the daypack she's been using and upends it on the zebra hide. Amid other detritus is Carter Goodman's business card, complete with phone number. Rose punches the number into her cell phone. On the third ring a familiar voice says, "Goodman here. What can I sell you?"

Rose laughs in spite of herself. Drat. Roughing up her voice to what she hopes is official-sounding, she says, "I'm calling about Anthony Brevard."

A moment of silence passes; then a sigh gusts out. Carter says, "What's he done now?"

Bingo, Rose thinks.

"It's regarding that truck you held for a Mr. Martinez."

Carter groans. "I really don't know anything about it.

"T. Brevard. You know about him," Rose presses. "Who is he?"

"My brother-in-law," Carter admits. "I know better than to get mixed up with any scheme of Tony's, but I always cave. Please don't tell me it's stolen."

"Where does your brother-in-law work?" Rose asks.

"He's got a job as an orderly for a hospital.

At least he had. If he got himself fired from this one, I'm going to kill him."

"Did he own the truck?" Rose asks.

"Like I said, I don't know anything about it. It was one of those friend-of-a-friend deals."

"And you don't know who the friend-of-the-friend is?"

"No. What's this all about?"

He doesn't sound like he is willing to talk anymore without a little quid pro quo, and Rose can't see any harm in telling him the truth. "The truck was payment for a hit job."

"Holy Christ!"

"Nobody died. Everybody lived — so far — not exactly happily ever after, but that's neither here nor there. I need to know who was paying the would-be assassin."

"You're the lady that stole the paperwork," Carter says.

"That would be me, yes."

"Was it you somebody wanted killed?" He sounds incredulous. This annoys Rose.

"They should have held out for a Hummer," Carter says, redeeming himself.

"Could you ask your brother-in-law for whom he did the favor?" Rose asks hopefully.

"Turn on family, and rat him out to a strange woman who didn't even buy a car?"

Carter asks.

"That would be a big help," Rose says.

Another puff of air gusts through the ether. "Shoot," Carter says. "What the hell. My sister can't be any worse off with him in jail than she is with him in the house."

"Text," Rose says. "I don't have voice-mail." She taps the red END CALL button.

T. Brevard, an orderly at the MCU, had arranged the payoff to have Rose killed. He was probably either Tweedle Dee or Twee-dle Dum. Neither one struck her as deep or cunning; not criminal mastermind types. Of course, she was drugged to the gills the few times she'd had any interaction with them.

She returns to the attachments Marion sent. The manager of the unit is a woman named Wanda Lopez. Rose remembers her. Mostly she remembers the new Corvette she'd driven so sedately, and the bright-colored suits.

Reading on, she finds the orderlies earn thirty-eight grand a year, the nurses seventy-two grand, and the manager one hundred twenty-nine grand per annum. Not enough for a Corvette, but Wanda might have other sources of income. Illegal income?

Then Rose sees the smoking gun. Not smoking exactly, but definitely warm. Before Wanda Lopez was promoted to manager she worked as a pharmacist, then manager of all the hospital's pharmacies. Wanda's was the bejeweled hand that gave her the spiked orange juice.

Rose sets the iPad down, lies back, and stares at the scrap of discolored sky. A pharmacist in a unit for hopelessly demented people, people with money, who might live a long time, long enough, all that lovely money will vanish into the black hole of elder care.

How easy would it be to help them along?

Easy as pie.

How easy to substitute meds?

Pie.

Getting drugs to not-yet-demented oldsters outside the facility? Rose can picture a close friend or family member working with Wanda. Easy to order capsules identical to the kind the victim takes — and all old people take something. Then Wanda substitutes the bad drug for the good. All unsuspecting, the victim goes on taking the medicine. The dementia-producing drug is upped slowly, maybe at a crucial time — like the death of a spouse — when people are expected to suffer mentally. The victim becomes less and less lucid. Then a flyer from a respected care facility is put front and center. An answer to the beleaguered family's prayers.

Rose is willing to bet that would work often enough that a few people could make a good living, everybody along the line getting a cut: the heir, the inheritance; Wanda, a druggist's fee.

There has to be at least one other person involved. A person in a position to interview family members, find those who are amenable to a little murder to help the money flow from generation to generation more rapidly. A person who procures the victims to be delivered to Wanda's kind ministrations.

Who could get to Flynn, Daniel, or Nancy, as well as the not-brother and/or Barbara Boster? Did the victims have a geriatrics specialist in common? A therapist? Psychiatrist? Car mechanic? Someone who routinely worked with, and was trusted by, elders and their family members?

Too many questions. Fatigue catches up with Rose. Closing her eyes against the pale orange, she relaxes her body.

Rose is sound asleep, the iPad on her stomach, when a scratching sound claws her into terrified wakefulness. Her first unworthy thought is that she wishes she hadn't left the gun behind.

"Gigi? You better be in there."

A moment of sleep-fog robs Rose of her short-term memory. It clears. Her night out with Eddie floods back. She renews her conviction that, lie though she must, she will not infect Mel with the truth about what she has done.

Mel opens the flap. At least, a creature with Mel's voice shines a blinding cell phone flashlight in Rose's eyes. From the clashing beams and the trampling of feet, Rose surmises Royal is with her.

Mel sits down with an audible thud. "You are in so much trouble, Gigi. I told you not to go anywhere without us." Mel is much aggrieved. Angry, but not curious. Maybe she is miffed because Rose didn't call her to let her know she was safely home from her fictional date with Brian the Lyft driver.

"What?" Rose says, hoping to sound innocent and slightly annoyed at being awakened. She glances at the glowing screen of Mel's phone, flashlight now blessedly turned off. Ten forty-seven. She's slept for over an hour.

"Dad's coming home. Grandma Nancy is on the warpath. Uncle Daniel is stoned. The police are all over with lights and stinking badges."

Rose's mind whirls. Has she told them and forgotten?

"It was all on TV," Royal explains. "They had hidden security cameras. They showed you doing . . . all that stuff."

"Hidden security cameras?" Rose gasps. "That's a trespass on patients' rights to privacy," she says indignantly.

"Maybe they thought they needed them now because somebody kept breaking in, drugging the night nurse, and snatching old men," Mel retorts. "Oh, Gigi! How could you? That poor nurse — you held a gun on her."

"Poor nurse, my aunt Fanny!" Rose flashes in self-defense. "That 'poor nurse' shot at me six times!"

"The gun wasn't loaded," Mel snaps.

"And a good thing, too!" Rose argues. "If it had been, somebody might have gotten hurt. I should at least get Brownie points for that." She looks from one young face to the other. If soft child-flesh can be said to be stony, theirs is. "No Brownie points?"

"No Brownie points," Mel says flatly.

"That guy in the Trump mask, who was he?" Royal asks.

Rose buries her face in her hands. "No one special," she mumbles through her fingers. She'd known the manure was going to hit the fan; she just hadn't thought it would be so soon, or so public.

"When you said you had to get Chuck out of there, I thought you meant you'd get a representative to walk in the front door and check him out like a civilized person. Not go all Rambo and gunslinging, with a *hench-man,* for God's sake. In a mask! This is so bad, Gigi."

It is. It is so bad. Rose feels her guts collapse inward, her stamina crumble, her plans implode. The wild hare chase she's been leading herself, and these kids, and the police, is over. She is so tired, she would weep, except it would only add to the crushing sense of guilt and failure.

"How did you get in?" Royal asks. "I thought the unit was locked from the inside."

Rose wonders if Karen destroyed the placards so she wouldn't have to admit she was tricked into losing her temper and opening the door to villains.

Before she has to answer, Mel asks, "Did you really leave the gun so the nurse wouldn't lose her job?"

"That was on the security tape?" Rose asks.

"Everything between the edge of what must be the reception desk to the hall where the Donald Trump guy went to get the old man," Mel says.

"That old man is Chuck Boster, my friend. I did this to save his life," Rose says. Cheap shot. Though it is true, she hasn't said it to communicate truth. She's said it to make Mel feel bad. Unfortunately, it works. Mel's face softens into guilty sadness.

Rose wishes she could take it back, but words spoken are actions done. No more lying. "Partly to save her job. Partly in hopes the police could trace it."

"Where did you get it?" Royal asks. He doesn't sit, but stands in the parting of the canvas, as if a sudden departure might be required.

"TMI," Rose apologizes. "It's probably untraceable, though. Numbers or something filed off — whatever experienced criminals do."

"You have to turn yourself in," Mel says.

Rose tries to think about that, but her mind is opaque, a recently clear pond choked with duckweed.

"The news reporters were interviewing the cops," Royal says. "Everybody is talking about you being . . . unstable."

"Criminally insane, Gigi," Mel declares. "That's what they said, that they think you might be criminally insane, and a danger to yourself and others. Nobody is supposed to talk to you, just call the police."

"You could get shot," Royal says. "Grandma had that happen when she was practicing criminal law. She had this guy who got shot because the cops were so scared of him, they didn't give him any time to comply. Just *bang!*"

"Please, Gigi, you have to turn yourself in." Mel is crying. Rose can barely stand being in her own skin.

"You could go in with Grandma," Royal suggests. "I think she'd do it if I asked her. She knows all the judges and attorneys. It won't be pro bono. Grandma doesn't do criminals for free."

Of course not.

And Rose is a criminal.

"Okay," she says finally. "Ask your grandmother. I'll turn myself in."

"Now?" Mel demands.

"Grandma goes to bed after the ten o'clock news," Royal reminds her.

"I bet she'd get up if she knew the star of the ten o'clock news was hiding out under her bedroom window," Mel says.

"Let her sleep," Rose begs. "Let me turn myself in tomorrow. Maybe a night free of drugs will clear Chuck's mind. Besides, there is one last thing I need to do."

Mel sucks in a breath. Probably to yell at her.

"Don't worry," Rose says. "It's safe, legal, and necessary. After that, I'll go to jail."

Everybody will be safer then.

CHAPTER 28

Greene and Associates will be glad to accommodate Mrs. Dennis at such short notice, and, yes, attorney–client privilege most certainly does apply to clients of estate lawyers. Rose warns Ms. Greene that her passport, credit cards, driver's license — all her ID has gone missing. Ms. Greene assures Rose the firm has everything on file from when she and Harley did their estate planning six years before. As Alma had met Mrs. Dennis on that occasion, there will be no difficulty establishing identity.

This is all done via email. After the previous night's video, until Rose has confirmation on the attorney–client privilege part of the deal, she has no intention of revealing so much as her phone number. The video from the MCU's security camera — Mel calls, half alarmed, half excited, to tell Rose — leaked and has gone viral. Already it has over seven hundred thousand hits. Mel also informs Rose that "about a zillion" related items come up if one Googles "Gun Granny."

Gun Granny.

Rose cringes. Could ageism and sexism have made a more unholy match than "Gun Granny"? What is wrong with Vixen Vigilante? Senior Siren? Armed and cantankerous? At this juncture, Rose would settle for Walker Woman. "Gun Granny" is horrid on so many levels, she might actually welcome solitary confinement.

Given this excrescence of notoriety, Rose has no doubt her estate lawyer is aware that consulting about the will after her husband's unexpected demise isn't the only issue her client has with the legal system.

The upside of the YouTube phenomenon is that Royal's grandmother, Elizabeth Pryor, has not only agreed to accompany Rose when she turns herself in but will also represent her in all things pertaining. Royal promises Rose can't find a better criminal defense attorney than his grandma. What better recommendation can Rose ask for?

Not that she has to ask. Now that she is a media sensation, everyone and his or her dog is clamoring to represent her. Mel calls to let her know Uncle Daniel had to unplug the house phone and that after her dance class, he and she will be driving to the Highlands. A friend of her dad's has a cabin there. She and Daniel are to hide out for a few days until, to quote Flynn, "I get this finalized."

Not a phrase that comforts a felon with a target on her back.

At two thirty, dressed in another of Izzy's outfits — a gray pin-striped skirt, a fitted cap-sleeved blouse in white cotton, black patent leather flats, and an ear-length auburn wig, shingled into gentle flying buttresses to either side of her face — Rose calls for a ride.

Once the will is changed, she will breathe easier. Flynn, Daniel, and Grandma Nancy will be removed, if not from suspicion, at least from the temptation to make any future attempts on her life.

Maybe it's because of the numbing effects of drugs working their way out of her system, but if the greedy murderous person is family, Rose doesn't want to find out who. If it is Flynn, Mel will be shattered. If Daniel or Nancy, the hit won't be as devastating, but it will hurt. Blended-family gatherings are hard enough to navigate without one member having literally tried to murder another.

Ms. Lopez and the provider of victims

might still want to kill Rose for what they imagine she knows. Oddly that doesn't frighten her as much as it should. That isn't personal. She is too tired to drum up any interest in deadly strangers. Spiritually and psychologically, Rose is exhausted, the kind of life-fatigue she occasionally glimpses in the eyes of the very, very old. Her mother-in-law at ninety-seven, her great-uncle at ninety-five, no sorrow, resentment, or despair, just a great weariness, a desire to leave this party and go home.

Unfortunately for Rose, though she is a lousy Buddhist, she is a believer. If she nods off with her karma in such a snarl, she'll just be born into another life and have to work the whole thing out over again.

From scratch.

A good reason to stay awake and alert, she thinks, as, on the screen of the cell phone, she watches the Lyft car stagger robotically through its paces as it zeroes in on her location.

The estate lawyer's office is twenty minutes toward the central, skyscraper-infested part of the city, near, but not in, what in New Orleans would be called the business district. Rose doesn't know what it is called in Charlotte. Like many other private practices, the office is in a repurposed home.

What was once the front lawn is paved to make an eight-car parking lot, prettily edged with planter boxes to soften the blow for a neighborhood in transition from residential to commercial.

The building is two stories, of the ubiquitous brick, painted pale yellow with forest-green shutters. A sign, imitating an old brass plaque, lists the estate lawyer and another law firm, JENSON & DAUGHTERS. An omen, Rose hopes, indicating that the world isn't going to hell in a handbasket, or at least not as quickly as she sometimes fears.

The driver lets her off. Rose takes a moment to gather herself, make sure that her costume — conservative Izzy elegance — is hanging neatly and that there is no lipstick on her teeth. Her objective is to look overwhelmingly sane and utterly harmless. To further this effect, Mel had brought her pearl stud earrings, a pearl necklace, and a clutch bag that matches the shoes. The clutch holds nothing but a cell phone and a lipstick. These are all the personal accoutrements Rose can lay claim to, unless one counts acrylic animal skins and three plastic arrows, one missing the feathers.

Inside the building, a receptionist, serving both firms, is seated behind a faux antique cherrywood desk that supports a discreet computer and phone. She directs Rose to the elevator. Given it is a two-story house, Rose requests the stairs. The receptionist emits a mildly irritated huff, then indicates a door marked EMERGENCY EXIT on the far side of the room.

The stairs, plain and shabby, are a dirty little secret the elevator aficionados are spared. As she emerges, she finds Greene and Associates to her right. The door is open. There are two rooms in the suite; the first, the paralegal's domain, guards the second, an inner sanctum where the lawyer holds dominion.

The paralegal's desk is untenanted. As Rose enters, a small, pleasant-looking woman, midfifties at a guess, with narrow shoulders and wide hips, comes into view from the inner office. A mischievous smile quirks her thin lips. The lenses of her oversized glasses reflect the gray of the walls. "Mrs. Dennis." She advances with a fine-boned hand, graced with an emerald ring, the stone too heavy for the delicate fingers, extended. "I was so sorry to hear about your loss." Her handshake is firm, her flesh cool and dry. "Come in, come in. My paralegal is out on an errand. Can I get you anything? Water? Coffee?"

Rose is ushered into the office. Lush

carpet, bookcases heavy and dark, leather chairs with high backs: little has changed. The woman doing the greeting and ushering, Rose realizes, is Alma, the old paralegal. The furnishings might have stayed the same, but Alma is changed. She looks younger than Rose remembers. Her hair is a different color and worn in a fashionable cut. She's lost weight. Where Rose remembers a bit of an aging drudge, there stands a polished, vibrant professional.

"Alma?" Rose says.

"Alma," the woman agrees with a smile. "When I met you I was finishing up law school. I was promoted to junior partner. When my mentor — and friend — passed away several years ago . . ." She shrugs and smiles as she gestures at the room. "I left the manly décor because it reminds me of him. And it seems to comfort people." Alma raises her eyebrows. "We have tea, if you prefer."

Tea sounds good, civilized. "I would like some tea," Rose says.

Alma leaves to fetch refreshments. Rose studies her surroundings. The furniture mimics antiques but is probably no more than twenty years old. Boilerplate, as if the importance of male professionalism has been captured by a franchise designer, and sold as Big Deal Lawyer in a Box. As one would expect, gigantic framed diplomas and certificates cover the wall behind the desk. Alma Mae Greene, magna cum laude, Tulane University. Much in the way of olde-fashioned script and gold foil. In lesser frames, on a lesser wall, are the memorabilia of the firm's founder.

Rose remembers him, a slight man with thinning white hair. There was a genuine kindness about him that settled the inevitable queasiness stirred up by deciding who would benefit from one's demise. Rose notes he also graduated from Tulane, sixty years to the day before his protégée.

"Choices," Alma says, returning with a tray bearing an honest-to-England tea set complete with matching sugar and cream servers.

"Perfect," Rose says. She chooses Lady Grey. Alma pours steaming water over the bag. Not quite in keeping with the classics, but close enough.

They settle down to the arduous business of rewriting the will. Alma, the professional woman Rose hadn't seen when she was the firm's paralegal, doesn't ask Rose why she is cutting Harley's sons out of the will less than three months after their father died. Undoubtedly stepparents do that sort of thing all the time, which is probably why someone in Harley's family wants Rose too crazy, then too dead, to make the aforementioned changes.

Mel, too, is cut from the will. Though it can be changed back at any time, it feels like a betrayal. To alleviate her conscience, Rose leaves three million to Mel's favorite charity, a no-kill shelter for animals of all kinds on a big chunk of land in Arizona. The remainder Rose leaves to Planned Parenthood. Until overpopulation is curbed, addressing other issues is merely postponing the inevitable.

By four thirty the bulk of the work is finished. Mel's dance class lets out soon; then she will be heading to the Highlands with her uncle. Rose wants to see her before she goes, say goodbye, and hope Mel has forgiven her the lies and the gun.

Flynn is due in on an eleven-ten flight. Rose will not see him until after Elizabeth Pryor has negotiated her surrender. Hopefully this will keep everyone safe. With the will changed, Flynn won't suffer the temptation to strangle her for her money, but he might for the incredibly bad example she set for his thirteen-year-old daughter, not to mention showing her a severed finger and dragging her along on quasi-criminal adventures.

Rose signs, reads, drinks tea, signs more papers. Outside the light changes. Alma reviews and explains, makes copies, and heats water for fresh tea. Periodically both women check their cell phones, the lawyer writing necessary texts and Rose hoping for one.

The afternoon drags on. Alma murmurs explanations and types into her computer. Rose's mind is fixed on her upcoming role in *Orange Is the New Black: The Golden Years,* the coming booking, mug shot, cavity search, and she knows not what else.

Long after everything is signed Alma still shuffles paper assiduously. Rose sips tea and wonders if the lawyer is waiting for something. Or wasting time, padding an already substantial bill. Alma's mentor, Phil Miller, would have hated that. He and Harley were associates from when Harley worked in Charlotte — long before he met Rose. Mr. Miller was on Harley's board of directors, hence the choice of him as their estate lawyer, that and the fact Flynn, their executor, lives in Charlotte.

Phillip Miller.

Miller and Associates.

Alma killing time.

Rose takes the cell from her bag and texts her sister.

Five minutes pass while Rose, like Pavlov's friend, waits for the bell. Finally her phone pings.

The text reads: "There was a Miller on our dead MCU list. Phillip Marsden Miller, age eighty-two. Rapid onset. Died six weeks after incarceration. No early onset, hence dropped from core study group."

Miller is a common name. Even Phillip Miller is a common name. Rose stands, stretches, and wanders around the room pretending to read book spines, books that computers have turned from precious information venues to wall décor. Miller's diploma is tucked between bookcases. Phillip Marsden Miller.

Four months after Alma graduated from law school her beloved mentor suffered rapid-onset dementia and was put in Longwood's MCU under the kind auspices of Wanda Lopez. Six weeks later he was dead, and the newly minted Alma inherited a lucrative law practice. A branch of law that specializes in the knowledge of precisely who will benefit from the death of whom.

The skin on the top of Rose's head creeps as the hairs try to stand on end beneath the wig. She needs to leave this office. She sets her teacup down on the desk. First she needs to use the restroom.

Returning, she is girded for battle; no argument, she is walking out regardless of how the will is situated. Striding into the office, she doesn't sit down. "I'm sorry," she begins.

"We're all done," Alma announces with a bright smile, as she moves her phone off a folder. "Bet you thought you'd die before we finished your will."

Rose smiles. "It did cross my mind."

"No one dies until after Greene and Associates finishes the will. Company policy." Alma rises from her chair and hands Rose her copy of the papers in a thick creamy folder embossed with the firm's name. Rounding the desk, she retrieves Rose's clutch, tucks it under Rose's arm, and walks her to the elevator, evidently as anxious to have her go as she was to have her stay five minutes before.

Rose wants out badly enough that she doesn't even start an argument about taking the stairs.

The elevator arrives. "You're the last out tonight," Alma says as Rose steps into the elevator.

CHAPTER 29

The elevator is small and old, probably installed when the house was a home. It is also slow. Though the descent is no more than fifteen feet, it inches and creaks along like an old man afraid of falling. Usually, Rose would suffer a few pangs of claustrophobia. Today her mind is such a tangle of thoughts, reality is as inaccessible as Sleeping Beauty's castle before the lawn boy came.

Alma stirred up countless memory fragments from a life Rose hasn't visited since she first became aware of the fog machine installed in her skull — a machine that still periodically manages an obscuring puff. Drugs don't clear out immediately, nor without leaving residue. In the old days, it manifested as flashbacks. This time around, it manifests as confusion.

You're the last out tonight, Alma said.

Rose suffers a disorienting sense that a

memory, a name, is teetering on the edge of her mind, an important revelation on the tip of her tongue.

The elevator slows to less than its arthritic creep and begins groaning as it settles onto the ground floor. Rose waits while the doors decide whether or not to open this one last time. They manage it in halting lurches. The receptionist has gone home for the day. Rose lets herself out.

Last out tonight. Alma's words niggle and tickle.

She is standing on the wide doorstep, juggling the fat folder and the slippery clutch, when she hears a familiar voice.

"Gigi! Over here!"

Mel is leaning out the passenger window of a flame-orange Jeep Wrangler Sport. Rose's heart lifts so strongly, she rises up on her toes. Mel loves her. Mel has forgiven her. Mel has come to say goodbye.

Smiling like a fool, she trots over to the Jeep and climbs into the rear seat.

"What a treat," she says. "I was afraid you were going to leave before I got to see you again." She is about to give the driver the address of Royal's house, where she is to meet with Elizabeth to strategize her coming surrender, when the driver leans around the seat.

"Hello to you, too, Rose," Stella says.

"Stella! What are you doing here?" Rose's voice is tart, bordering on rude. The sudden appearance has startled her, as does the orange Jeep. She's never seen Stella drive one.

"I would have texted," Mel says, "but Stella took my pack and phone. She shoved them under her seat."

"There is no possible way to have a civilized conversation when you're glued to that thing," Stella says.

"Uncle Daniel told her to pick us up," Mel continues. "But she won't tell me why."

"I did tell you," Stella says, maneuvering the Jeep into traffic. "I told you I don't know why. I just got this hysterical text from Dan. Don't let's go through this song and dance again."

"You and Daniel are split up," Mel insists stubbornly.

"Eleven months and thirteen days," Stella says.

"I'm surprised you'd do any favors for Uncle Daniel," Mel says.

"I didn't do it for him." Stella meets Rose's eyes in the rearview mirror. "I did it for you two. Regardless of Dan's being a prick, I couldn't leave you stranded, now, could I?"

"We aren't exactly stranded," Mel says.

"Jesus!" Stella bangs a palm on the steering wheel. "What is it with you Dennises? Never say 'thank you.' Just expect everybody to hop when you say 'jump'."

"Uncle Daniel isn't a jerk," Mel says.

"I didn't say he was a jerk," Stella snaps. "I said he's a prick. And you're a twit."

"Where are you taking us?" Rose doesn't worry about sounding rude this time.

"To your new house on Applegarth. And don't ask me why. I'm just the fucking driver."

Rose settles back in the seat. Careful to make no noise, she opens the clutch. She will text Daniel and see what is going on. In Izzy's purse there is nothing but a tube of lipstick. She left the phone on the desk in Alma's office.

Or did she?

She thinks she remembers putting it in the clutch before using the restroom, but then she remembers a lot of things that never happened, and doesn't remember a lot of things that did. Could Alma have stolen the phone? To what end? So Rose couldn't call for Lyft?

Or dial 911?

Not *last out tonight* but *She won't last out the week.* It was Alma's voice in the hallway outside her bedroom in the MCU, the other participant in the conversation Rose heard as a threat to her life.

She reaches past the headrest and lays her hand on Mel's shoulder. The girl's fingers close warm around hers for a moment.

Eleven months and thirteen days. Daniel, too, was counting the days; Mel had said so. At the time, Rose thought he was merely celebrating his freedom.

The Greene and Associates gilded cream folder lies next to her empty clutch. An unpleasant premonition causes her to reach out and flip open the cover. The pages inside are blank.

"Eleven months, thirteen days," Rose says. "Why are you counting?"

Stella doesn't reply.

"In North Carolina you've got to be separated for a year before you can file for divorce. Uncle Daniel can file in seventeen days," Mel says spitefully.

Stella does not respond. A moment later, Rose hears the telltale thump as the doors are locked from the driver's seat.

Once the papers are served, the marriage is officially at an end. The marital property accrued during the union will be split. Daniel and his wife lived in a rental, have no children, no investments, no property, and a good bit of debt: Stella will get half of nothing. Unless Daniel comes into a windfall before he files for divorce.

"Stop the car," Rose orders.

"Keep your panties on. We're almost there."

Rose considers strangling Stella from behind but is afraid the ensuing car accident might hurt Mel.

The Jeep turns onto Applegarth and proceeds in the direction of Rose's house. Late-afternoon sun paints the white brick a burnt orange. Though it is prime dog-walking hour, the street, as usual, is empty of life, doors closed, windows curtained. In this moment Applegarth strikes Rose as a stage set for *The Truman Show, Our Town, The Stepford Wives*, a place real people don't reside. Where neighbors never notice murderers on the porch roof, or strange sounds in the night.

Stella conns the Jeep up the empty driveway and noses it in in front of the one-car garage.

"Who are we meeting?" Rose asks, trying the door handle and finding it still locked. "Where's Daniel?"

"Other people being here is not part of the plan," Stella says calmly.

"What plan?" Rose and Mel demand simultaneously.

"Mine," Stella replies, pulling on the parking brake. "Don't get freaked. I don't want to hurt anybody. I just need you two to be out of sight for an hour or two. Not even that long probably. Then I'll let you out. You can report me to anybody you want. It won't matter by then."

"Why? Why out of sight? Why won't it matter? What are you doing?" Rose's voice is rising with each question.

Stella's calm shatters. "Shut the fuck up! Melanie, do I have a blue-and-white tote in my lap?"

"What does —"

"Do I have a fucking bag on my lap?" Stella snarls.

"Yes," Mel answers.

"Is my hand in the bag?"

"It is, but —"

"Tell your fucking Gigi I have my hand in the bag," Stella snaps.

"Gigi, Stella's got a blue-and-white bag on her lap, and her hand is in it." Mel sounds confused, and a little scared. Rose doesn't blame her. Suffering is boiling out of Stella like ants from a burning nest.

"In this bag is a gun," Stella says.

Rose wonders if she is bluffing. "What kind of gun?"

"A big fucking gun, you stupid old bag. That's what kind of gun. My hand is gripping the butt of a big fucking gun that is aimed at your darling little Melanie's head. You hear me?"

"I do," Rose says, ice forming in her belly.

"If both of you don't do precisely as I tell you to, I could accidentally pull the trigger. Since it's in a bag, I might not hit cute little Mel, but in a small space, short range, a bullet could splatter your darling little Melanie's adorable little brains all over my nice clean dashboard. Are you listening, Rose?"

"I'm listening."

"Do you understand?"

"I do."

"Then nobody has to get hurt. That's what we all want, right? Nobody getting hurt. Right?" When neither Mel nor Rose says anything, Stella jerks her right arm, and Melanie cries out.

"Right," Rose says quickly. Shock is slowing her wits. Rose can't think of any way this can end without her death — and now Mel's — that will further Stella's interests. Unless she isn't after a marital share of the inheritance.

But she is.

There is nothing else. Nothing that locking Rose and Mel away for a couple of hours can facilitate. "Alma called you, didn't she?" Rose asks. "Told you when to be there so I wouldn't call a car. Mel was bait to guarantee I got in."

"Whatever you say, Einstein." Stella opens the driver's door.

"Okay. You got me," Rose says. "No need for bait. Let Mel out. She'll leave. All she knows is you gave me a lift home. Nobody believes kids anyway. Then you lock me up by myself for a couple of hours, and then come let me out. If you do that, I won't yell or be a nuisance." Rose tries to sound as if this situation is perfectly normal. She is just bartering. *I'll give you ten cents a pound for those carrots.* All good. All sane.

Stella ignores her. "I'm going to walk around the back of the car. If I see either head move, that head gets shot off. You get out of the car when I say." She climbs out, slams the Jeep's door, and presses the remote locking device. Her right hand is still in the tote bag, a bit of it crumpled as if she holds a wad of bag along with the gun butt to keep it covered.

"Do you think she really has a gun?" Mel asks without turning her head.

"I don't know," Rose says. "We better assume she does."

The locks thump open. "Get out," Stella

says. In the side-view mirror, Rose can see her gesture with the bagged gun.

"Wherever she's putting us has to be better for her and worse for us," Rose whispers hurriedly. "Otherwise she wouldn't bother. On three, we open our doors. I'll distract Stella. You run."

Rose sees Mel's head nod once.

"Seat belt off?"

A second nod.

"One, two, three." Both passenger-side doors fly open. Mel leaps out and darts toward the hedge and the house. Rose stands and whirls around. Stella is not where she'd been a moment before. As they'd opened the doors, she'd moved up next to the vehicle directly behind the rear passenger door.

Rose catches a flash of blue from the corner of her eye, then is driven to her knees, hanging on to the door to keep from pitching onto the concrete. Her brain is knocked to the far side of her head. Consciousness scatters onto a gray plane; vision works but doesn't connect things to thoughts.

The blue bag comes up. There is an odd phwump and a ping. Mel pitches forward, striking the ground with tremendous force. Stella's gun has a silencer.

A silencer, Rose thinks stupidly.
Mel has been silenced.

CHAPTER 30

"No!" Rose thinks she screams, but she emits only a pathetic bleat. Cheek on the concrete, she can see the bottoms of Mel's running shoes and one knee, scraped and oozing blood. Grabbing the armrest, she drags herself up. Despite the blow to her head and the shredding of her own knees, there is no physical pain, no bodily sensation at all. Vision narrows to a long tunnel. As Rose peers over the bottom edge of the car's window, only Mel is visible in her eyes. Mel, looking no bigger than a cat, curls in the only sunlight in the world.

Rose tries to get to her feet. Her legs are as unresponsive as the cloth legs of a rag doll. Letting go of the door, she falls to her side, blackness beating in great raven's wings against her eyes. Rolling to all fours, she holds her neck rigid, her head still, trying to make sense of the images. Her eyes find Mel. Rose starts to crawl.

Groaning and clanging, as if all the ghosts who've ever trod the boards are having a jamboree, fracture the air. Behind Mel, the earth moves. Rose shakes her head. This time there is pain, sharp where the pistol struck, dull behind her eyes, flickering in her skull as the scattered cerebral matter falls back into place.

The earth is not moving. The garage door is opening. Stella, using the rusty old pulley-and-chain the original owner installed, hauls it up. The racket is short-lived. When the door is a foot and a half from the concrete, Stella lets go of the chain and starts shoving, then kicking Mel's body under the door into the garage.

Mind and body stunned, Rose is paralyzed. She can't even draw breath.

Then Mel whimpers. A mewl, scarcely louder than the whine of a mosquito, but Rose hears it. Mel has not been silenced. Mel is alive.

The toes of Izzy's ballet flats find the concrete; Rose launches herself at Stella. Her shoulder slams into the younger woman's knees. Stella reels back. Rose hears her hit the door and hopes she's cracked her skull. She hasn't. A fist strikes Rose on the side of the face. Holding tightly to Stella's bare legs, Rose tucks her chin down and sinks her teeth into a ropey calf. Fists hammer at Rose's cheek and neck. She focuses on one fact: The jaw muscles are the strongest muscles in the body. Rose hangs on like a puppy with a sock, biting and shoving, hoping to knock Stella off her feet so she can sink her teeth into her jugular.

Blood bubbles around her nostrils. A little trickles into her mouth. If she swallows, she really will be a cannibal, finger or no finger.

Doubled fists pound her temple. Rose's body topples, lax and senseless. Another blow, and her vision fades. The only sense that doesn't abandon her is hearing, Stella muttering ". . . got to pry the damn thing open. Mouth like a badger trap."

Rose does not completely lose consciousness. There is a vague awareness of her body being kicked and rolled, the sound of chains, a sharp banging, then silence. Rose is on her back on the concrete inside the garage. The only light comes from a two-inch slit between the bottom of the door and the ground. Rolling to her side, Rose tries to get to her knees, but cannot.

"Here," Stella says from outside. A piece of paper is shoved through the opening. "Read this. Bite me, you bitch. Jeez!" Rose looks at the paper in the narrow spill of light. Thick creamy bond, her signature at the bottom. The upper half has been cut away. On the bottom half, above her signature are the words *I can't go on. Life is too hard. I'm taking Melanie with me.*

"This is so trite!" Rose hollers. Then she realizes what it is. "No one will buy it. Mel's got a bullet in her foot. That's going to blow the whole scene. Let us out. Let's talk. It's about money. I've got lots. Don't you think I'd gladly give you a few million for my life and Mel's? Don't be an idiot."

"A little late, Gigi," comes a sneering voice. "Maybe you and Harley should have thought about Dan and me five years ago. You forgot he had two sons. We didn't have a little grandchild to dandle on your arthritic knees. A week in the mountains, a vacation at the beach. Nothing too good for little Melanie."

"We invited you!" Rose wails.

"Right, like we were going to come be an audience to the perfect family, while you and Izzy warbled over Miss Cutie-pie. Melanie, Grandma was going to cut you out of the will. Good old Gigi was going to leave you high and dry."

Something metallic clatters to the ground. "Doggone it!" Stella grumbles. Rose puts her eye to the crack, ear to the concrete. The magazine of the gun has slipped through Stella's fingers and lies on the cracked paving near her feet. A hand clutching a gun enters Rose's field of vision. The gun slides under the door. Before Rose can react, the door falls with the finality of a guillotine blade.

So sudden and complete is the darkness, she can't tell if her eyes are open or closed. Reaching up, she touches her face. Open. The sturdy, windowless little brick bunker has no chinks where ambient light might penetrate.

"Mel," she breathes. "Grasshopper?"

"Gigi?"

What a wonderful sound. "Are you okay?" The stupid question. It is the only kind Rose can think of.

"Aunt Stella shot me!" Mel sounds more aggrieved than dying. That gives Rose heart. "I didn't even hear a bang."

"The gun has a silencer."

"That's icky professional."

"I saw you go down. You weren't moving. I thought . . ." Rose decides not to tell her what she thought. "Where are you hurt?"

"My foot. It felt like somebody hit the side of my foot with a crowbar. I hit my head when I fell. I think I passed out for a minute. Are we in the garage?"

"Yes."

Harley's truck is idling, the metallic rumble familiar, almost reassuring. For a moment, Rose is confused. The truck, the darkness, the door, the engine running: It hits her with unnerving force. Carbon monoxide gas. Stella is going to gas them, make it look like suicide.

"Stay here," she says to Mel. "No, wait. Keep talking. I'm going to have to find you by sonar."

"I bet Aunt Stella got Dad's keys to your house. She got in, did the drug switch. Made you seem crazy. I should have seen it." Mel's voice is thin, more air than sound. She is probably in shock: gunshot, blow to the head, kicking. The kicking bothers Rose — though probably not Mel — almost more than the gunshot. It betokens such a visceral form of hatred.

"Ack!" Mel squeaks as Rose shuffles into her.

"It's me," Rose says, and reaches down. "What part of you have I got?"

"My right elbow."

"Hang on. I've got to get you away from the exhaust pipe." It might buy Mel a few seconds or minutes, but the garage is full of fumes, and more pumping in. She grabs the girl under the arms and uses all her strength to drag her away from the back of the truck.

Mel makes muffled whimpering noises. Rose knows she is doing her best not to scream like a scalded cat as her wounded foot is dragged and bumped over the uneven concrete of the old garage floor. Rose talks to distract both herself and Mel. This is one moment she does not want to be in.

"How bad does your foot hurt?"

"Not like it was shot exactly. It burns. It hurts, but not screaming hurts." Mel's voice is full of catches where pain snatches at her breath.

"I heard a ping. I think the bullet ricocheted off the pavement. Might not be all that bad." Rose knows that half of surviving is thinking one will. Gunshots are considered deadly even when they're not, then they are. "Stella was shooting to scare us."

"You just want to believe she was only trying to scare us," Mel mumbles.

"True."

"Should we yell for help?"

"In a minute." Rose doubts the sound will carry through brick and heavy wood. Or that anyone can reach them before they succumb to the fumes.

"Stay low," she says as she abandons her granddaughter near the front tire. "Breathe as little as possible."

"No breathing," Mel manages.

Rose wraps her fingers around the door handle and tries to thumb down the button. It doesn't move. Old trucks are as stiff and hard to manage as old women. Rose backs up one thumb with her other fist.

"It's locked," she says. "I'm going to try the other door. Don't let me step on you."

There is no hint of dawn or dusk, no spark of sunlight through a chink in walls or roof. Shuffling so she will not accidentally stomp on Mel, or trip and fall, Rose makes her way around the hood of the truck, her hand on the smooth metal for guidance. The garage is so small, there is barely room for her to squeeze between the front bumper and the back wall. Moving in the darkness — *stygian,* she thinks, *absolutely stygian darkness* — is peculiar. If she didn't hurt in so many places, Rose would feel disembodied.

For a moment there is only the rumbling of the engine, as oppressive as darkness. "Talk to me, Mel. I need to hear your voice," Rose says as she half floats around the bumper.

"What about?" Mel is hard to hear.

"Anything," Rose says. Fear that Melanie will fall asleep and never waken is making her insides cold.

"Why don't you ever want to talk about

402

how Granddad died? Because it was so awful?" Mel asks after a moment.

No light, little hope, and this is what Mel
wants to know. Rose didn't realize she made
such a mystery of it.

"No," she admits. "It's stupid, really."

"I like stupid," comes Mel's reply.

"Okay." Rose feels the headlight against
her middle. "Your dad might know some of
this."

"You tell me."

"You knew it was your granddad's eightieth birthday?" Rose thinks she hears an as-
sent, but she's not sure. She goes on. "Well,
for his big day he and some of his old hiking buddies — and I mean old; Phil is older
than Harley, and Alex has to be at least late
seventies — decided to do a trail in Glacier
National Park."

"Gigi! Granddad was eighty! Why didn't
you stop him?"

Mel's voice is strengthened by outrage.
Hope flutters in Rose's chest.

"It's a park. These guys have been hiking
together for half a century. They all have
cell phones and Apple Watches. One call
and they'd have rangers running from every
direction with the latest carry-out gear. Phil
and Alex are — or were before they retired
— doctors. Mostly, though, Harley and I

didn't cotton to making the other guy curtail his activities because it scared us."

"I bet you pushed that. It doesn't sound like Granddad," Mel says.

"Mouths of babes," Rose says. Her hand slides along the hood, the round smooth metal soothing. "It was on the day of your granddad's birthday. They were high up, camping in a valley. After dinner Harley walked to the stream to wash, and a grizzly bear attacked him."

"Dad said he was mauled by a bear. That's bad, but not like something yucky, dying in flagrante delicto with a goat or something." Mel's voice is both husky and air-filled. Rose can feel her head beginning to lift, to float above her last cervical vertebra.

"Ish," she says.

"You can't blame the bear." Mel's words barely clear the mutter of the engine this time. "Granddad got between her and her cubs, Dad said. Do you feel bad because you let him go and he got killed?"

"No. Bears are not ageist. Young people get mauled and eaten, too," Rose says, the foggy drift of carbon monoxide poisoning feeling unpleasantly familiar. "It's that Harley being . . . you know . . . it's just not real to me. I doubt it was real to me then. Harley was killed and eaten by a bear." Rose laughs. "See? Not real."

"Because you didn't see the body?"

"I don't think so. Maybe because that is how Harley would have wanted to go. You know how he loved the wilderness, the animals. It was too perfect: eightieth birthday, best friends, good food, then a bear. It's like a deus ex machina. Except in reverse. Too perfect. I can't make it real."

"I bet Granddad gave that bear as good as he got," Mel says stalwartly.

"I bet he did," Rose agrees. "Except for the killing-and-eating part."

"And you didn't want to talk about it because nobody would understand why you thought your husband being eaten alive by a carnivore was some kind of wonderful?"

"Exactly," Rose says. A weight lifts from her chest. Somebody understands her. She is not alien to all humankind. "That is it exactly."

"Or why you find it excruciatingly funny."

"That, too. That more than anything. I was afraid I'd laugh, and people would think I was crazy."

"I guess that whole not-looking-crazy thing didn't work out for you."

"Karma." Rose lifts her shoulders in an invisible shrug. Her fingers find the door handle. Nothing moves.

"The passenger door is locked. Are you still there?" she calls to Mel. The smell of exhaust is strong. Rose knows it's poisoning her. The only symptom of carbon monoxide poisoning she can remember is red lips. In the dark, that's not a big help.

"Still here." Mel's voice trickles over the truck's low rumble. "What can I do to help?"

"Sit tight. I've got to bust out the window."

"With what?" Mel asks.

That's a good question. Rose is clad in faux ballet slippers. No kicking the windshield out. The truck is vintage, mint condition, without the safety glass that will politely shatter if a window is tapped firmly with a ballpoint pen in the proper corner. Closing her eyes to see through the choking darkness, Rose "looks" around the garage. Harley's toolbox is in the house. Nothing but an inflatable mattress has been stored in the building. The garage is scarcely big enough to contain the truck.

Aluminum lawn chairs, the plastic mesh seats and backs rotted off — she remembers seeing two of them pushed in between the studs. "Maybe something," she says encouragingly. "Keep your face near the floor. That's supposed to help."

"That's for smoke," Mel returns. "Maybe

exhaust is heavier than regular air."

Maybe it is. Rose doesn't know. She's running her hands along the rough wood, knuckles cracking into studs, then over, and along the next stretch. Skin tugs as splinters embed, but she feels no pain. There is too much to feel for pain to penetrate. *Spiders beware,* she thinks, *or it's on to a better life.* "Got it!" she calls as her fingers run into a cold smooth tube. Rose grabs what she can and yanks. The chair comes free of whatever it was attached to with such ease, she stumbles back and hits the fender of the truck.

"What happened?" Mel calls.

"I'm good," Rose says. "Stumbled is all." Her head is beginning to ache, but then she was pistol-whipped. That might cause it. "You?"

"Not breathing over here," Mel says. "Am I supposed to be feeling dizzy or something?"

"Do you?"

"Hard to tell on the floor in the dark. Where does dizzy go when you can't fall?"

Scooting sideways, belly to the truck, back to the wall, Rose feels her way back up to the window in the passenger door. There isn't room to swing the aluminum chair frame. Holding it awkwardly in both hands, she shoves it hard against the truck. The first blow strikes the metal of the door. "Sorry, Harley," she says. The second blow strikes the window. It has as little effect on the thick glass as it did on the truck's body. Maybe less. She's probably at least scraped the paint on the door.

"Gigi! The pistol." She hears Mel's voice, weak and breathy.

The pistol. Rose worms her way down the body of the truck. Her head is splitting in two. Her body feels heavy and cumbersome. Her mind spins. If it weren't for the unforgiving dark, she knows, the world would be spinning as well. When her hands hit the tailgate, she drops to her knees and begins sweeping the floor with her hands. She hits the pistol, and it skitters away. Another sweep, and she has it. Not daring to try to rise, Rose crawls back around the truck on hands and knees, shoulder brushing the metal, then the rubber of the tire. Finally she's reached the door.

Bless running boards, she thinks as she levers herself up, one hand occupied with the pistol, and scrabbles onto the hood of the truck. It feels as if she is sliding across, sliding down, sliding up. Breath is hard as granite pebbles in her lungs. Grasping the pistol by the barrel, she hammers on the windshield. The gun butt bounces off. Getting to her knees, she raises the pistol over her head and brings it down with all the weight of her body behind it. A crack. This is not safety glass; this will break into a field of knife-edged shards. She strikes again. The butt goes through. Rose bashes and swipes, trying to clear as much of the glass away as she can.

No time. No light. Rose knows she will soon pass out. Then they both will die. Tossing the gun into the truck, she follows it with her body. Clothing snags; skin snags; a leg is captured, then released with a searing pain. She is in. Wriggling to the door, she opens it. "Can you get in?" she asks, not seeing Mel, not seeing anything, not even sure she's opened the door on Mel's side.

"I think so." This is followed with a cough.

Then Rose feels a hand. She grabs it and pulls. Mel comes with it, her limbs and head tangling with Rose's until they are lying atop one another like wrestlers. Rose wants to stop there, lie there, die there, but she can't. She pushes Mel off of her and runs her fingers over the steering column. There is no key in the ignition, or it's been snapped off. She waves her hand, hoping to hit the gearshift. Her hands pass through empty air. Sliding down between the seat and the gas pedal, she feels along the floor of the truck's cab. A lump, a cone of rubber, the gasket around the gearshift staff. The shift rod has been broken off, leaving nothing but a stump and a bit of rubber.

Frantically, Rose claws at it.

"What are you doing?" Mel gasps.

"Stella broke off the gearshift," Rose says. Her eyes are burning; her head feels as if it is going to explode. The smell of exhaust clogs her nose and throat, devours the gray matter in her skull.

She feels Mel's hands join hers around the cone. With strength born of necessity, they rip away the rubber. Rose's hand clamps around the few inches of metal rod remaining. Necessity's strength has been used up. "Help me," she whispers. Mel's fist closes around Rose's.

"What now?"

Rose presses the clutch pedal down with her knee. "Toward you." They force the small rod an inch toward Mel. "Up an inch." It moves up. "Now toward me."

When it's done, Rose lifts her knee from the clutch and, with both hands, jams the gas pedal to the floor. There is a lurch and a crash, then the scream of tires spinning on concrete. Rose's head hits the console. In the black of the dark, she does not know if she is conscious or unconscious. For a moment she cannot remember where she is, why she is.

A scream brings her back to herself — wherever that is. Her hands are not on the gas, but the truck is still running. It hasn't coughed and died.

"Gigi! Are you still here?" It's Mel.

"Here," Rose gasps.

"Help me. The gas pedal."

"Right." Rose finds the hands at the ends of her arms and forces them to sweep the floor of the old truck. "Ah!" Her hand closes around one of Mel's.

"Hold down," Mel says. Rose finds the gas pedal. Together, their hands squash it into the floor. The shriek of tires fills the world with a howl of power too long kept silent. The truck shudders around them as if it will explode, blowing them and the garage to rubble and bone.

"It's not working!" Mel wails.

"Keep on!" Rose shouts. Four hands hold the gas pedal to the floorboard of the ancient truck. Harley's beloved old cherry-red darling merges in Rose's heart with the strength of his arms and force of his smile.

Suddenly there is a crack and crunch of rotting wood. A splinter of daylight pierces through, a dusty sword that cuts into the

411

grave. Rose can see Mel's face. Tears run down her granddaughter's cheeks in contrast to the determined set of her soft mouth.

The truck hurtles backward with a grinding roar. Light shatters with a volcanic eruption of wood and the cry of metal torn loose. Shards of wood and dust fly by the edges of Rose's vision as if they are on a land-bound ship that is somehow sinking in a storm of beams and splinters. Seemingly bent on vengeance, Harley's truck tears through the wood of the garage door.

Then there is all the light and air Rose could dream of.

"We are out!" Mel yells.

This new world ends abruptly as the truck smashes into an immovable obstacle. Rose's head smacks into something solid and she is slammed into the absolute darkness of oblivion.

Silence calls her back. After the cacophony of destruction, silence is a healing force. Shuddering racks Rose's entire being. She is afraid to open her eyes. "Mel?" she whispers.

Nothing. She has killed her granddaughter. "Mel? Please . . ."

"Here," Mel answers as if her name has been called in homeroom.

"Breathe," Rose says. "Just keep on breathing."

Fresh air is clearing her mind with reassuring rapidity. She can see Mel, crumpled in the footwell opposite her. "Are you okay?" Rose croaks.

"I think so. Are you?"

"I think so."

Another horrific jar of metal on metal. Both Rose's and Mel's heads snap on their necks, Rose hitting the seat this time. The driver's door is yanked open.

"You are like a nasty old cat!" screams Stella.

Rose's feet are grabbed, and she is dragged half out of the truck.

"Coming back and coming back," Stella mutters. Rose's hips hit the running board. Her torso slides over the bench seat. The pistol is still where she's thrown it. Her hands close around the butt.

Her elbows hit the doorsill. Then her chin, and she is on the ground, Stella still dragging her by the ankles. Stella's Jeep, engine running, driver's door open, has rammed its bumper into the side of the truck bed, slewing the vehicle around perpendicular to the driveway.

"Mel, get to the Jeep. Go!" Rose cries. She hears the other truck door open. Stella lets go of her ankles. Rose's toes hit the concrete hard.

"God damn it!" Stella yells.

Rose rolls to her back, the pistol in both hands now. "Don't you move!" she yells at Stella as the woman turns to stop Mel's escape.

"I ejected the clip," Stella sneers, and starts to move.

"You left one in the chamber," Rose says, not knowing if it's true.

The flicker of alarm on Stella's face lets Rose know Stella doesn't know either. *Do you feel lucky?* Clint Eastwood asks in Rose's mind. Hysterical giggles bubble past her lips. It is the maniacal cackle as much as the threat of a bullet that stops Stella.

Mel yelps. A body hits the ground.

"You okay?" Rose calls.

"Can't do it. Can't walk," Mel sobs.

In the second that Rose's mind is on her granddaughter, Stella kicks the truck door. Automatically, Rose's finger tightens on the trigger. The gun clicks emptily. The bottom edge of the pickup door hits Rose's shoulder. Not hard, but in her condition it doesn't take much to knock her over. Toppling to her side, she rolls underneath the truck.

"Mel! Can you get under the truck?" She

hears a body sidewinding over the mix of concrete and dirt into which the old driveway has disintegrated.

"God damn it!" Stella says again. Feet appear, then knees, then hands, then Stella's face, her red hair swinging below her ears. "Come out from under there!" she says as if Rose is a bad dog.

"Go away. You've lost. The neighbors will be coming home from work soon. This place becomes like Grand Central Station. Get away while you can. Mel? You under? You okay?"

"Under. Okay," comes a patchy response.

"You are going to ruin everything!" Stella gets down to her elbows and reaches beneath the truck, grabbing at Rose. Using the pistol like a hammer, Rose pounds the intruding fingers. "Damn you!" Stella changes hands, grabbing with the other. Rose bats at it, sending Stella's knuckles cracking into the undercarriage of the truck.

Hands flat on the ground, Stella pushes back. Rose hits every part of hands and arms she can manage with her limited range. "I'm going to kill you," Stella says viciously.

You and whose army? Rose thinks. It makes Rose laugh. She's always had a soft spot for the theater of the absurd.

Hands, knees, and feet move out of Rose's range of vision. Laying her cheek on the ground, she listens. Not a sound. Down near Rose's feet, toward the front of the truck, she hears Mel move.

"Listen," she says to Mel. More silence.

"Is she gone?" Mel asks. Then she yelps.

"I've got you, you little shit!" Stella gloats.

Crabbing around, Rose sees Mel, face contorted with pain, being dragged out from under the truck by her injured foot. Commando-style, Rose propels herself with elbows and knees, trying to catch the girl's outstretched hands.

"You come out from under there now!" Stella says.

Rose lies still, not sure what to do.

Mel screams. "Don't come out, Gigi," she cries, and screams again.

"Out," Stella says, "or I shove a goddam stick in this bullet hole and move it around."

"I'm coming!" Rose yells. "Here I am. I'm coming."

"No!" Mel yells. Rose ignores her. Scrabbling through loose dirt and rock, Rose slithers from under Harley's old Ford. "I'm out," she pants. Mel's hands and chest are on the ground, at eye level with Rose. Her right foot is held up in the air in Stella's two hands.

"Drop the gun," Stella orders.

"It's got no bullets," Rose says.

Stella wrenches Mel's foot to the left. Blood begins dripping from the rim of the shoe, a beautiful shade of red in the last of the day's sunlight. Rose drops the gun. "Put her foot down. She's bleeding!" Rose begs. "I'm here. You've got me. I've got the money. I'll write you a check; ten million bucks to let Mel go. Swear to God, I'll never tell a soul."

"You don't believe in God," Stella sneers.

She's got Rose there.

"I can sign things," Rose pleads.

"Turn around. Face the truck," Stella says, her grip tightening on Mel's foot. White-faced and sweating, Mel puts both hands over her mouth to keep the sounds of pain from escaping.

Rose staggers to her feet. Her front is a mess of blood and torn cloth. She turns and faces the truck.

"Put your hands on the fender. Assume the position," Stella says.

Like anyone who has watched cop shows, Rose knows what the position is. She puts her hands on the polished red fender of Harley's truck, spreads her feet a little wider than her shoulders, and waits for Stella to kick them wider, because that's what she's seen on TV.

"Gigi, turn around!" Mel squeaks.

Before Rose can respond, Mel cries out and Stella says, "Don't even think about it."

Rose's eyes fix on the rich cherry-colored paint. Had she the ears of any proper animal, they would be turned to catch any noise from behind. What she hears is a crunch, a grunt, a gasp. Then Mel yelling, "Turn around! Turn around!"

Whirling, Rose sees Stella, close behind her, a concrete garden gnome held high above her head, ready to bring it crashing down on Rose's skull.

There is no time to do anything but throw one thin arm up to protect her face.

Eyes squeezed shut, Rose hears rather than feels the awful crunch as an inanimate object strikes hard against flesh and bone. An exhalation of breath and a soft thump as a body hits the dirt.

Rose waits to wake up dead.

Finally, she opens her eyes. Harley's ex-wife, Nancy, is standing where Stella had been, her eyeglasses flashing fire from the setting sun, her neat hair in place, her clothing pressed and tailored. Stella is lying prone, the garden gnome circled in one arm, the other outflung, her face to the ground.

"What did you hit her with?" Rose asks stupidly.

"A fifteen-pound box of kitty litter," Nancy retorts. Rose sees the box, leaking litter, to one side of Stella. She wonders if Stella is dead, but finds she doesn't care as long as the woman stays down.

Rose pushes away from the truck. "Mel . . ."

Nancy has moved and is talking with Melanie. "I've called 911," she says. "They will be here shortly. I asked for an ambulance as well as police." On cue, sirens sound a few blocks distant.

The setting sun is painting the world umbers, golds, and oranges, the colors of the autumn leaves. Blood runs down Rose's forearm, more down the outside of her right leg. Wounds she must have gotten when she shinnied through the broken windshield. One of Mel's shoes is dyed dark red. The knees of her skinny jeans are no longer artfully shredded but torn open, the skin beneath scraped away.

"Oh, Grandma!" Mel cries, sounding like a very young girl. "It's so lucky you came."

There is a moment of silence as Rose sinks down onto the running board, no longer able to stand.

"It wasn't luck, was it?" Mel says shrewdly.

"You were tracking my phone!" The affront in Mel's voice makes Rose smile. Mel will be all right.

Nancy snorts, an action not in keeping with her appearance. "Flynn off half the time, Rose going off the deep end, Daniel being Daniel, I couldn't think what else I could do."

Lights and siren running, the first police car arrives. Moments later a second, and an ambulance, fill the long driveway with noise, red and blue streaks of color, and men and women in uniform bustling efficiently.

Rose drops her guard. Bonelessly, she slips from the running board to the ground.

CHAPTER 31

Rose wakes to the murmur of voices. She opens her eyes. A hospital room; a virulent sense of déjà vu sweeps over her. Has it all been a dream? Is she still in Longwood?

"Gigi?" Mel says her name.

Rose turns her head. In a single bed next to hers is her granddaughter. One leg is elevated, the foot in a cast. Mel is propped on pillows holding court. Around the foot of her bed stand her dad, Nancy, Daniel, Royal, his grandmother, and two people Rose assumes are medical professionals.

"Is this a dream?" Rose asks in a whisper.

"You always tell me life is a dream," Mel teases.

"Yeah. It is. But is this a life dream or a dream dream?" Rose asks.

To the medical personnel, Mel says, "Gigi's okay. She's just being Buddhist." To Rose she says, "This is real. You conked out, and they brought us here. You've been asleep for all night and this morning."

One of the medical people says, "Mrs. Dennis, you've been diagnosed —"

Rose cuts her off. "Let Mel tell it. You might be imaginary. Or worse."

Mel makes a face. "You've been diagnosed as suffering from malnutrition, severe exhaustion, dehydration, and muscle strain. They had to put thirteen stitches in your leg, and seven in your forearm where you cut yourself on the windshield of Granddad's truck. You had a concussion . . . Is that had or has?" Mel asks the doctor.

"Let's say 'has' to be on the safe side," the woman answers. "Head injuries in the elderly —"

"Got it." Rose cuts her off again. "Concussion." The diagnosis of "elderly" is damning enough; she doesn't want to know if she's also been diagnosed with dementia. That's a worm can she's not ready to open. "I'm good," she says firmly. "Are you okay, Mel?"

"She filled me in on what happened," Flynn answers before Mel can. "She's going to be fine." In his tone Rose distinctly hears *No thanks to you.*

Evidently, the doctor can't stand being left out. "The bullet cut a furrow along the outside of her foot. There will be a scar, but she should regain full use of the foot."

For some reason Rose doesn't want to talk to the doctor, doesn't want to hear the doctor talk. "Do you have a concussion?" she asks Mel.

"Nope. Harder head than you," Mel says smugly.

"I doubt that," Nancy murmurs.

Rose looks at Harley's ex, her co-grandmother. Nancy appears as cool and collected as always. "You saved me," Rose says. "After that email I thought . . ." Saying that she thought Nancy would let her be murdered by a crazy woman wielding a garden gnome seems harsh, so Rose leaves the sentence unfinished.

Nancy sniffs delicately. "I assumed you were grieving for Harley, and under stress, so I forgave you."

"You got a nasty email from me," Rose says.

"Nasty is your word, not mine," Nancy replies, "but I won't disagree with it."

"I got a nasty email from you," Rose says. For a few seconds, they digest this. Then Nancy nods. They realize who sent them. The woman cutting Rose from the herd for slaughter, the one who had keys to both their houses, the woman who exchanged Rose's drugs and put the prescription bottle through the dishwasher.

"Aunt Stella is the queen of nasty emails," Mel says.

"Stella's been arrested," Elizabeth, Royal's grandma, says. "She will be held at County until the arraignment. She is cooperating."

"Ratting out everybody she can possibly think of," Royal says. His grandmother lays a repressive hand on his shoulder.

"Alma Greene has been detained; charges are pending," Elizabeth says.

"Stella got to know Alma when her father made a new will after he remarried," Flynn says. Rose remembers that. He left everything to his new wife. Stella went ballistic. When he died in an automobile accident a couple of years later, Stella's fury was reignited. "It looks like, after Dad died, Stella and Alma Greene got together and hatched this plot."

Rose is afraid to ask any of the questions she needs to know the answers to. Mel helps her out. "Gigi, you're going to be charged with some things, but Royal's grandma thinks it won't be too bad."

"Longwood doesn't want this kind of publicity," Royal explains. "You know, patients poisoned, murdered, people breaking in, snatching old guys." Elizabeth's fingers tighten slightly on his shoulder and he stops, but the grin doesn't leave his face.

"No offense meant."

"None taken," Rose assures him.

"You have to produce this Chuck of yours, the one you made away with so flamboyantly," Flynn says. He looks a lot like his dad did when dealing with a difficult situation. Rose knows that she is that difficult situation, and will be dealt with. With Mel's intervention, she might be spared banishment. "Without a living, healthy Chuck, Ms. Pryor says all bets are off," Flynn finishes. It's possible her stepson hopes she will be safely locked away for a while — at least until Melanie is thirty and can take care of herself.

"This is better discussed in private," the lawyer says. Elizabeth speaks in such a way that they all feel the threat. Rose doesn't know what it is exactly, but she believes lawyer–client privilege, and plausible deniability for possible deposition questions, might be involved.

"Where is my phone?" Rose asks.

Mel pushes it toward her from where it lay behind a box of tissues on the table between their beds. "The police found it on Alma Greene's desk and gave it to Dad. The nurse put it on airplane mode so you wouldn't be disturbed."

Rose takes it off airplane mode. Immediately it begins to buzz and chirp as messages download. Three are from Marion. Half a dozen or more are from Eddie's phone. Rose starts to call, then stops. She looks at Elizabeth Pryor. "Can you handle another client?"

"Are you referring to Edward Martinez?" the lawyer asks. By the look on Royal's and Mel's faces, Grandma has been filled in on Eddie's involvement so far as they know.

"Yes," Rose says.

Ms. Pryor looks at her Apple Watch. She tucks a stray strand of blond hair behind her ear. She will have guessed Eddie was the masked man in the kidnapping. "I will speak with him if you both do exactly as I say," she concedes.

Rose is fine with that. She pushes REPLY without bothering to listen to messages or read texts.

After a single ring Eddie answers. "Hey!" There is the sound of a mild scuffle; then a deep baritone says, "Yes?"

"Eddie?" Rose asks. It doesn't sound like Eddie. Rose wonders if he's gotten himself arrested for something in Brevard.

"May I ask who is calling?"

"Speaker, please," Ms. Pryor says flatly. Rose puts the call on speaker.

She doesn't know what to say, whether to

answer. "May I ask who's answering?" she asks cautiously.

"Charles — Chuck — Boster." In the background Rose can hear a voice raised in protest. Slightly muffled, the baritone says, "Take it easy, son. Have another Fig Newton." Mouth back to the speaker: "Now. Who is calling?"

"Chuck, it's me, Rose." There is a muffled discussion on the other end of the line. Then Chuck is back.

"The woman who took me out of . . . what? Longwood. The woman who took me out of Longwood?"

Chuck doesn't remember her. Though Rose understands — he was drugged nearly to obliviousness when they were together — still she is a little hurt. "Yes. We knew each other in the MCU, the Memory Care Unit."

"Eddie here has told me a little about that. I am not a man who enjoys only being told a little about why he is in the woods in the middle of nowhere without so much as a change of clothes."

"Charles Boster?" Elizabeth Pryor says.

"Speaking," says the voice.

"The Honorable Charles Boster, Court of Appeals?"

"Retired."

"This is Elizabeth Pryor. I have been in

427

your court many times."

"Counselor Pryor, I remember you."

Rose hands the phone to Elizabeth, who immediately leaves the room in search of privacy. A policeman is stationed outside the hospital room's door. Rose doesn't think he is there to ensure her safety.

No one speaks for a while. "I guess it's all about lawyers now," Flynn says. "I'll see if I can't arrange to reduce my travel."

"I've got to . . . go . . . somewhere," Daniel says vaguely. "Find an apartment. Like that." He drifts out of the room.

"Let me know where to deliver your dratted cats," Nancy says. "The big one has ruined my sofa. I'll send you the bill."

"Thank you," Rose says to the ramrod-straight retreating back.

A nurse appears to shoo Flynn and Royal from the room. In the doorway, Flynn halts like a freeze-frame in a movie. Mel and Rose wait.

Without turning to face them, Flynn says, "Rose, I'm sorry I let this happen to you. Dad . . ." He clears his throat. "Dad was the guy who could fix anything, make things work, make them whole. When he died . . . I guess that guy is me now."

"Us," Rose says. "That guy is us."

Flynn looks at her. "Us," he agrees. "I'll

be home a lot more," he says to Mel.

"Promise or threat?" she teases.

"Both," he answers with a crooked smile. "I'll be back later. You two get some rest."

"Wow," Mel breathes when her dad is gone.

"Yeah. I thought I was in big trouble," Rose says.

"Me, too."

Rose and Mel sit quietly, both on their cell phones. Too tired to talk, Rose texts Marion a brief update. *Got to love a happy ending,* Marion texts back. It is a happy ending. Rose knows that; she just doesn't feel that. What she feels is emptiness. Emptiness is good. She breathes it in for a while, balancing in that lovely space between thought and death where the knowledge that one is made of stardust becomes visceral.

After a time, she says to no one in particular, "Chuck doesn't remember me."

"He will," Mel says comfortingly.

"It'll be good to have my cats back. Do you think Honey Cat really shredded Nancy's sofa?"

"It's pretty shredded."

"The cats must not like Nancy."

Mel doesn't comment.

"I'll bet you are really going to miss

Granddad now," Mel says.

Mel is astute, and not just for her age. When the emptiness fills with the detritus of life on earth, Rose will long for her husband, her friend, her sweetheart.

"Death should be called graduation. Life leaves this form and goes into the next," Mel says. Mel has learned the dharma by osmosis. Rose doesn't know if she knows the dharma that can be known, or if Mel is secretly enlightened. She suspects the latter.

"That is true," Rose says. "But it's hard to hold hands with the truth when you go to the movies."

Mel sighs. "The truth doesn't teach you to build things."

"The truth won't pretend it's his fault when you screw up."

"The truth won't toss you the remote when you're too lazy to get off the sofa," Mel says.

"The opposite of one profound truth is an equal and opposing profound truth," Rose says.

Silence settles along with the dust motes in the afternoon light that slants through the window.

"Do you think Granddad will come back?" Mel asks softly.

"I do," Rose says.

"You'll have to become a vegetarian," Mel says, "so you won't accidentally eat him."

"It's not like he'll come back as a pig or a chicken." Rose spreads her arms out. "He'll be, you know . . . one with everything."

"Granddad is coming back as a hot dog?"

Rose turns her arm so Mel can see the IV tube. "Pretend my pillow has just been thrown firmly at your head."

"Oof!" Mel whuffs, and falls back laughing. Rose hears Harley in his granddaughter's laugh.

Orange light turns to blue, then gray. Rose watches the incremental miracle as Mel dozes in the bed beside hers.

"You are very wise, Grasshopper," Rose whispers.

"This is so, Gigi Rinpoche" trickles back on an exhalation.

EPILOGUE

Hoping to avoid bad publicity, Longwood did not press charges against either Rose Dennis or Edward "Eddie" Martinez. Despite management's efforts, the story was leaked. Following the exposé, the waiting list for families wanting to place their elders in the MCU increased exponentially. Nurse Karen Black and Anthony Brevard were fired.

Ms. Elizabeth Pryor, citing the lack of charges from the facility, along with the circumstances of Rose Dennis's illegal incarceration, and diminished mental capacity stemming therefrom, got the State to drop all charges against Rose.

At Eddie's trial, Rose testified that she had met Mr. Martinez when he was working on her roof and convinced him Chuck's life was in danger. Judge Charles Boster appeared as a character witness on Eddie Martinez's behalf. Charges of kidnapping were reduced to reckless endangerment. Eddie was sentenced to six months' community service. Ms. Elizabeth Pryor got his mother released from detention and is representing her pro bono.

Wanda Lopez was found guilty of conspiracy to commit murder, the murder of Phillip Marsden Miller, Camilla Reynolds, and James Madding. She received two life sentences and is currently appealing the verdict.

Stella Dennis was convicted of assault and battery, assault with a deadly weapon, attempted murder, and kidnapping. She is currently the captain of the North Carolina Correctional Institution for Women's volleyball team. She will be up for parole in eight years.

Alma Greene was disbarred and found guilty of conspiracy to commit murder and of fraud. She turned state's evidence in consideration of a lighter sentence, testifying that Wanda Lopez had broken Camilla Reynolds's femur by shoving her against a sink, then used the morphine drip prescribed for pain to induce heart failure via overdose. James Madding was choked by a Vienna sausage Wanda pushed down his throat when he was too feeble from drugs to defend himself. Phillip Marsden Miller was smothered with a pillow. Alma was sentenced to eleven years in the state penitentiary.

Marion Bliss, Rose's sister, is presently obsessed with 5G.

Carter Goodman sold the painting of the truck in the desert for twelve hundred dollars. The business is now Goodman's Used Cars and Fine Art.

Anthony "Tony" Brevard was indicted as an accessory. He jumped bail. Whereabouts are unknown.

Nurse Karen Black sued Rose Dennis for assault, deprivation of civil liberties, and psychological trauma. The suit was settled out of court for an amount rumored to be in the low seven figures. Ms. Black is on her sixth luxury cruise, this one to Antarctica.

Nancy Dennis received a new couch and adopted a rescue Chihuahua.

Daniel Dennis was promoted to manager of the Starbucks. Finding it too stressful, he quit and got rehired as a barista.

Chuck Boster went back to his wife, remarking that both he and Barbara needed someone to look after them.

Derek Pound, the not-brother, disappeared before he could be arrested. Derek had worked as a personal trainer for both Alma Greene and Charles "Chuck" Boster.

Melanie Dennis, though starting her first year of high school, still hangs out with Gigi occasionally. She and Royal remain best friends. In a short, and less than solemn, ceremony, Mel, Royal, and Rose interred Eddie Martinez's finger in the backyard of the Applegarth house. The grave is marked with a cracked garden gnome.

ACKNOWLEDGMENTS

Don, Carter, Kendall, Marsden Jr., Brooks, London, Helen, Lee, Charles, Liz, Jason, Marsden Sr., Logan, and Jacques for letting me join the wild and delightful world of extended family.

ABOUT THE AUTHOR

Nevada Barr is a novelist, actor, and artist best known for her *New York Times* bestselling, award-winning mystery series featuring Anna Pigeon. A former National Park Service Ranger, she currently lives with her husband in Ashland, Oregon.

The employees of Thorndike Press hope you have enjoyed this Large Print book. All our Thorndike, Wheeler, and Kennebec Large Print titles are designed for easy reading, and all our books are made to last. Other Thorndike Press Large Print books are available at your library, through selected bookstores, or directly from us.

For information about titles, please call:
   (800) 223-1244

or visit our website at:
   gale.com/thorndike

To share your comments, please write:
   Publisher
   Thorndike Press
   10 Water St., Suite 310
   Waterville, ME 04901